THE WELCOME WAGON

THE WELCOME WAGON

JAMIE ADAMS

THORNDIKE PRESS
A part of Gale, a Cengage Company

Thorndike Press, a part of Gale, a Cengage Company.

**LIBRARY OF CONGRESS CIP DATA ON FILE.
CATALOGUING IN PUBLICATION FOR THIS BOOK
IS AVAILABLE FROM THE LIBRARY OF CONGRESS.**

ISBN-13: 979-8-8857-8185-5 (hardcover alk. paper)

Published in 2022 by arrangement with White Rose Publishing, a division of Pelican Ventures LLC.

Printed in Mexico
Print Number : 1   Print Year : 2023

This book is dedicated to my family, immediate and extended. Thank you for all the love and support you've given me through the years.

PROLOGUE

Owen Somers counted fifty-three heads, not including his own.

Stationed beside the door to the judge's chambers, he had a clear view of the proceedings. The crowded courtroom buzzed like a swarm of bees ready to defend the hive whatever the cost. Pretty much everyone within the city limits of West Ridge showed for the short-notice meeting called for by Mayor Todd.

The early summer heat combined with scents from the different professions represented in the room permeated the air. Owen fought back a sneeze until his eyes watered. The sweet smell of fresh baked bread from Swenson's Pastry Shop mingled with the subtle reminders of the livery stable's residents. The windows on the west wall of the building were raised, but until a breeze came through there would be no relief.

"What's this all about, Mayor?" Rudy

Brown's deep voice rose above the murmuring crowd of spectators. The burly blacksmith sat in the front pew of the jury box. After the chairs filled, he was one of the first to migrate to the benches on the left side of the room. By then folks were taking a seat anywhere they could.

"Everyone, just calm down." Mayor Todd took the judge's chair. The circuit judge wasn't due in town for another couple of weeks. "There's no sense in anyone getting riled up."

"Why are we just now finding out about this?" Someone from the back of the room called out. Owen suspected the new schoolteacher. Hard to tell what with the way his voice cracked when he spoke.

Like a flame that refused to go out, Rudy rose from his seat this time. "We don't want no mail-order brides in West Ridge."

Rita Todd, the Mayor's wife, jumped from the bailiff's chair and planted her hands on her hips. Her eyes were wide. She thinned her lips and her words shot out like a round of bullets during shooting practice. "They are not mail-order brides."

"Well then," Rudy refused to back down, "what do you call a wagon load of single women invading a quiet little town like ours?"

8

A series of gasps spread throughout the room. Reverend Irvin's wife, Betty, pulled a large white lacy fan from her purse and waved it back and forth in front of her face.

"Rudy, if you don't watch your tongue, I'll have to ask you to leave." Mayor Todd glared over the top of his spectacles until the blacksmith returned to the pew.

"Please, let's keep this civil." Mrs. Todd sat on one of the more comfortable chairs in the room.

"Rita, dear." Mrs. Irvin spoke so softly Owen was forced to stretch his neck to hear what she said. "What did you have in mind when you agreed to house these people?"

"I believe it's our Christian duty to do something to help." Mrs. Todd's gaze dropped to the sheets of paper in her hand. She cleared her throat and turned her face toward the crowded chamber. "Besides, the women in this town are sorely out numbered."

Owen gave the room a quick glance. At last count there were sixty-two men, twelve children and twenty women living in West Ridge. Made up of predominantly confirmed bachelors, women made many of his neighbors nervous. From outside the building the sound of a donkey's loud whinny ended with a sharp hee-haw.

"Don't forget to count Dan's donkey." Someone from the back yelled, bringing snickers from several of the younger men in the room.

Mayor Todd turned his eyes upward and shook his head slightly as if looking for help from the heavens. "Whatever the reason, we've got to figure out where to put these people." He glanced at his watch. "The welcome wagon assigned to our community is due to arrive this afternoon."

"That's if the stage in Batesville arrived on time." Rudy had a way of finding the dark side to every situation.

"Lord willing, they'll be here before night fall." The exasperation in the Mayor's voice sounded more like a prayer than a reply.

"How many did you say would be coming?" Dale Sanders, the bank manager, stood at the back of the room beside the window with the best view of the savings and loan building across the street.

"Six, maybe nine." Mrs. Todd took a moment to peruse her notes but apparently, they didn't have an answer. "I'm not sure."

Mrs. Irvin stilled her fan and lowered it to her lap. "We have no work here to offer them."

"They aren't looking for work." Mrs. Todd raised her chin and pressed the palms of her hands together. "These women and children are the victims of the horrible attack that took place in Missouri nearly two weeks ago. The incident left them alone in the world and penniless. Several other towns have offered to house women and children left without any means of support. It's part of a relief program organized by the local churches."

Owen flexed his arms before crossing them over his chest. The news had been in all the papers. A group of settlers taking the Southwest Trail to the Red River Valley were forced to stop in Missouri when some folks got sick with cholera.

Two days after stopping, they were attacked and robbed by outlaws. No match for the bandits, those who survived were forced to stand by and watch the wagons burned to the ground. Single men and families with a male head of household were allowed to continue on to Searcy, Arkansas, to regroup. Women and children without family to return home to, were being relocated to Batesville where they were assigned to a community willing to take them in.

Owen looked past the faces of people he'd known all his life and then out the front window. Their concern wasn't unwarranted. West Ridge didn't often see strangers.

11

Travelers didn't pass through their out-of-the-way community. If someone new wandered into town, most likely, they were lost.

"Sheriff?" Mayor Todd cleared his throat with three sharp hacking sounds.

Owen raised one brow and waited for the mayor to repeat what he'd missed hearing. The mayor's wife invited these women, but Owen would be the one called upon to find a fix.

The badge he wore symbolized the law to outlaws, but there weren't any such persons in West Ridge. Over time, his duties quickly turned from keeping the peace to fixing the problems. Cow got out of its pen? Call the sheriff. Can't open last year's jar of beets? Call the sheriff. Foliage-eating caterpillars feasting on your tomato plants? Call the sheriff.

"What do you suggest we do with the ladies?" Mayor Todd nodded several times and then shrugged his shoulders as he waited for an answer.

Giggles came from the back of the room where Anna Grace and Sadie Mae Swenson sat side by side. The elderly spinster sisters were never seen apart. There was no telling what mischief they would get into next. The mayor banged the judge's gavel on the desktop and shot a harried glance toward the ceiling. "Sheriff Owen?"

All eyes were on him. Owen lowered his arms and stood to attention. He'd held the office of town sheriff for the past four years. His friends and neighbors, the community, counted on him.

Reverend Irvin raised his hand and stood. The tall gray-haired man tugged on the hem of his coat jacket and squared his shoulders. He gave both Mr. and Mrs. Todd a brief nod before turning to face the crowd. "For the time being, we can let them stay in the old meeting house." The minister's soft reply seemed to bring a sense of calm over the group. "The empty office and living quarters in the back of the building should be enough room to shelter them comfortably."

"That's a wonderful idea." Mrs. Todd clapped her hands together. Her voice dropped as she continued speaking out loud. "It has a kitchen, and the outhouse isn't very old. It even has an indoor pump. Why didn't I think of it?"

It was a good solution if only a temporary fix. Since the congregation moved to the new church house last spring, the old building remained abandoned, unused, and stood right next door to the sheriff's office.

1

Tuesday June 2, 1867
Northeast Arkansas

"Hold on!" The wagon driver's warning snapped Maggie from dozing. Her eyes flew open and her stomach roiled as the front wheel hit a rut in the road. The rig tilted dangerously to the right. She held tight to the child in her arms and prayed.

The driver got them back on level ground. The danger passed, but her heart didn't stop racing. She blew out a deep breath to calm her nerves, careful not to wake Esther. Her four-year-old niece clutched her favorite yellow blanket as she slept undisturbed. The bench seat was hard, but the discomfort kept Maggie from totally falling asleep. A tumble from this height would be disastrous. Her head bobbed along as the wagon wheels gained a steady rhythm. Her chin dipped toward her chest as she fought to keep her eyes open. The sun's heat mixed with the humidity made everything sticky. The bodice of her dress clung to her sides. Her skirt stuck to her legs. A cool breeze would be nice or, better yet, a dunk in the river.

"Maggie, I'm scared." Katie's timid voice came from the back of the wagon. The teenage girl's words tugged on Maggie's heartstrings. At seventeen, Katie was almost an adult but in so many ways still a child.

"Don't fret." Maggie shifted her body and craned her neck to check on the three passengers sitting in the back. The two children and Belinda were huddled tight against the bench seat. Esther's twin, Hannah, sat on Katie's lap playing with her favorite rag doll.

"There's nothing to be afraid of." Maggie forced herself to display confidence. "We're all in this together. Remember, you're not alone. Think of it as having a new family that loves you and will take care of you."

The words came easy, but she was a bit nervous herself. She'd never heard of West Ridge, Arkansas, until they stepped off the stage in Batesville. Little more than strangers, she and her companions were headed to an unknown future together. Maggie returned to facing forward and pulled Esther closer.

"You heard what the man from the way station told us." A slight pause followed the sound of Belinda clearing her throat.

Maggie could imagine the dark-haired woman resting her hand on the teenage girl's arm.

"He said the people in the town are nice. We'll all be fine. Just you wait and see."

Belinda was a few years older than Maggie. Small in stature, with dark eyes and dark brown hair, she looked younger than her late twenties at first glance. Worry lines etched her face. Smiles were few and often feigned. Only a lifetime of suffering could be responsible for the sharp features hiding such a soft and caring heart.

"The road's a bit twisty for my taste." Mrs. Lamb sat beside Maggie. The elderly woman adjusted the strings on her bonnet before a brave smile spread across her face, "but the hills here are quite beautiful."

For the first hour or so of their journey, they'd rolled past green fields dotted with longhorn cattle and wide-eyed calves. Half an hour ago, the landscape began to curve upward, with towering cliffs on the right and a sheer drop off on the left. Below, a rushing river carved a path through the Ozark Mountains.

"Yes, they are beautiful." Maggie reached out and gave the elderly woman's hand a quick squeeze. She admired Mrs. Lamb's sweet spirit.

The sound of a shotgun blasted in the distance. Mrs. Lamb gasped and grabbed onto her arm. Maggie held back a scream. *Not again! Dear Lord, please this can't be happening again.*

Mr. Gentry gave the woods a sharp look. He scratched the back of his neck and glanced toward Maggie and Mrs. Lamb without any sign of concern. "Just someone out hunting for deer."

The rolling scenery speeding alongside them captured Maggie's attention and calmed her racing heart. Tall pine trees lined the top of the craggy ridge. Above the rock wall, layers of leaves from autumns past covered the forest floor. Shrubs she'd never seen before sprouted among the foliage. The land formations in this part of the country were filled with caverns, so different from her home in Boston.

Nestled in her arms, Esther smiled in her sleep. Maggie stroked the angelic child's soft cheek and smiled. Tears filled Maggie's eyes. Her breath hitched in her chest. She was single, jobless, but determined to find a way to care for the children of her deceased relatives.

"West Ridge is around the next bend." Mr. Gentry's voice vibrated from somewhere deep in his chest. When he met them at the way station, the man introduced himself as Rob Gentry and had little else to say. He looked to be in his late forties.

Either he was a quiet man by nature, or he wasn't happy to be handed the task of driving a wagon filled with females. Maggie suspected the latter.

They passed by what may have been a tall wall or gate at one time. Broken chunks of bricks lay scattered on the ground next to what was left of a structure.

"Don't pay those old bricks any mind." Mr. Gentry waved his hand toward the eyesore. "A few years back, a feller who owned a lot of land around these parts thought he'd build a fancy sign to let folks know they'd reached West Ridge. He hired a bunch of townsfolk to drag boulders up from the river. The cement he used wouldn't dry in the humid air, so he finally gave up. That's what's left of his gate."

Mr. Gentry didn't seem to think it odd no one bothered to clean it up. There wasn't time to ask because just on the other side of the broken gate was a town.

"There she is!" their driver said with enthusiasm, or maybe it was relief, as he pointed toward the scattering of buildings ahead of them. The excitement in his deep voice roused the sleeping child in Maggie's arms.

A mixture of fear and excitement sent a shiver through Maggie as they drew closer to the town. She wasn't surprised by the size or number of structures. The Women's Church Committee representative in Batesville warned them West Ridge was a small community.

Esther wiggled. Maggie took a deep breath and forced herself to smile. Esther blinked several times before she sat up and yawned.

A fair-sized gathering of people congregated in the center of the street. Were they blocking the path on purpose? Maggie held her breath. What would become of her and the children if they weren't allowed to stay? Mrs. Lamb and Belinda were on their own, as well. A tall man with broad shoulders and a gun belt strapped around his trim waist stood front and center of the crowd. Their gazes met and held. Her cheeks warmed, and she lowered her gaze.

He wore a badge.

Resentment welled up inside her. Not having some sort of control over her destiny was unnerving enough without coming face to face with a sheriff. The last person she wanted to see was a lawman.

Their driver brought the team of horses

to a stop and set the brake.

Belinda and the young girls in the back scrambled closer to her. Mr. Gentry stood where they could all see his face and waved his hand toward the crowd of people. "Welcome to West Ridge, ladies."

Owen joined the mayor on the boardwalk in front of the old church building. The welcome wagon had finally arrived. The women and their sad tale were the talk of the town. A group of settlers taking the Southwest Trail were forced to stop in Missouri when illness struck. Two days later they were attacked and robbed. No match for the bandits, those who survived watched their wagons burned to the ground. Women and children without family were relocated to Batesville, where they were assigned to communities willing to take them in.

"Get off the street," Mayor Todd ordered the crowd of curious onlookers. "Give them room to breathe."

Owen motioned for Buster, his Blue Heeler, to sit as Mayor and Mrs. Todd took their rightful place as the town greeters. Buster wagged his tail.

Rob Gentry hopped down from the driver's side of the wagon and grinned. The look of relief on his face was almost comical. A confirmed bachelor, he ran the livery stable. The new wheels on his buckboard earned him the task of riding out to Batesville to meet the stage. He owned the best rig in town.

"Welcome." Mayor Todd stepped forward, waving until he reached the side of the wagon. "Welcome to West Ridge. I'm Thomas Todd, the mayor of our beautiful town. We're pleased to have you all joining us."

Mayor Todd gave Owen a sharp nod when he was ready for him to help the women from the wagon.

Owen took a step forward, and Buster rose to join him. "Stay." He raised the palm of his right hand. The dog sat and watched, waiting for his next command.

A silver-haired woman, carrying a drawstring purse that matched her calico dress, held out her hand. He steadied her as she lowered herself to the ground. Next came a tall, thin, dark-haired woman. She held something in her arms, covered by a thin yellow blanket. When he reached out to help her, a fist came out from under the cloth, followed by the face of a beautiful, blue-eyed little girl. Owen reared back and nearly lost his balance on the edge of the walkway. The little angel gave him a playful grin. An abundance of blond curls covered her head.

The woman holding the child cleared her throat. Owen looked into a pair of dark-blue eyes so striking his jaw dropped open. The woman's dark hair was tied in a bun, but loose strands draped the back of her neck. Her lovely eyes reflected a wariness he attributed to the horrific events of the past two weeks. The woman's lips tightened into what appeared to be an attempt at a smile. She pulled the child close to her chest. He took her by the waist and swung her and the youngster to the walkway.

"Thank you." The woman kept her gaze trained on the young girl, adjusting both the blanket and the little one in her arms until she had them propped steady on her hip.

"Look! It's a dog." The child pointed at the ground behind Owen.

Buster's tail thumped against the board-walk in response to the little girl's excited greeting. The compliant canine didn't move from the spot where he had been told to stay. The good dog would receive an extra treat when they returned to the jailhouse.

Owen tipped the brim of his hat toward the woman and child before he moved to the back of the wagon. Another blond-haired, blue-eyed youngster, nearly identical in appearance to the other, stood holding her arms out toward him. This one tilted her head as if sizing him up. Her shy grin put a smile on his face. He swung her to the ground, where she hurried to join the woman with the beautiful blue eyes.

A third woman clambered out of the wagon before he could get to her. Last was a teenage girl with bright red hair pulled back into a tight bun. Freckles covered her fair skin. She moved back when Owen reached out to help her.

"It's all right, Katie." The elderly woman came to stand beside him, as if to reassure the girl she was safe. "Let this nice man help you down from there."

The young lady squared her shoulders and took a deep breath before she timidly came to the side of the wagon where Owen stood. He reached up and gently swung her stiff form to the ground. Once she was on her feet, she scurried to stand beside the others in her group.

"Welcome to West Ridge." Mrs. Todd's warm greeting was directed at the newcomers huddled together on the boardwalk. "I'm Rita Todd, wife to the mayor and president of the Women's Church Committee."

Owen exhaled a quick breath and stepped

24

back, happy to let her take control of the situation. He stood next to Buster, rubbing the dog's head while he watched and listened.

"We are so happy to have you join our community."

"We appreciate your kindness." The dark-haired woman juggled the girl on her hip while the one on the ground clung onto her skirt. Apparently, the spokesperson for the group, she held out her free hand and shook Mrs. Todd's. "I'm Maggie Lynn. This is Esther and her sister Hannah."

The sisters looked so much alike, if not for the difference in the shape of their faces and noses, they could be identical twins. The one being held grinned happily while the other shyly hid her face in Mrs. Lynn's skirts. The little girls didn't resemble the woman caring for them, other than the color of their eyes. Owen remained quiet but kept his full attention on the proceedings.

Mrs. Todd bent down and smiled sweetly as she reached her hand out to the little one standing beside Mrs. Lynn. "Hello, there."

The girl shook her head and turned a pleading gaze at the woman holding her sister while the other one squirmed in her arms. One wanted up and the other wanted down. The woman had her hands full.

Mrs. Todd straightened and returned her attention to the spokesperson for the group. "Are these your children?"

"They're my nieces and have been entrusted in my care." Moisture filled the woman's eyes, and her voice quivered. She took a deep breath. "By their parents."

In all the excitement and commotion, it had been easy to forget the emotional ordeal this group of travelers had endured. A lump formed in Owen's throat as an awkward silence settled over those assembled.

Before Miss Lynn could explain more, the eldest of the women stepped forward. "I'm Martha Lamb, sixty-five and from New Jersey."

"I'm sorry for your loss." Mrs. Todd's lips thinned, and her brow wrinkled. The edges of her mouth pulled downward, but her attempt at a heartfelt reply was cut short.

"My husband died twelve years ago."

Owen's attention snapped toward the eldest member of the welcome wagon. What was a sixty-five-year-old woman doing headed west on her own? Each new introduction brought more questions. To protect these people and keep the peace, he would need answers sooner or later.

"How did you come to be part of a wagon caravan, if you don't mind me asking?" Mrs.

Todd's train of thought seemed to coincide with Owen's.

"My nephews planned to start a ranch out West. They convinced me to sell everything and join them. They said that with my money they could start big and promised to take care of me." Mrs. Lamb shook her head slightly and turned her hands palm side up. "As they're my only living relatives, I had no choice but to agree rather than be left alone."

"Oh my. Were they lost in the attack?" Mrs. Todd pulled a handkerchief from her skirt pocket. She dabbed the edges of her eyes as the crowd waited to hear more of the woman's sad story.

"No. They decided to go on ahead. They promised to come for me once they got their ranch started. I don't expect I'll be hearing from them anytime soon."

Mrs. Todd clutched the hankie in her fist and trained her attention toward her papers for a moment before acknowledging the third adult woman in the group. Her lips curved into a friendly, if not somewhat feigned, smile. "And you are?"

"Belinda Jones, twenty-eight, from New York City." She answered the standard questions without pausing to take a breath.

"You have no family back in New York?"

"None who would take me in. I was on my way to California with my business partner. He disappeared the day before the attack on the wagons."

"He disappeared?"

"Yes. The wagon master sent men out looking for Brent, but there was no sign of him." The woman crossed her arms. She looked more annoyed than saddened by the loss of her friend. "They figure he either got lost, got killed, or returned to the East."

After making a mark on her list, Mrs. Todd gave Miss Jones a nod before stepping over to the young girl in her teens. "And how about you, young lady?"

"I'm Katie," she spoke so soft, Owen strained to hear, "from New Jersey."

"What about your family, Katie?"

The young girl lowered her head and shuffled her feet.

"Do you have any relatives back home we can contact?"

Like a wall of protection, the three adult women shuffled to position themselves around the one called Katie. Miss Lynn stood front and center, while the other two women flanked the girl on either side.

"She's with me and my nieces." The firmness in Miss Lynn's voice startled Owen. These weren't fragile women as he'd first imagined. They were as tough as one of the blacksmith's anvils and ready to fight if needed.

Maggie squared her shoulders and held her breath. The reception had turned from a welcome to an interrogation without warning. Katie's story was complicated and not one to be shared in public. Maggie glanced toward the sheriff. A surprised look was followed by one of pure confusion.

"All right, then." The smile on Mrs. Todd's face never wavered. "Let's get you all settled before nightfall."

Maggie relaxed. They must have passed inspection because, after sizing them up, the sheriff bid them farewell with a tip of his hat and the mayor's wife took them to the place where they were to stay.

Mrs. Todd led them into what appeared to have once been a church building. A picture of a large waterfall and white doves were painted on the vestibule partition. A large table and a tall chair sat beside the door, leading to an empty auditorium.

Maggie put Esther down and took each of the twins by the hand. It was almost impossible to carry one child with the other wrapped around her leg. She wished she were strong enough to hold them both at the same time as their father once had. The children didn't fully understand the changes taking place in their lives. They needed her comfort and guidance.

Now that she was all the family they had, it fell on her shoulders to feed and clothe them, as well as give them moral support. Not that she minded. She looked forward to watching them grow. The only problem was how she'd be able to care for them financially.

Windows lined the outer walls of the building where church members once gathered to worship. Marks on either side of the room showed where pews must have stood. Unsure of where they were being taken, she turned and looked at their guide. "This looks as if it used to be a church building."

"It was, not too long ago. We built a new church on the other end of town." There was pride in Mrs. Todd's voice. "These will be your living quarters for the time being. I believe you'll be comfortable in the old church house. Some of the ladies and I spent most of the morning cleaning. There wasn't much that needed to be done, mind you. A good dusting and a few shakes of a broom fixed it right up. You'll find everyone in town is looking forward to helping out."

Their footsteps echoed off the empty walls

as they passed through the large room to the back of the building.

"Wes Porter built a chicken pen out back. His brother, Jack, added some laying hens and a rooster. You'll have plenty of eggs. Aaron Miller supplies milk for some of the folks in town. He'll leave a couple of quarts in the vestibule for you each morning." Mrs. Todd came to a stop when they reached the other side of the room. She pulled open the door and led them down a long shadowy hallway. "It took some doing, but we were able to collect bedding to put in the living quarters. There are three rooms and a kitchen. I'm not sure how you'll want to divide them up. We found plenty of pillows and blankets to spare."

Maggie and her companions didn't have many belongings. Most of their things perished in the fires. She shuddered at the memory of wagons set aflame while people around her wept. They'd been left with little more than the clothes on their backs.

"I realize you don't have much in the way of personal possessions. If you'll write down your clothing and shoe sizes, I'll see what we can round up."

The kindness of Mrs. Todd and the small community touched Maggie's heart. The citizens of West Ridge willingly chose to

31

disrupt their day-to-day lives to help total strangers. It was reassuring to know there were still good, kind people in the world.

"This was once the church office and is the biggest of the three rooms." Mrs. Todd moved to the window on the far wall and pulled back the curtain, allowing light to flood the airy chamber. She leaned closer and looked out the glass pane. "As you can see, the outhouse is a short distance from the door at this end of the hall."

After taking a tour of the building, they took turns writing the information needed for clothing and thanked their host for her kindness. Mrs. Todd stuffed the slip of paper into her skirt pocket and waved before she hurried from the sanctuary.

"You and the three girls should take the office, Maggie." Although only her nieces were legally her responsibility, the group silently agreed Katie was to become a part of her mismatched family. Mrs. Lamb turned to look at Belinda. "Which room would you like?"

"I'm fine with the one at the far end of the hall." Belinda appeared to have already sized up the situation. "You should be comfortable in the middle room, Mrs. Lamb. It's right next to the kitchen, and we all know how much you enjoy your cup of coffee in the morning."

"Then it's settled." Mrs. Lamb clasped her hands together as she surveyed their new house. "Let's get to work and see what we can do about making this place feel like home."

"It does seem kind of strange living in a church building." Belinda gave the empty hallway walls a dubious look.

"With a few extra touches, we'll make it feel like a home." Maggie was comfortable with the situation.

Her father had been a preacher, and her mother had played the piano at church. After her parents died, she went to live with her sister, Sarah, who was six years older than her and newly married. A year later, Sarah gave birth to the twins. It had been some time since Maggie had lived in one place for very long. When they started for California, she dreamed of finding true love, marrying, and having a home of her own. So far, nothing was working out as planned.

2

Owen thumbed through the newest batch of wanted posters. He didn't expect to find any of the names or faces of those from the welcome wagon, but perusing the circulars was part of his job.

A muffled bark broke the silence. Buster lay curled up on his favorite rug between Owen and the nearest wall. The dog's hind legs jerked slightly as if the animal were running in its sleep. He was probably after another raccoon in his dreams.

A nap in the middle of the day sounded tempting, but Owen had work to do. Whoever thought of sending one of the Welcome Wagons to a town made up predominantly of bachelors must have a funny sense of humor.

The group of women and children sent their way were a curious bunch. The one with the two little girls . . . what was her name? He pulled his notepad from his shirt pocket and glanced at it before placing it on the desk in front of him. She identified herself as Maggie Lynn. She was single and not married, as he'd first assumed. Although she didn't give her age, she looked to be about twenty-two or so and perhaps the most beautiful woman he'd ever seen.

Owen tried to shake that pointless thought from his mind, but it was hard to dismiss the way her dark blue eyes caught and held his attention. She was from the city and far too refined for someone like him. Besides, she had her hands full with a family to raise. The two little girls were as cute as a button and looked to be doing well, considering the attack on the wagons and the loss of their parents.

Rather than dwell on the horrific crime the ladies had survived, he rose from his chair and walked across the room to the cook stove in the corner.

Buster lifted his head. The dog's gaze followed Owen's movements, and his ears stood at attention.

"Stay." Always at the ready, the dog was a good companion and one he could count on for help any hour of the night or day. "I'm just getting some coffee."

A small fire kept the coffeepot warm. Steam rose from the kettle as he filled his cup. Owen took a long, slow sip while looking out the window. It was quiet outside. The excitement over, most folks had returned home or to their places of business.

From here, there was a clear view of Swenson's Pastry Shop across the street. One of the elderly Swenson sisters flipped the open sign in the window to let customers know they were closed for the day. The elderly sisters were a pair of independent women who did fine on their own.

The pastry shop had been serving the community for as long as he could remember. The only type of eatery in town, the Swensons started baking early in the morning before sunrise. Their hard work kept the population of mostly bachelors supplied with fresh bread and pastries.

Owen gripped the handle of his coffee cup and returned to his desk. He took a seat and patted Buster on the head before giving the list of newcomers another look. The one called Belinda was a curiosity. With the figure of a young woman, her facial features were hard and lined with years of worry. She spoke with a mix of worldly confidence and sarcasm, which was foreign to the friendly, laidback lifestyle of most citizens of West Ridge. She wasn't likely to feel comfortable around town.

He hadn't been given much opportunity to size up the teenager. The women called her Katie and didn't give him or Mrs. Todd a chance to talk alone with the child. There was something there, something he couldn't put his finger on. It might not be any of his business, but he planned to keep a close eye on these ladies.

The older woman's sobering tale got to him the most. He'd like to get his hands on those nephews of hers. How could they leave an old woman stranded after she'd given all her money to help them? The irresponsibility of it set his teeth on edge.

Footsteps outside the door caught his attention. Buster stood and wagged his tail. Owen gathered the wanted posters and stuffed them into the top desk drawer as the door swung open.

Rudy Brown entered the office. The burly blacksmith took a wary look around the room before crossing the floor to stand beside the desk. "Howdy, Sheriff."

"Good afternoon." Owen gave the empty chair across from him a quick nod. "Have a seat. What brings you by at this time of the day? Did you close up shop early?"

"Didn't have much to do today. I got all my orders filled early." Rudy lived by himself in the back of his shop. The only blacksmith in town, he was good at what he did, and his prices were reasonable. "I just wanted to see what you thought of the town's newest residents."

Rudy wasn't one for small talk, and he never kept his opinions to himself. He said what he thought and anyone listening could take it or leave it. The blacksmith was a bit impetuous but, for the most part, he was a good man. A little rough around the edges maybe, but that came from living with no one to give account to. He was honest and could be trusted.

Rudy leaned forward and placed the palms of his hands on the top of the table. A stern look appeared on his face. "Do you think they're trouble?"

Owen stifled a laugh. The thought of three grown women and three innocent children causing him any trouble was ridiculous. He wasn't a detective, a lawyer, or a judge, but he was good at reading people. His job was to keep the peace and make sure everyone in his district stayed safe. Enforcing the law in West Ridge required little effort, and he didn't expect anything to change because of their new residents.

"No. I think they're just a bunch of women and children in a hard spot." Owen glanced toward his desk. The list of names he'd made earlier caught his eye. He cleared his throat and stealthily slid a book on top of the slips of paper. "I think it's a good thing our community can help them out in their time of need."

The ladies were just a handful of those who'd been resettled and were in the process of being relocated across the Ozarks. There was nothing for Rudy or anyone else to fret about. He understood their concerns. Living in a secluded area made folks suspicious of outsiders.

"There's nothing to worry about." Owen leaned back and crossed his arms. "Trust me."

Rudy raised one brow and, after a moment of hesitation, nodded. "If you say so. The town's counting on you to keep an eye out for any trouble."

"Have I ever let you down?" The question was a loaded one, but he couldn't think of a time when he'd failed to do his job for the community. The badge he wore symbolized the law to outlaws, but there weren't any such persons in West Ridge. Over time, his duties turned from keeping the peace to fixing the problems.

"No." Rudy pulled a handkerchief from the pocket of his work overalls and wiped his brow. "But we've never had anything out of the ordinary happen before."

This was true, but the idea of a few women causing trouble was plain silly. He and Rudy grew up together and had gotten into a few scrapes as kids. The best way to put a stop to Rudy's critical thinking was to redirect his train of thought. "Are you going down to the river today? I hear the fish are biting."

"I might just do that." Rudy loved to fish. Big in size, he was known to polish off a slew of fried catfish all on his own. He rose from his chair. "I've got a can full of worms out behind the shop. Do you want to come along?"

"It sounds tempting, but I'll have to pass this time." Owen walked Rudy to the door and gave him a friendly tap on the back. "I've got some paperwork to do. Maybe next time."

Owen returned to his desk, closed his eyes, and leaned his head against the back of his chair. An overwhelming rush of responsibility weighed on his shoulders. Buster came and rested his chin on Owen's leg. Owen stroked the dog's neck.

Rudy wasn't the only one in town upset over what Owen considered a minor event. His duties might not match those of most lawmen, but he did have his finger on the pulse of the community. *"Lord, I know I'm not much, but I could use some of Your wisdom."*

"This is a big house, Aunt Maggie." Hannah twirled in a circle, her arms out and her face pointed toward the ceiling. Shy around strangers, she was a happy, outgoing child when alone with her family.

"It's the biggest house I've ever seen." Esther's eyes were wide with awe as she moved about the room, inspecting every detail. She took one look at her sister and watched for a moment before joining her. "Why are we going around and around?"

"Because we're happy." Hannah finally stilled her steps and stumbled onto the nearest mattress. Esther soon followed suit.

Maggie made their beds with Katie's help, while the girls entertained themselves. Noise coming from the sanctuary caught her attention. She motioned for Katie to keep an eye on the girls. "I'll be right back."

The sheriff and three teenage boys stood in the empty auditorium. Each held a large box. One lad shifted his weight from one foot to the other while the other two kept glancing toward the lawman.

"Sorry to disturb you, Miss Lynn." The sheriff's hazel eyes focused on her as she crossed the room.

A blush warmed her cheeks.

He nodded toward the packages he and the boys carried. "The mayor and his wife asked us to drop these off."

Mrs. Todd entered the building, followed by a woman Maggie didn't know.

"Thank you, Sheriff," Mrs. Todd motioned for them to set the boxes on the platform that once served as an altar. "That will be all. I'll let you know if we need any more help."

"Yes, ma'am." One of the teenagers mumbled as he and his two friends hurried toward the door.

"They're a little bit shy around women." The sheriff chuckled as he watched them go. Laughter lit his eyes when his gaze returned to Maggie. "If you ladies don't need me for anything else, I'll be heading back to the office."

"Thank you, Owen." The mayor's wife nodded in his direction and smiled. "We'll be sure to call if we need anything."

The lawman tipped his hat before he followed the path taken by the boys. His strides were long and steady. He wore his gun belt low on his waist. Holstered, the weapons swayed with each step he took.

A flash of relief filled Maggie when he was

gone from the building.

"I'm Betty Irvin, the pastor's wife." The woman with Mrs. Todd placed a smaller box on top of the pile. She gave Maggie a warm smile as she pointed at the stack. "These are a few items we thought you might be able to use."

"Thank you. That's very kind." Maggie struggled to fight back the tears. "Please let everyone know we appreciate all you've done for us."

"Just let us know if you need anything else." Mrs. Todd nodded toward the boxes before looking at her sheaf of papers. "We have a school in town as well. The teacher is new this year, and classes will be starting in the fall."

"The twins turn five this summer." Where had the time gone? The memory of two newborn baby girls wrapped in linen entered her mind. "They will be old enough to start school this year."

"What about Katie?"

"She's seventeen and finished school two years ago."

"Oh, well then." Mrs. Todd made a checkmark on her list. "I suppose we don't need to worry about school supplies for a few months yet."

Maggie hoped to be able to support

herself before it came time for the girls to start school. She didn't plan on being at the mercy of the community any longer than necessary. All she needed was a steady income and a place to live and raise her nieces. The girls were young, and she had been their main caregiver since their birth. Her sister, Sarah, never fully recovered after the delivery of her babies. Her husband, Chester, was under the impression the air quality out west would be better for his wife. Unfortunately, neither of them lived long enough to find out. Sarah succumbed to her illness, and Chester died while riding with the posse of men who went after the bandits.

"If you ladies feel up to it, my husband and I thought it would be nice to take you all out to the river tomorrow afternoon." There seemed to be no end to their benefactor's thoughtfulness and kindness. "It will give you all a chance to see more of your new home."

"That sounds wonderful." It would be nice to relax and forget their troubles for a while. "The girls and I will be happy to join you. I'll let Belinda and Mrs. Lamb know as well."

"Perfect. The more the merrier." The mayor's wife jotted a note and smiled. "I'll bring a picnic lunch for all of us. There's a lovely area by the river, which is a favorite eating spot."

"Thank you. You've all been so kind to us." She was beginning to feel like a parrot repeating the same words. She didn't know what else to say other than to thank them over and over.

"You're most welcome." Mrs. Todd tucked the papers under her arm and shot a sideways glance toward the preacher's wife.

"It's getting close to supper time. There's food in one of the boxes." Mrs. Irvin responded to the less than subtle message with a gentle smile. "If you all are set for the evening, we'll get going."

"Yes. We'll be fine. Thank you."

"Good-bye, then." Mrs. Todd led the way to the foyer. "We'll be by to pick you up around ten tomorrow. Until then, if you need anything, the sheriff is always available."

"Thank you. We'll be sure to speak with him if anything comes up." Maggie waved and closed the door behind them.

She wasn't about to seek help from the sheriff. It was bad enough they were right next door to the jailhouse. Maggie blew out a slow breath and reached for the door lock, but there wasn't one. An uneasy feeling crossed over her. Back home, her family and neighbors all locked their doors at night. The door in the back of the building had a board that swung down into latches to secure it, but the front entrance was left unsecured. Life was different out in the woods, but still, she'd feel better with some sort of protection.

"Girls, come look at all the boxes."

Belinda must have been waiting for their hosts to leave before venturing out into the sanctuary.

Mrs. Lamb, Katie, and the twins filed out from the back rooms.

"Oh, it's like Christmas." Hannah clapped her hands together.

"I wonder what's inside?" Esther's face glowed with anticipation. "Are they for us?"

"They're for all of us."

The looks of joy on her nieces' faces filled Maggie's heavy heart with hope. She'd tried her best to shelter them from the ordeal they'd experienced. Being like a mother to them all these years helped ease their confusion.

Belinda sat on the edge of the platform, and the twins climbed up to settle on either side of her. Mrs. Lamb and Katie gathered around Maggie as they all watched with anticipation.

"Let's start with this one." Belinda pulled

46

back the lid from the largest box.

"Oh," Hannah squealed as she raised the palms of her hands to her cheeks. Two cloth baby dolls wearing identical outfits lay on top. Belinda gave Hannah and Esther each a doll. Each girl hugged her new toy close.

Belinda continued to dig through the box. "Esther, look." She pulled out a slate board and chalk. "You love to draw. With this, you can make pictures whenever you want. Oh, look, there are two of them."

More tears filled Maggie's eyes. The ladies of West Ridge were so sweet and kind to think of the little girls. Hannah and Esther played with their new toys while the older women continued to inspect the boxes.

"Will you get a look at this?" Belinda giggled as she held up a long pink-and-white checkered dress with ribbons on the sleeves. It wasn't something anyone would wear back East, but Maggie refused to laugh at the gift.

"I don't think it looks so bad. It might be comfortable." Mrs. Lamb took the dress and held it in front of her body. "I believe it will go nice with my rose-colored shawl."

She was right. The gown would look lovely with her favorite wrap. Mrs. Lamb had a way of finding good in everything. The woman's positive outlook on life reminded

Maggie of her mother's favorite verse. "In everything give thanks: for this is the will of God in Christ Jesus concerning you."

This life lesson was easier said than done. Maggie was thankful for the outpouring of kindness from the people of West Ridge, but she couldn't bring herself to be thankful for the events which led to their needing support from strangers. What good was there in so many women and children being left alone and homeless?

"Oh, look," Belinda pulled several pairs of shoes from a box. She passed them around until everyone found a pair matching their size.

There were shoes for each of them. Most looked new, except for those for the two little girls. Maggie sat next to the twins and helped them put on their shoes. With only a slight bit of wear and tear, they would do until they had money to buy new ones. Maggie was happy to see there were some children's storybooks included as well. One box was full of kitchen supplies as well as food. It did feel like Christmas in June.

The sound of a sharp gasp caught Maggie's attention. She looked up from the book she had been showing Hannah.

Katie's eyes were wide with wonder. Among the clothes was a beautiful dark-blue dress with mid-length sleeves and lace on the hem. The teenager reached out and touched the cloth. "It's beautiful."

"And it's your size." Belinda held the dress in front of Katie.

"I've never seen anything so pretty." Longing filled the girl's eyes for a moment before she shook her head and backed away.

"Take it," Belinda insisted. "The color looks lovely with your auburn hair."

Maggie agreed. The coloring was flattering. "It will look very nice on you."

Katie took another step away from Belinda and the seemingly intimidating dress. "I couldn't wear something as lovely as this."

"Of course, you can." Belinda looked at Katie. "Why shouldn't you look just as nice as anyone else?"

"I don't know." Tears welled in the teenager's eyes, and her chin trembled.

Maggie's heart broke for the young girl who'd been mistreated by those claiming to be her family. She thanked God she'd been raised in a loving home with parents who made her feel loved. She would do everything in her power to give Katie and her nieces the type of home she'd grown up in.

"Belinda is right." Mrs. Lamb took the dress and draped it over her arm. "Let's go into the back, and I'll help you try it on."

The sweet woman wrapped her arm around Katie's shoulders and led her from the room.

Belinda looked at Maggie with raised brows.

A weary sigh escaped Maggie's lungs before she turned her attention to her nieces. Their innocent laughter echoed off the walls of the empty chamber as they played with their new baby dolls.

Careful not to waken the sleeping children, Maggie backed into the hallway and pulled the bedroom door shut. Her nieces and Katie had fallen asleep soon after finishing supper. Mrs. Lamb had managed to find enough supplies from the food box to make a simple meal of beans and cornbread for them.

Maggie tiptoed down the hall to help with cleaning the dishes. The kitchen was across from Belinda's room and next to Mrs. Lamb's. The room was well supplied with a stove, and several cupboards lined the wall closest to the door leading to a walk-in pantry. There was also a washbasin with an indoor pump. It was a bit of a surprise to find such a modern luxury so far out in the country and in a church building.

Maggie slipped into the kitchen and found

Mrs. Lamb stacking canned goods on a shelf in the pantry. When she finished, the woman used her apron to wipe off her hands. "It's nice to have an organized kitchen to work in again."

Living out of a wagon hadn't been easy. It took time to set up for meals and their limited supplies had to be portioned with considerable care if they wanted them to last until they reached their destination. They had just started the journey when the trip was cut short.

"Excuse me." Belinda entered the room with a pail of water in either hand. She carried them to the sink where she set one down on the floor and proceeded to pour the other one into the basin.

"Is there something wrong with the sink pump?"

"It dried up after a few pumps." Belinda heaved a heavy sigh and set the empty pail on the floor. "This is my second trip bringing water in from the outside well. There's water heating on the stove."

"Oh, that is a shame." It was unfortunate, but they didn't have any reason to complain. The Women's Church Committee had provided them with much more than they ever expected. She never dreamed of finding an indoor pump in the old building.

"What can you expect so far out in the wilderness." Belinda shrugged as she took a bar of soap from a dish beside the sink. She scraped shavings into the water to make suds. When she had a good amount of foam, she wetted a cloth and scrubbed one of the battered-looking pans they had used to cook their meal. Some of the plates were chipped, but all their gifted supplies were usable. "When something stops working out here, there isn't much you can do about it."

Maggie dried the plates. From the window over the sink, they had a perfect view of the alley behind the jailhouse. The lawman's dog barked at something up in a tree. A door opened, and Sheriff Owen stepped outside. The tall, lean man clapped his hands, and the canine ran over to him. The dog's tail wagged with excitement. The sheriff pulled something from his pocket and tossed it in the air. The dog jumped and snapped the treat in his mouth. Sheriff Owen threw back his head and laughed. As he reached down to pet the dog, his gaze wandered toward their window before he opened the door and ushered the dog inside.

Had he seen her watching him? She turned her attention to drying the dish in her hand.

"Maggie?" Mrs. Lamb touched her arm.

"I think it's dry now."

She handed the dried plate to Mrs. Lamb, who placed it on the shelf next to the pantry. They worked in companionable silence. Mrs. Lamb began to hum "Amazing Grace" as they continued working. There was a feeling of family as they labored together. When they were finished, Belinda poured what was left of the rinse water over the last pan and handed it to Maggie. Mrs. Lamb pulled out a chair and sat down.

Maggie set the dried pan on top of the cold stove. Mrs. Lamb had created a delicious meal with a few simple ingredients. They had all eaten their fill.

She joined the older woman at the table. "Where did you learn to cook so well?"

"Many years ago, my husband and I cooked for a lumber mill outfit. It was Jeff who taught me to make do with just a few ingredients but still create food people could enjoy."

"So, you're used to feeding a crowd of people." Belinda joined Maggie at the small table and chairs they used for eating.

"Yes. We were expected to feed a couple dozen men at a time all day long." Mrs. Lamb folded her arms and rested them on her waist. "They came in shifts, and the food had to be hot for the men. That was part of the deal."

Belinda's brow raised slightly, and she held up three fingers. "Breakfast, lunch, and dinner?"

"Yes. Breakfast was the most important meal of the day, followed by supper." A faint smile spread across Mrs. Lamb's face as she seemingly stared at a memory only she could see. "Lunch was usually a cold sandwich and fruit prepared the night before by our crew. Suppers were the most complicated, but we had more time to prepare them."

This was news to Maggie. Each day she learned something new about her companions. "Did the two of you ever consider running a restaurant?"

"No, not really. When we were finished there, we were ready to settle down and live quietly by ourselves." She chuckled softly. "It was hard at first to adjust to cooking for only two people after feeding twenty to fifty a day for so long."

A heavy silence fell over the room, and Maggie started to excuse herself. They'd stirred up enough memories for one night. She pushed back her chair, but Mrs. Lamb apparently wasn't through speaking.

"My sister's boys were like sons to us." She continued staring into the distance as she told her story. "After Jeff died, they were constantly checking in on me."

"I hope you hear from them soon." Belinda stood and pushed her chair up to the table.

Maggie followed suit.

"I'm not sure I ever will." Mrs. Lamb stifled a yawn as she joined them. "I imagine they'll end up cowhands for some outfit out west. Well, good night, girls. I'll see you in the morning."

They all three stepped out into the hall. Mrs. Lamb fought another yawn as she slipped into her room, leaving Maggie and Belinda outside Belinda's room.

"How are you doing?" Belinda held the doorknob but didn't attempt to enter the room.

"Other than feeling exhausted, I'm fine. How about you?"

"It's not as bad as I expected." A weak smile tugged at the corners of Belinda's lips, without reaching her eyes. "Do you think you'll like it here?"

"I think so." It wasn't much different than crossing the country to start afresh, just not as far. Life was full of new beginnings. This was just another part of the journey. She'd lost her parents and then her sister and brother-in-law. Things couldn't get much worse. A stab of guilt pierced her heart. Her parents taught her to look on the bright side, no matter the situation. "It does seem like a nice place to raise the girls."

"I'm afraid it'll be a little too quiet for my taste." Belinda had no problem sharing her true feelings.

"Have you had a chance to look around the town yet?"

"No. Only the part we saw when we rode in."

"There was a telegraph office, a post office, and, of course, the sheriff's office." Maggie listed the businesses she'd observed when they arrived in town. "I'm pretty sure I saw a bakery."

"I heard someone mention a bank and a mercantile as well."

"They did say they have a new church." She hadn't seen any such building when they arrived, but she had yet to see any of the structures east of the jailhouse.

"I haven't had much use for church recently." Belinda bowed her head and poked at the tan rug with the toe of her shoe. "Or maybe I should say church hasn't had much use for me."

"This is a new start for all of us." She didn't know Belinda well, but, from her comments, Maggie gathered life hadn't been easy for her. "A fresh beginning. I've always enjoyed going to church."

"I did too when I was a little girl." A smile softened the worry lines around the edges of her mouth. "Especially the dinner on the grounds my grandmother's church had once a month."

"I'm looking forward to giving this one a try." The townspeople would expect them to attend. It was, after all, Mrs. Todd and the Women's Church Committee who'd reached out to help them with food, shelter, and clothing.

"I suppose it won't hurt." Belinda started to enter her room and then paused. "Maggie, what do you think happened to Brent?"

"Brent?" Brent Cooper disappeared the day before the attack on the wagons. Maggie hadn't given him much thought after the men who'd searched for him returned empty-handed.

"I can't believe he just left me like that." Tears moistened the abandoned woman's eyes. "But, at the same time, I don't want to believe he's dead."

"Try not to worry." Maggie reached out and squeezed her arm. "I know we aren't much, but you have us."

"Yes, and I'm thankful for that." Belinda glanced toward the room where Katie and the girls were sleeping. "I wonder whatever became of Mr. Maxwell."

Maggie shuddered at the mention of Katie's so-called uncle. Katie's aunt was one of the first to die from the cholera outbreak. Loud and outspoken, the woman hadn't made many friends along the trail. Still, they'd done their best to keep her comfortable during her illness.

There was only one word to describe Mr. Maxwell. Mean. He was unkind to animals, his wife, and his wife's niece, Katie. A retired lumberjack, he still wore the tall black boots common among those used by men who felled trees for a trade. There had been no sign of him when the women and children were assigned to the communities willing to take them in. They couldn't leave Katie behind. Maggie was happy to bring her along.

"I have no idea what might have happened to him and don't want to know."

Both Mr. Maxwell and his wife treated Katie like an indentured servant, only they were cruel as well. Maggie suspected Mr. Maxwell drank in excess. She only spoke with him one time on the trail but smelled whiskey on his breath. There were scars on the back of the child's legs from past beatings. Poor Katie. Their treatment of the child made Maggie's stomach sour. Katie would turn eighteen in November and would no longer be his ward.

"Me either." Belinda shook her head as she pushed her bedroom door open. "I hope we never hear from him again. Katie is better off without him."

"If he ever does find her," Maggie prayed he wouldn't, "I'll put up a fight."

"You can count on me being by your side." Belinda slipped into her room, and Maggie continued down the hall.

What would Sheriff Owen think if he knew about Katie's uncle? Mr. Maxwell wasn't the child's blood relative. According to Katie, she didn't know of any papers or formal adoption proceedings ever being made. She'd lived with the couple since her mother died. Maggie wasn't sure if the law would side with them or Mr. Maxwell, and it was too risky to find out. Mr. Maxwell had no business raising a child. Maggie vowed to keep Katie safe as long as it didn't jeopardize the twins.

3

"Ready, Buster?"

The Blue Heeler rushed to the door and wagged its tail. Owen grabbed his Stetson from the hat rack and placed it on his head before stepping outside. The sun peaked over the hills to the east. He filled his lungs with a deep cleansing breath and surveyed the empty street. There weren't many people out at this hour when he made his scheduled rounds. The early morning air was crisp and cool. By noon, the humidity would rise enough to drench a dried-out piece of leather. The best time to move around in the Ozarks was before the saturating summer heat set in.

He took long strides as he moved westward. Buster's legs were short, but the dog had no problem keeping pace. Their first stop was the old church house. The door was secure and there was no sign of trouble. Most likely the women were still sleeping.

This time of year, folks rose early to get chores done before the heat of the day hit. Mrs. Todd may have filled them in. If not, they would figure it out soon enough.

A redbird swooped overhead before landing on a high tree branch across the street. The chatter of birds welcoming the sun's return never failed to lift his spirits. The joy in their singing was contagious. Next came the telegraph office. Mitchell didn't open up for another hour. Owen twisted the knob. The door was locked. He pressed his face against the front window. The little space inside looked undisturbed. He marched down the road a piece to check on Lee's Saddlery. The building was quiet as well.

Then he and Buster crossed the street and turned eastward. Other than the sound of a horse nickering from inside the barn, Rob's livery stable was quiet. Next door, the blacksmith lived in his quarters, and there was little need for him to check the premises. Other than a quick glance, he continued making his rounds.

Buster sniffed the ground and zigzagged a few feet ahead. The dog was onto an intriguing scent of some sort. Owen caught a whiff of fresh dough and let the dog follow his own interests.

The Swenson sisters were inside the pastry shop preparing bread for their customers. Owen climbed the steps to the building as he did every morning. It was part of his routine, and the sisters seemed to look forward to his visits.

The bell over the door announced his entry. "Howdy, ladies."

"Good morning, Sheriff," Anna Grace called from the kitchen area. "How are you today?"

"I'm doing fine. How about you two?"

"Couldn't be better. What will you have this morning?" Sadie Mae Swenson entered the room and came to stand behind the counter. She wiped her hands on a cloth she kept draped over her shoulder. More outgoing than her younger sister, Sadie Mae took most of the orders. She was good at making small talk. "Anna Grace just pulled a fresh batch of blueberry muffins from the oven. We know how much you love those."

Owen stepped past the table and chairs lining the front windows and moved closer to the counter. "Sounds perfect. I'll take two."

He was the only customer in the shop. Before long, most of the town's bachelors would be lined up waiting for their turn to place an order. One good thing about his job, he got the pick of the day's batch.

"Is it still nice outside?" Sadie Mae opened a small bag and placed the muffins inside before handing them to him.

"It's not too bad yet." He accepted the package and pulled some coins from his front shirt pocket. "But looks like it'll be another scorcher."

"It's warm in here all year round." The weariness in her voice drew Owen from counting money. She looked tired. He couldn't recall how old they were and wasn't feeling brave enough to ask. Most folks their age would be ready to retire but the town would be lost without them and their shop.

"You ladies have a good day." He finished paying for his food and left the pastry shop. There was still the bank, the courthouse, the new church building, and the mercantile to check on.

He took a big bite from one of the still-warm muffins and headed for the mercantile. Anna Grace and Sadie Mae Swenson made some of the best pastries he'd ever eaten, although it seemed age and the early hours were taking their toll on the sisters. Perhaps one of the women from the welcome wagon could help them. Maggie would be a good choice, only she was tied down with youngsters to look after. Mrs. Lamb appeared to be able-bodied, but what they needed was someone who could step in and take their place. Mrs. Lamb was around the same age, perhaps older. The only other choice was Belinda, and he still wasn't sure about her. Something about the woman from New York didn't sit right with him. He wasn't about to recommend someone he wasn't sure he could trust.

By the time Owen reached the mercantile, he'd polished off the second muffin. Next door was the Savings and Loan. The bank required special attention. Owen surveyed the alley and windows before moving to the front where he took hold of the door handle and tried to make an entry. The building was secure.

Buster rejoined him when it came time to cross the street and check on the courthouse. Mayor Todd came from around the corner headed for his office. He had on a pair of overalls and carried a stack of papers.

"Howdy, Mayor Todd."

"Good morning, Sheriff Owen." The mayor tipped his hat. He made it a practice to use their official titles when in public even though they went to school together and were fishing buddies from way back.

"You're headed to work early this morning." The courthouse didn't open for business for another hour, and he didn't seem dressed for work. The town's only true dignitary, he wore slacks, a pressed shirt, and a bow tie when he went to work.

"I've got some paperwork to finish, and then the wife and I are taking the welcome wagon folks down to the river."

Owen glanced toward the sky, which was clear and dry. The temperature would be nice by the water. The Spring River was the pride and joy of West Ridge. Some of the best fishing spots were on the west bank a quarter of a mile from the lookout. He and his brother had spent many summer mornings pulling catfish from the deep waters.

"You're welcome to join us if you have a mind to."

Buster barked and wagged his tail as if he understood. Owen was tempted to accept the invitation but had other plans. "Thanks for the invite, but I promised to help Fred Barkley get the mail ready for the weekly run. If we finish soon enough, I might ride down there and join you."

"See that you do." Thomas quirked his brow. "I'll be sorely outnumbered."

"Hello, are you ladies ready?" Mrs. Todd's voice came from outside the door leading from the sanctuary to the living quarters.

"We'll be right there." Maggie took hold of Esther's hand and Katie held Hannah's. The girls were full of energy and looking forward to this trip to the river. Maggie was thankful for all the help she could get. "Belinda, are you ready?"

"Yes, I'm all set." Belinda came from her room to join them in the hall.

They met Mrs. Todd in the sanctuary and followed her outside. The mayor looked them over, his chin bobbing as he counted heads. It was amusing to watch, but Maggie held back her laughter.

She waited until he was through taking inventory to explain they would be one short. "Mrs. Lamb won't be joining us this trip. I hope you don't mind."

"No, of course not." The man's brows creased, and he gave his wife a quick glance. "Is she ill? We can send for the doctor."

"No. That won't be necessary. Her arthritis is bothering her this morning. She said to warn you it will most likely storm before the day is over."

They all glanced upward. There were a few fluffy clouds in the sky. It didn't look like rain. Maggie recognized the wagon as they boarded. It was the same one Mr. Gentry used when he'd picked them up the day before in Batesville. The bench seat was painted an odd shade of brown, darker than the rest of the buckboard. The horses were the same pair he'd used to bring them into town.

The mayor must have sensed her confusion. "Rob runs the stable. These horses and the wagon see a lot of the country around these parts."

"Is it far to the river?" Belinda insisted on sitting in the back with the girls again. This time Maggie rode in the back as well, letting the mayor and his wife have the bench seat to themselves.

"It's just up the road a piece, but the spot we like to visit is about two miles when you take the river road." The mayor shook the reins and the horses moved forward. "Other than the ridge, the road is level for the most part, without any curves."

"The ridge?" Maggie used her hand to shade her eyes and looked in the direction of the river.

He spoke as if it were a landmark. "Yes, the west ridge is how our town got its name. Some people believe east ridge would be a more accurate description." He laughed at a joke she didn't quite understand. "What with us being closer to the eastern part of the state and all."

"I see." Maggie nodded. Although they had their backs to her, she tried to keep the confusion from her voice. She appreciated the mayor's explanation, but it still wasn't clear as to how the ridge they were headed for earned the town its name.

Mrs. Todd laughed and then cleared her throat. "What Thomas started to explain is that West Ridge is named for the ridge on the west side of the river. As with any body of water, there are some access points that are easier than others. At this elevation, you'll find most of them impossible to go down. In fact, this ridge is the best way and, for more than a few miles in either direction, the only way to get to the water. Years ago, when folks were explaining how to get to the fishing hole, they would refer to it as the west ridge."

"Oh, now that makes perfect sense."

"Look, a bird." The awe in Hannah's voice drew Maggie's interest.

She turned sideways so she could see what the child was looking at. "It's a bluebird."

"How come it's blue?" Esther had an inquisitive nature and blue was her favorite color.

Mrs. Todd glanced over her shoulder and gave the child a quick grin. "That's the way God made it."

"Look." Katie pointed to the other side of the road. "There's a red one."

The woods were full of birds. Some of them she recognized, as they were native to Boston as well. There were several others she couldn't identify. Since West Ridge was to be their new home, she would make it a point to find out more about the wildlife living in the Ozarks.

"Why did God make one blue and one red?" Esther's questioning phase had been going on for several weeks. Her eyes wide with wonder, she stared at the flying activity going on overhead.

Mrs. Todd's laughter was genuine as she seemed to enjoy the girl's curiosity. "I suppose it's so we could tell them apart."

"Oh." Esther nodded, as if the explanation made all the sense in the world.

Maggie marveled at the innocence of her nieces. The changes they'd encountered in their young lives would seem unbearable to some. The only constant figure in their life, it was important for her to remain confident and positive, but it was like a weight on her shoulders at times.

The humidity in the air wasn't as heavy when they reached the river. The mayor stopped the rig under the shade of a trio of tall pines and pulled the brake. A path of worn-down grass led to a large clearing in the center of the plentiful undergrowth. It looked like a popular place used by many people. A path wound through the foliage leading to the water.

Mr. Todd carried the picnic basket while his wife laid a blanket under a large shade tree. The land was flat and the grass smooth, almost as if maintained for the purpose of having a picnic. One thing which set the Ozarks apart from most any other place Maggie had seen was the terrain. Most of it was covered with rocks, some large but most small. It had to be hard to grow crops in this part of the country.

"I hope everyone likes chicken." Mrs. Todd motioned for them to join her on the blanket. "There's tea to drink, and I picked up some rolls from the pastry shop. If you haven't noticed, it's across the street from where you're staying. You'll love the ladies who run the bakery. The Swenson sisters are two of our town's most memorable characters. Thomas brought up a couple of watermelons last night and left them cooling in the river."

"Please, let us help you." Maggie took the stack of plates. She gave everyone a dish to hold their food while Belinda poured tea into several cups. "The food looks delicious."

Katie sat between the twins and kept them entertained by pointing out a chipmunk underneath a nearby tree.

"I hope I'm not too late." The sound of the sheriff's voice surprised Maggie. He rode into the clearing on a white horse with a dark mane and tail. His dog ran alongside them.

"You're just in time." Mayor Todd waved. His face brightened with a smile. "Come sit down and join us."

Maggie's shoulders tensed and her stomach twisted, but she forced herself to smile and stay calm. The tall man with the shiny badge dismounted and joined them. The mayor moved over to make room for the lawman. The sheriff lowered himself on the blanket between the town leader and Maggie. Buster sat off to the side and wagged his tail until Sheriff Owen tossed him what appeared to be a bone.

"We're glad you could make it after all, Owen." Mrs. Todd leaned across her husband and handed the lawman a glass of sweet tea.

"Thanks, Rita." Sheriff Owen took a long sip. "I wasn't sure I would for a while there, but we managed to get the mail wagon off in time."

"I thought he was the sheriff." Esther never hesitated to question things she didn't understand. More outspoken than her sister, there was no telling what might come out of her mouth.

"He is the sheriff." Mrs. Todd spoke over the sound of laughter. "There are a lot of things the sheriff does that people don't realize."

"Like take care of the mail?"

"Not exactly. Our sheriff helps wherever he's needed, and today the mailman needed help."

"Oh." Esther nodded before turning her attention to a pair of squirrels racing to the top of a walnut tree.

Maggie handed the sheriff a plate and then the basket of fried chicken.

"Thank you." His palm brushed against her fingers and sent a warm spark racing through her hand. He took a chicken leg and then passed the basket to the mayor.

The conversation ceased while they handed out the food. It was a nice day for a picnic. They ate off tin plates and drank sweet tea. It was one of the finest meals Maggie could recall, even if the presence of the law hung over her like a dark cloud. Tree limbs swayed in the light wind, making it much cooler by the river than it had been in town. When the two men cleaned their plates, Mayor Todd focused his attention on the sheriff. "I left two melons in the river last night. Do you mind getting them for us?"

"Sure thing." He stood, and the dog went to his side. "Usual spot?"

"Yep." The mayor reached into the basket and pulled out a large knife. He set it beside him and leaned toward the young girls across from him "We have some of the best watermelons in the country."

"Oh, goodie." Hannah clapped her hands.

"Watermelon is my favorite." Esther smiled, closed her eyes, and let out a slow sigh. Then she sat up straight and added. "Next to ice cream."

Sheriff Owen returned with the fruit and proceeded to cut them into slices for the mayor to hand out. After everyone had a piece, Mr. Todd nudged the lawman's arm with his elbow. "How about we go check out that old fishing hole of ours?"

"Sounds good to me." Sheriff Owen rose from the blanket and joined the mayor but paused to look at Mrs. Todd. "Thank you for the fine meal."

He tipped his hat as the two of them and the dog turned to walk toward the river.

When she and the girls finished eating, Maggie rested her head on the trunk of the tree behind her and closed her eyes. A gentle breeze brushed her cheeks. The twins sat on either side of Katie, still eating their slices of watermelon.

"What lovely flowers." The awe in Belinda's voice was evident and unusual for one not easily impressed. "I've never seen anything like them."

Maggie peeked under her lashes. Belinda rose and walked a short distance toward the woods. Purplish-blue flowers lined the path near the river. The buds were small but plentiful.

"Those are wild crocus." Mrs. Todd called out from her spot on the blanket. Her voice seemed to always fill with pride when she talked about her community. "They only grow in the Ozarks."

Belinda knelt beside the blossoms and took in a deep breath. It was nice to see this softer side of the somewhat cynical woman. The day was turning out to be a blessing. Maggie closed her eyes again. The sun warmed her face, and she took a deep breath.

"Aunt Maggie," Hannah stood and tugged on her arm. "I want to go in the water."

Maggie's heart raced. She opened her eyes

and straightened. She didn't want the girls to go near the river without her. "Just a moment. I'll go with you."

"Me, too." Esther looked up from what was left of her watermelon and grinned. Red sticky juice dripped down her chin.

"All right, let's all go to the water." Maggie sighed as she pushed up and stood.

Katie joined her and the twins on their walk to the water. She let the girls clean their faces and hands in the cool liquid. They took off their shoes and sat on a flat rock which lay partially in the river. The little girls splashed their legs in the cool stream and laughed at the water cascading off their bare feet.

At the sound of crunching leaves, Maggie looked at the path behind them. Belinda came to stand beside them without saying a word. She bit down on her bottom lip and squinted her eyes. Maggie considered whether to say anything. Between Mrs. Lamb and Belinda, Belinda was the hardest for her to figure out.

"Do you need to wash your hands too?" Katie looked at her and giggled. "The water is cold, but it's better than being sticky."

"What?" the bridge of Belinda's nose wrinkled, but she kept her gaze on the woods, which lay in the direction of town.

Katie turned to Maggie and shrugged.

"Is something wrong?" Maggie followed the woman's gaze but couldn't see anything out of the ordinary.

"No. Well, yes. I'm not sure."

Maggie raised her brows and shared a quick glance with Katie. The teenager shrugged and covered her mouth with the palm of her hand.

Belinda lowered herself onto the empty spot on the rock next to Maggie. "I thought I saw someone watching us."

"Well, this is the Spring River after all." Maggie scanned both sides of the riverbank. She didn't see anyone about. "They say it's a popular place, especially during the summer months."

As hot as it was outside, the water was the perfect place to be. It was perhaps the only place to find relief. It seemed stranger to her that they hadn't seen anyone. Seemingly bored with the conversation, Katie slid from her perch to help the twins stack pebbles in the clear, shallow water.

"People use the river for fishing or swimming." Maggie tried to assure her new friend.

"I suppose you're right." Belinda's brown eyes narrowed, and her gaze never wavered from the opposite side of the river. "There's nothing to worry about in a small community like this."

They were safe. There wasn't any reason for them to fret unless they allowed the lawman to get too close. He was a nice enough person and seemed genuine, but he also enforced the law. None of them had broken the law, not really. Maggie shifted her focus on the children playing on the riverbank. Esther and Hannah took turns splashing water on Katie. It was good to see all three of them laughing and carefree.

4

Owen took a good long look at himself in the mirror. He had taken extra care this morning while he shaved. Last night he found a few spots along the sides of his chin he'd neglected. A town sheriff shouldn't look scruffy. He rubbed his hand over his smooth skin, satisfied he was ready to start the day.

After he was done making his morning rounds, he planned to pay the welcome wagon crew a visit. The mayor asked him to keep an eye on them, and he'd been ignoring his duties.

"Ready?"

Buster rushed to the front door and waited.

They stepped outside to another sunny day in the Ozarks. To mix things up, he turned right instead of left. Buster sat on the boardwalk. Owen watched and waited to see what the dog would do. Buster tilted his head to the right and then to the left before deciding to join him.

It was still too early for most of the shops to be open. Over the years, he learned the best way to occupy his mind as he took this lonely journey was to admire God's handiwork as he walked. West Ridge was one of the prettiest towns in the county, with the river on one side and the bluffs to the south. Other than the birds praising God for another sunrise, Owen and Buster were the only two out and about.

It was still a bit early when he finished checking the businesses on Main Street, so he made a special trip to the pastry shop.

"Stay." He motioned for Buster to wait as he climbed the steps.

If the sisters were surprised to see him again so soon, they didn't say. There were a few men at the counter. The shop was about to get busy. Owen bought some cinnamon rolls to take to his new neighbors.

"Ok, Buster." Back out on the boardwalk, they crossed the street, and he rewarded the Blue Heeler with a treat. "Go ahead."

The dog gobbled his piece of bread and then looked at Owen.

"Go on."

Buster wagged his tail and trotted off to the alley separating the jail from the old church. He was headed for the backyard where he liked to play and chase squirrels.

Owen pounded hard on the vestibule doors, loud enough for them to hear him from the back of the building. He didn't feel right walking through the sanctuary uninvited. It took a while but eventually, Miss Lynn answered his knock.

"Hello, Sheriff." She tilted her head to the side and gave him a sharp look. Her dark-blue eyes were just as striking as the first time they met. "It took me a while to figure out where the noise was coming from."

"Good day, Miss Lynn."

"Please call me Maggie."

"OK, Maggie." He liked the sound of her name. It reminded him of a field of wildflowers in spring.

The woman with beautiful blue eyes stepped back to allow him room to pass through the doorway. She didn't appear bothered by his gawking at her face nor did she seem aware of his fascination with her eyes.

"I wanted to stop by and see if there is anything you all need." Owen's face heated up. He thrust the box of rolls toward her. "These are some cinnamon rolls from the pastry shop, if anyone's hungry."

She took her time looking at the box after

accepting it before turning her face to him. Her cheeks were flushed, and wariness lined her lips. "Thank you. Come on back to the kitchen. We were just sitting down to eat breakfast. You're welcome to join us."

He matched his steps to hers. Even with his long strides, he had to work at keeping the pace. She seemed to be in a hurry to return to the kitchen, or perhaps it was to get away from him. When they reached the door on the other side of the room, he jumped ahead and held it open for her. She mumbled something which sounded close to "thank you" as she passed into the hall.

He wasn't hungry, but the savory smell of eggs, along with ham and biscuits, wafted out into the hall. The pastry he'd eaten earlier, much earlier, hadn't been very big. His stomach rumbled in agreement.

"Welcome, Sheriff Owen." Mrs. Lamb stood in front of the cook stove scooping scrambled eggs and ham with a spatula. The elderly woman's cheerful greeting lifted his spirits and put a smile in his heart. "Have a seat and join us. The little ones have already eaten, and there's more here than we can finish off."

Owen sat down. It had been some time since he'd eaten in a warm, cozy kitchen. She placed a plate of steaming hot food in front of him before taking a seat at the other end of the table.

"Thank you." Remembering his manners, he pulled his hat from his head and contemplated what to do with it. He should have taken it off in the vestibule and left it on the table. Anxious to sample the food in front of him, he shoved the Stetson on his lap before picking up his fork. He bowed his head in a quick, but silent prayer. When he looked up, the ladies were watching him.

"We said grace earlier with the girls," Maggie explained.

The food was delicious. The eggs were fluffy, and the ham was cooked exactly right. It was one of the best meals Owen had eaten in a long time.

"Here, help yourself to a biscuit or two." Mrs. Lamb slid a platter filled with biscuits in his direction. "Take as many as you please. We have plenty."

Belinda rose from the table, with a coffee cup. The early morning sunlight filtered through the window, casting shadows across the room as she moved to the big stove in the corner of the kitchen. She poured herself a cup and turned to look at him. "Would you care for some coffee?"

"Sure, so long as it isn't any trouble." For a man who never learned to cook for himself, he was in heaven.

"We are blessed." Belinda set a cup of coffee down for him and returned to her seat. "Mrs. Lamb does all our cooking."

Owen glanced up to give the elderly woman an appreciative smile and then paused. Maggie was no longer in the room. Perhaps she went to check on the children.

"I brought some rolls from Swenson's for you all." At least she had set the box on the table before leaving the room. "Help yourselves."

"Thank you. Don't mind if I do." Belinda opened the lid and removed a pastry from the container. "I love having a cinnamon roll with my morning coffee."

"Good, I'm glad." His gaze strayed toward the door. *Will Maggie be coming back?* He turned his attention to the women being so kind to him. "I sure do appreciate your sharing your breakfast with me this morning."

"You're welcome. I enjoy cooking." Mrs. Lamb helped herself to a cinnamon roll. "I've cooked for large crowds and small. Honestly, I've found it's easier to cook for a large group."

"Is that your dog I saw out back behind the jailhouse?" Belinda finished her roll and worked at brushing loose crumbs to the center of her plate.

"It is if you're talking about the Blue Heeler. His name is Buster."

"He's a nice dog." Belinda looked toward the window above the sink. From the west side of the building, the back of his office was visible, as well as the eastern wall of the jailhouse. "I wasn't sure what to think at first, but he wagged his tail and came right up to me the other night."

"He's a well-behaved dog. One of the best I've ever had." Buster was a good judge of character. If he presented himself to Belinda, then she must be all right. Owen glanced toward the door. It didn't look as if Maggie planned to join them. It didn't make any difference. She wasn't the reason he'd stopped by. "Thank you for the meal. If there's anything I can do to help, please let me know."

"I'm so glad you came to visit." Mrs. Lamb rose and poured herself another cup of coffee. "We're having trouble with the water pump."

"What seems to be the problem?" There had never been any trouble with the church pump before as far as he could recall.

"Well, we managed to get a few drops to come out the other night but ended up going to the well for water since."

"It sounds like the leathers have dried out.

That can happen when the pump goes a long time without being used." Owen glanced around the room until he spotted a pail. "If that's all it is, it will only take a moment for me to get it started again."

He carried the bucket to the outside well and filled it before returning to the kitchen. "If this doesn't work, we may need to replace a rod or two."

This would be an easy fix. The other would require most of the day to repair. The check valve kept the suction pipe full of water. The suction pipe was attached to the bottom of the hand pump and was easy to reach.

"We tried priming the pump." Maggie appeared from out of nowhere.

Owen paused to give her a nod. All three children were with her. She looked doubtful as she watched him return to the hand pump.

"If a check valve isn't used, the water in the pipe will drain back into the well. For it to work, it must be kept filled with water. When priming doesn't work, it may be the leather checks have dried out."

Owen poured water over the leathers and waited a moment to allow the liquid to soak into the dried-out rings. He set the pail onto the table and then shot the ladies a playful shrug. "Let's hope this works."

He pumped the handle several times until a trickle of water started to flow. Determined to make the device work for them, he continued to pump until a strong, steady flow of water poured out from the pipe.

"Hurray!" The two little girls waved their arms over their heads and cheered.

"Thank you, Mr. Somers." The smile on Mrs. Lamb's face was contagious. "How can we ever thank you?"

"There's no need to thank me, but I'd appreciate it if you called me Owen or Sheriff. It's what all the folks in town call me." He almost added it was his job, but it wasn't. He was the sheriff, not the handyman. The memory of the savory meal was still fresh in his mind. "Thank you again for breakfast. It's been a while since I ate a decent home-cooked meal."

"We'll need to remedy that again sometime soon." Mrs. Lamb headed for the door. "I noticed a little rose bush in the alley. I plan to see what I can do to get her to grow."

The two little girls began to giggle and chase after each other. The room wasn't very large and being filled with people made it seem smaller. One of the twins bumped into a chair, ramming it into the table. A fork and spoon landed on the floor.

"Katie, is it time to finish the story you started reading this morning?" Maggie gave the teenager a hopeful look.

"It sure is." She reached her hands out, and the girls each eagerly grabbed on to one. "Let's go to our room and find out what happens next to the little bunny."

"Hurray." One of the twins hopped on one foot as they headed for the door.

The other tried to imitate her sister but fell. Katie scooped the little one up and all three left the kitchen.

Maggie lingered. "We really do appreciate your help."

"It wasn't much. I just put some fresh water into the well."

"I've noticed there aren't any restaurants in town, but still I find it surprising you haven't had a home-cooked meal in a while."

"I don't have much in the way of a house. As the sheriff, I'm allotted living quarters in the back half of the jail." The simple life they lived out here in the woods must seem strange to these city folks, but he wouldn't trade it for anything. "I do have a stove, but the most cooking I do is to open a can of beans."

"Don't you have any family in town?"

"I was born and raised right here. Last

year my parents moved over near Hot Springs for my father's health."

Her face paled when he mentioned his father's health. Doubt? Surprise? He couldn't tell which.

Some folks thought the healing powers of the mineral springs were a hoax. "The springs are supposed to help his arthritis pain. I get down to see them every so often. It's only a three-day ride from here."

She cleared her throat and gave him a polite smile. "So, you don't have any brothers or sisters?"

"No. I only have one brother. He's married and lives up north." Owen needed to send a letter to him with the next mail run. There was plenty of news to share. "How about you?"

"What about me?"

"Do you have any brothers or sisters?"

Maggie opened her mouth to answer, but Mrs. Lamb returned to the kitchen, followed by Belinda, who carried a large box. "Look what we just received."

"Here, let me help you with that." Owen took the box from Belinda and set it on the kitchen table.

"Thank you." She pulled back the flaps and peered inside. "It's another delivery from the Women's Church Committee."

Maggie and Mrs. Lamb moved closer to the table. All the excitement brought Katie and the twins back into the kitchen. The two little ones smiled with anticipation as they watched the unveiling. Owen got his first glimpse of what a difference the town's generosity made in the lives of those who had little or nothing.

"This looks like a box for Mrs. Lamb." Belinda looked at Hannah and Esther and shook her head. She batted her eyelids and her mouth drooped with an exaggerated look of sorrow. "It's full of food items."

"Oh, let me have a look." Mrs. Lamb's interest was evident as she sifted through the supplies. She pulled out a jar of canned tomatoes and a can of lima beans and then dug deeper. "Here's some pork. I see everything I need to make a nice pot of Brunswick stew. It's been a while since I've eaten any. Why don't we have stew for dinner tonight?"

Maggie smiled as if the woman's joy pleased her. The blue-eyed beauty appeared to be the one who held them all together. He was surprised she'd spent time speaking with him. Until now, he'd gotten the impression she wanted nothing to do with him.

Maggie picked up one of the can goods and took a long look at the words on the label. "I've never heard of Brunswick stew."

"My grandmother used to make it when I was a little boy." Owen's mouth watered at the memory of Granny's cooking.

"Well, then, in that case, you be sure to stop by for dinner tonight." Mrs. Lamb pulled more items from the box. "We'll be eating around six."

"I'll make sure to have my evening rounds finished by then." He returned the bucket to the corner where he found it and then tipped his hat before leaving. He let himself out and walked through the sanctuary. The women had a nice setup and seemed to get along. It was hard to believe less than two days ago the town had been in an uproar over a few folks needing a place to stay.

Maggie cleared off the table while Belinda heated a pan of water to clean the dishes. Katie and the twins had already finished off the last of the cinnamon rolls. It was nice to have the pump working, but it meant they would be spending an evening with the sheriff. So long as he didn't ask too many questions, everything should be OK.

Belinda was tight-lipped and wary of strangers, so there shouldn't be any problem there. The twins were likely to ask a lot of questions as they often did, but they didn't know anything out of the ordinary. Katie's shyness would keep her quiet. Mrs. Lamb was the only weak spot. So friendly and folksy, she might let something slip unintentionally. Maggie would have to keep a close watch over everyone while their guest was present.

"The community is very generous when it comes to giving away food." Mrs. Lamb sorted through the newest box. She organized the items and stored them in the pantry. "We'll have to find a way to repay their kindness."

"I agree." Maggie placed a stack of plates and silverware next to the sink. She glanced around the small kitchen. It was cozy and they seemed to spend a lot of time together in this room. Her gaze fell on Katie and the twins. Katie was helping Esther draw the letter "A" on her new slate. Beside them, Hannah yawned widely as her head began to bob.

"It looks as though someone is ready for a nap." Maggie pointed at Esther, who fought to keep her eyes open as well. "Make that two someones."

"Why don't we put them down in my room?" Mrs. Lamb picked up Esther and hummed in the sleepy-eyed girl's ear. "I believe it's cooler in there, and I plan to do some reading for a while."

Maggie scooped up Hannah and followed Mrs. Lamb into her room. The window had been left partway open, and a nice breeze flowed into the room. Both girls nodded off as soon as they were put on the bed.

"Are you sure you don't mind having them in here?" Maggie kept her voice low.

"Of course not. I'll sit here and read one of the books we found in the boxes."

"Which book is that?"

"It's called *Recipes from the Ozarks.*" Mrs. Lamb grinned and gave Maggie a wink. "Learning what people like to eat tells you a lot about them."

"Well, in that case, since we're having company for supper, I think I'll visit the pastry shop across the way and see what they might have for us to serve for dessert."

Maggie had been able to keep some money hidden on her person when the wagon train had been robbed. She kept it quiet because the twins, and now Katie, were counting on her to feed and care for them. It wasn't much, but she could afford a simple treat for them to share with the sheriff.

"Since Esther and Hannah are asleep, can I come with you?" Katie stood in the doorway. The teen was such a help to all of them.

Hannah and Esther looked up to her as a big sister. She was their sister now.

"Of course you can if Mrs. Lamb doesn't mind keeping watch until we get back." Although it wasn't the largest room, Mrs. Lamb's was the most comfortable. The girls would nap for at least an hour, maybe two.

"They'll be fine." The older woman waved her hand toward the door. "Go on. We'll be here waiting when you get back."

Swenson's Pastry Shop was still open, but it was late enough in the day that there were no customers. Maggie led the way across the street after a buckboard filled with a load of straw passed by. Set back from the boardwalk, three steps led up to a porch where two chairs faced the street. The front entrance of the building was narrow, but inside, a pleasant and inviting appearance welcomed customers. The aroma of baked bread flooded Maggie's senses with a warm, happy sensation.

"Well, good afternoon." A gray-haired woman about Mrs. Lamb's age approached the counter. She turned and called toward the back. "Anna Grace, come on out. We have visitors."

"Hello." Maggie couldn't help but smile as she drew closer to the display of bread and cakes.

Katie stayed close by her side.

"I'm Sadie Mae Swenson, and this is my sister Anna Grace."

"It's nice to meet you both." Everyone she'd spoken with had only praise for the two elderly sisters. "I'm Maggie, and this is Katie."

"Well, it's nice to finally get to meet you. We haven't had an opportunity to come by to say hello. Our hours here make us early to bed and early to rise."

"You must be healthy, wealthy, and wise then." Katie spoke in an audible voice not much louder than a whisper.

The Swenson sisters laughed in unison. The sound was pleasant to the ear, like a duet.

Maggie was surprised by the girl's humor and willingness to speak to strangers.

"I'm not sure about wealthy or wise, but we are healthy." Anna Grace pulled several cookies from one of the displays and wrapped them in paper before handing them to Katie. "Here's a treat for you and the little ones. I planned to take them over later. You've saved me a trip."

"Thank you." A rare grin brightened Katie's face. She took the gift and carefully placed the cookies into her dress pocket.

Sadie Mae turned her attention toward

Maggie. Her eyes sparkled with humor and kindness. "How can we help you?"

"We thought we'd purchase something for dessert after our dinner tonight." Maggie examined the display of food on the counter and tables. "Do you have any cakes or pies?"

"Of course. Is it a special occasion?" Sadie Mae waited patiently for her to make a choice. "Like someone's birthday?"

"No. Mrs. Lamb has invited the sheriff to eat supper with us tonight. We have staples for a meal but nothing to make sweets with."

"I know for a fact Sheriff Owen loves blueberries." Sadie Mae came around from the other side of the counter and showed Maggie a table with pies. "We have one blueberry pie left, if you'd like that."

"It sounds perfect." She followed the shop owner back to the register.

"How can you have so many different foods at one time?" Katie's eyes were wide with wonder as she surveyed the loaves of bread and desserts.

"It does take some planning. We come in early in the morning and get the dough started. We always have bread, but our treats vary from day to day." Anna Grace remained at the counter and glanced behind her. "Would you like to take a look around?"

"Yes, I would." Katie looked at Maggie

for approval.

"Why don't you both come on back with me." Anna Grace waved her hand, inviting them into the large kitchen. "It won't take but a moment."

"We start early in the morning, long before the sun rises, to make the dough." Anna Grace pointed toward two cots near the back door. "We take a nap while the bread rises. Kneading the dough is the hardest and takes a lot of time, but we take turns. Preparing the rolls and loaves is my favorite part of the job."

Pots and pans hung from hooks on the wall next to two large cast-iron ranges. Bags of flour and sugar were stored on shelves. The floor looked freshly swept, and the smell of sugar and cinnamon still lingered in the air.

"Your kitchen looks so well organized." Maggie was impressed with how clean they kept their shop. Preparing the food and waiting on customers must take a great deal of time, and yet the kitchen was spotless.

"We've been doing this all our lives, and it runs smoothly, thanks to the things our father and mother taught us."

"It must take a lot of preparation to prepare so many different treats."

"Our range requires a great deal of maintenance. The sheriff keeps us up and running. The oven doesn't have a reliable thermometer, but, with Owen's help, we've created a way to check the temperature."

"How do you do that?" Katie moved to stand in front of the range. Her eyes sparkled with interest.

"We place a sheet of paper in the oven before we light it. Once it turns a dark shade of amber, we know the oven is hot enough for baking breads and cakes."

Anna Grace led them back out to the display counter. "Feel free to request some of your favorite desserts, and we'll see what we can do to make them."

"Thank you for letting us see how you make your pastries." Katie gave a short curtsy, and her face warmed with awe.

"You're most welcome, dear." Anna Grace's smile glowed with delight as she leaned in to hug the teenager. "Come back anytime. We have a little house behind the shop, but, as you can imagine, we spend most of our time here."

Maggie held the door open and waited for Katie to exit first. They were met by a cool gust of wind. It was nice to have a break in the weather. The air outside was warm, as usual, but dry for a change. The smell of what she assumed was wild crocus carried on the gentle breeze. A red bird flew over-head and landed on the top branch of the walnut tree outside the old church building. For the first time, she was thankful for hav-ing found her way to West Ridge.

Maggie studied her reflection in the small mirror above the dresser in her room. She wrinkled her nose. The high humidity energized her unruly curls. She pulled a brush through her hair and then pinned the sides back, letting the remaining locks hang free. Her face looked too round when her hair was pulled up into a bun. Thankfully, the people in West Ridge didn't seem to be fixated on how women should dress or wear their hair.

"Aunt Maggie, you look pretty." Hannah held up the picture she was drawing to show her. There was a smiling face with squiggly circles above it and on both sides. Maggie smiled and nodded. It was a perfect depic-tion of how her hair looked.

The slate board was one of Hannah's favorite toys. Esther still napped on the bed they shared. The twins didn't always take a second nap in the day, but, with so much going on, it was no surprise the little girl was worn out. As much as Maggie enjoyed the quiet, if she let the child sleep much longer, she wouldn't be able to fall asleep at bedtime.

Maggie took a seat in the chair beside the bed and motioned for Hannah to sit on her lap. "Would you like me to fix your hair?"

"Will you make me pretty, too?" Hannah dropped the piece of chalk she'd been using and crawled onto Maggie's lap.

"You are pretty." Maggie ran the brush over the child's hair as she prepared to fix it like her own.

"Am I pretty like my mommy?"

"Yes." Maggie blinked away the moisture in her eyes. "Just like your mommy."

She missed her sister. How proud Sarah would be to see how well her girls were adapting to the changes in their lives. Both Hannah and Esther were young but had seen their fair share of heartache. They were close and had each other as well as Maggie. And Katie.

Maggie and Sarah had been close too, but their age difference had been greater, making Sarah more of a mother figure to Maggie. Maggie had looked up to her sister and was grateful for her help when their parents died. It was her turn to repay the favor by raising Sarah's little girls. An honor she didn't take lightly.

Thinking of her sister reminded Maggie

of what Owen said about his father moving so he could take advantage of the hot springs' healing warmth. It had been her brother-in-law's idea for them to head west for California to see if the warm weather would cure Sarah. They never got the opportunity to find out.

The door opened, and Katie entered the room. Her cheeks were rosy, and her eyes beamed with happiness. "Mrs. Lamb is pleased with the pie we picked out."

"I think we all will be when it comes time to eat dessert."

Maggie enjoyed teasing the somber teenager. Anything to make her smile. The child was much too serious for her age. Life had given her a tough row to hoe. It was something Maggie vowed to rectify.

Esther started to stir. Maggie glanced at the watch piece she wore on a chain around her neck. It had belonged to her mother. Their guest would be arriving soon. Her heart skipped a beat, but she brushed off any such foolishness. Sheriff Owen was nice-looking and easy to like, but a lawman was the last person she or any of them needed. He seemed determined to learn all he could about them, and if he did, it would mean trouble for her and the girls.

■ ■ ■ ■

"Welcome, Sheriff," Maggie answered the knock at the door. It was nice of him to announce his presence rather than march into the sanctuary.

The old church building was a familiar place for the citizens of West Ridge. She feared some would have no problem walking right in as if they didn't understand it was now someone's home.

"How are you this evening?" He removed his hat and held it.

"We're fine, thank you." Maggie cleared her throat and started across the sanctuary. The sound of his boots pounding the hardwood floor echoed off the walls as they marched through the empty auditorium. He reached the other side of the large room first and waited for her before opening the door leading to their living quarters.

They paused halfway down the dimly lit hall, just outside the kitchen entrance. Chatter and children's laughter drifted through the open doorway. A whiff of Mrs. Lamb's cooking filled her senses with pleasure.

"I certainly appreciate you all inviting me to supper." Sheriff Owen twisted the brim of his hat and looked around as if unsure what he should do with it.

"Here, let me take care of that for you." She took the battered Stetson from him and placed it on a table they'd moved to the hall. A flower vase and Bible were placed there to give the long corridor more of a homey feel.

"Thank you." Their gazes met and held until Maggie looked away.

"Come on in, Sheriff Owen," Mrs. Lamb called from the kitchen. "You're right on time."

"It sure does smell good in here." A smile spread across his features, and a dimple appeared along the right side of his face.

They entered the kitchen.

"That's the food you smell." Esther glanced up from her drawing.

"Is that right?" The lawman walked over to where the twins sat and looked over Esther's shoulder. "Hmm, what are you working on?"

"It's a . . ."

"Wait. Don't tell me." He raised his right hand. "Let me guess."

Esther lowered her piece of chalk and waited.

The sheriff tilted his head to one side and then the other while he wriggled his lips. "Looks to me like a jackrabbit sitting on a rock overlooking the river."

"What?" Esther gasped, and both girls broke into giggles.

"No?" His brow creased, and he tapped his finger against his lips for a moment. "Oh, I see now. It's a cow grazing out in the pasture."

Esther slapped the palm of her hand against her forehead and groaned. Hannah threw back her head and laughed. It was nice to know the sheriff was good at entertaining children. He seemed to be a man of many talents. Maggie glanced around the room. Everyone in the kitchen was smiling. The sound of laughter was something they all needed. It had been a long time since she'd enjoyed a lighthearted moment with her family and friends.

"You can sit here, Sheriff Owen." Belinda motioned toward the chair at the head of the table as she set down a plate.

"Thank you." He left the twins and took the seat assigned to him.

"You're most welcome." Mrs. Lamb put a plate of rolls in the center of the table. "We're happy to have you join us."

He shot Mrs. Lamb a grin, which brought his dimples back to life. "I don't recall ever passing up a home-cooked meal."

"You don't get to eat out much, I gather."

"We don't have a restaurant in West Ridge." The sheriff took a deep breath and grinned. He seemed pleased by the smell of Mrs. Lamb's stew. "Never have had one, either."

"That is surprising." Maggie took a seat next to Esther, far from the lawman. She found it hard to believe a town this size didn't have a place for people to dine.

"The town's full of bachelors. Those blessed enough to have a wife cook for them aren't about to share." Owen took his napkin and placed it on his lap. "There's only the pastry shop. You'll notice a long line of customers there each morning. The Swenson sisters are getting up in age, and I expect they'll be looking to sell out or hire help eventually."

Maggie helped Esther set her drawing tools aside and then motioned for both girls to fold their hands and put them in their laps.

Mrs. Lamb took a seat next to the lawman. "Katie is good at making loaves of bread and pastries."

A rosy hue spread along the teenager's cheeks as she took a seat between Belinda and Hannah.

"Sheriff?" Mrs. Lamb placed her hand on his arm. "Why don't you lead us in blessing our meal."

"Certainly. I'd be honored to." He bowed his head. "Lord, we thank You for this food we're about to eat and ask that You please bless it for the nourishment of our bodies. Amen."

"Amen." The ladies spoke in unison.

Belinda stood and scooped steaming hot stew into bowls and passed them around. The sheriff seemed comfortable sitting at a table full of women he didn't know. The man was good-natured and likable. If not for the threat his position held over them, she wouldn't have minded the thought of getting to know him better.

"This stew smells delicious, Mrs. Lamb." He raised his spoon in her direction before taking a bite. A smile stretched across his face as he chewed. After he swallowed, his eyes filled with admiration. He set his spoon next to the bowl and picked up his napkin. He wiped his chin and then looked directly at Mrs. Lamb. "Have you ever considered starting a restaurant?"

"I'm afraid I wouldn't know how to run a business." The older woman sounded a bit disappointed, as if she missed cooking for a crowd. "Fixing the food itself is what I know to do best."

"How has the pump been working?" The

sheriff looked toward the sink he'd worked on that morning. "Has it given you any more trouble?"

"No. It's been working fine since you fixed it."

"Good. If there's anything else you need help with, just let me know."

"There is one thing," Maggie spoke up, thankful for the opportunity to address the one thing heavy on her mind.

The sheriff stopped smearing butter on a roll he'd chosen from the bread platter and gave her his full attention. "What is that?"

"Would it be possible for us to have a lock installed?"

"A lock?" His mouth fell open. He couldn't have looked more flabbergasted if she'd asked him to board up all the windows. His eyes narrowed, and he set his knife onto the table. "Has anyone been bothering you?"

"Yes. I mean no. No one has bothered us, but I think we would all feel more comfortable at night if we were able to lock the place up." Maggie squared her shoulders and glanced toward the twins and Katie. She didn't want to sound unthankful or suspicious of their new neighbors, but she was responsible for the care and safety of half the people in the room. "Maybe it just comes from living in the city. Everyone has a lock on their door."

"I understand." The look of doubt on his face contradicted his words, but at least he seemed willing to take care of it for them. "I'll see about having one put in tomorrow."

"Thank you." She was relieved he would get to it so soon.

When they finished their food, Belinda cleared away most of the dishes while Katie carried the pie over to the table. Maggie picked up a knife and cut a large slice for their guest. She handed the plate to Belinda and nodded for her to pass it to the sheriff.

"Thank you." He inhaled deeply and set the plate in front of him. "This pie smells as good as the ones the Swenson sisters make for the pastry shop."

"It is from the pastry shop." Katie's sweet giggle warmed Maggie's heart. The teenager looked pleased by his accurate assumption.

"Blueberry is my favorite." Owen forked a large bite from his plate.

"They let us look around and told us how they make the bread." Katie gushed. It was unusual to see her comfortable around new people, especially men, but the friendly lawman seemed to have put her at ease without any effort. Their visit to the pastry shop sparked a light in the teen as well. "My mother loved to bake."

"I'm sure she made wonderful treats for you and your family." Mrs. Lamb smiled.

"I hope Miss Swenson and her sister will let me visit them again."

"I'm sure they will." The sheriff forked another bite. "They love having visitors."

At least he didn't ask more about Katie's family. The less anyone else knew, the better.

5

Owen crossed his arms over his chest and bit back a sigh. What started as a simple task was taking longer than expected. He had been so sure Carter's Mercantile would have what he needed.

"Just what sort of lock are you looking for?" Jessup Carter's face scrunched up like a prune whenever he was confused. The shopkeeper seemed surprised by the unusual request. Folks around these parts didn't have much call for security devices. There was the bank, of course, and a few other businesses on Main Street needing to secure their business after hours, but, for the most part, West Ridge was a lock-free community.

Owen took a deep breath to keep his irritation at bay. It wasn't Jessup's fault he'd promised Maggie to take care of her problem so fast. "You know, just an average everyday lock and bolt."

Carter's Mercantile was well stocked with every imaginable type of food, a dozen or so bolts of different colored cloth for sewing, pots and pans galore, as well as most types of general equipment required to meet his customers' needs. Owen knew this for a fact because he had just perused every shelf in the store without finding what he wanted. "I'll need the complete doorknob and key."

"But the jailhouse already has a lock." Jessup scratched the back of his balding head, a sure sign he was getting perturbed.

It was true, the door to Owen's office had a lock, although he never used it. The front door could be locked if there were ever a prisoner behind bars and he had to leave the building unattended. There wasn't a lock on the back door of the building, which led to his sleeping quarters. So, in theory, anyone could walk in the back door and into the jailhouse, even if the front was locked. It wasn't something he needed to be concerned about. The last time anyone was locked up in West Ridge was long before he became sheriff.

"Are you thinking about putting a lock on the back door too?"

"It's not for me." Hopefully, Jessup would be able to find something. If not, they would have to order one and it would take a few weeks to arrive.

"Oh, all right then." Jessup gave the top of the counter a quick tap with the palm of his right hand before he pivoted to go into the storeroom. "I'll see what I can find."

The sound of boxes being shifted and rearranged in the other room intensified while Owen waited. The only customer in the store, he stared out the side window. He could see the jailhouse across the street and part of the large oak tree out in front of the old church building. Maggie's request for a door lock puzzled him. Just when he thought the ice was starting to melt, she went and asked for the least friendly item he could imagine. Did she need a lock to feel safe or was she sending him a message to keep his distance?

"Found one," Jessup called from the storeroom. There were more sounds of boxes being shuffled before the owner returned to the counter. Sweat on his brow and his glasses skewed, he plopped a box next to the register. "I knew I had one back there somewhere."

Owen paid for his purchase and stepped outside. Buster waited for him on the boardwalk. It was warm out but not yet hot enough to keep the birds quiet. The constant sounds of chirping reminded him of his parents, especially his mother. She kept bird feeders filled throughout the year to keep her feathered friends fed. His father could identify any variety of bird that happened to cross his path. The cardinal was Owen's favorite. His grandmother said whenever he saw a red bird it was a reminder from God that He cared.

The idea might sound silly to some folks, but the message stuck and took root in his heart. He couldn't help thinking of God's amazing love every time a rosy-hued bird flew by. A gust of warm air blew in from the south. It looked like a good day to slip down to the river during his lunch break.

"Let's go, Buster." Owen slapped the side of his leg, and they crossed the street.

When they reached the old church building, he paused. There had never been a lock on the church door before, but the women needed to feel safe. He debated whether to knock or just start installing the lock when the door opened.

"Good morning, Sheriff." Maggie stood in the doorway. She stepped back to allow him into the foyer. The dark-blue dress she wore drew his attention to her striking eyes. They would be an amazing sight if the smile she pasted on her face ever reached them. There was a calico cat in her arms. "The girls and I were watching for you."

Esther and Hannah peeked out from behind their aunt and waved.

Buster waited outside. His tail wagged, and he let out a whine. "Mind if my dog joins us?"

"Of course not." Maggie tilted her head and smiled at the dog. "So long as he doesn't mind cats."

"It looks as though you've found yourselves a pet." Owen set the lock on the table and motioned for Buster to enter. The dog was good around cats. Owen had seen the stray kitten around town and set milk out for it on more than one occasion.

"Mrs. Lamb found him." Maggie rubbed her hand along the animal's furry back. "She wanted us to ask if it was all right to keep an animal inside."

"I don't see why not." He had no claim on the creature and was glad it had a home. "Does he have a name?"

"We call him Cinnamon." One of the twins, he couldn't tell them apart, spoke up proudly.

"When he sleeps, he curls into a ball and looks like a cinnamon roll." Her sister grinned as if eager to join in with an explanation.

"Oh, there's your dog." One of the twins

knelt and held her hand out toward Buster. The Blue Heeler wagged his tail.

"OK." Owen nodded and the dog timidly walked toward the children. Both girls patted Buster on his head, and he took turns licking their hands.

"Hannah and Esther have some artwork they would like to show you."

The twins wore matching grins. Each one flapped a piece of paper in the air.

Buster stepped back and sat. The curious canine tilted its head to the side and kept a close eye on the girls.

One of them thrust a drawing in Owen's face. "What do you think this is?"

He peered at the interesting markings on the page and took a moment to speculate on the artist's intent. "Looks like a snowman lost in a blizzard to me."

Their aunt's snicker caught him by surprise. He swung his gaze in her direction. There was laughter in her eyes. Loose strands of dark-brown hair framed her face.

His heart stilled and then raced.

"Mine next." The other twin hopped up and down, demanding her turn.

Owen tore his focus from Maggie and acknowledged the little girl's work of art. It took him a moment to clear his thoughts and come up with an amusing title. "I do believe that is a red bird singing from a treetop."

The child's brow creased, and she took a long look at the drawing. She and her sister shared a glance and shrugged. Before he could explain his love of red birds, the cat jumped from Maggie's arms and dashed toward the hall.

"Girls, we better be going so Sheriff Owen can get his work done." She took her nieces' hands and started for the door. After taking a few steps, she paused and looked over her shoulder. "Thank you. We appreciate your help."

Alone with the lock and a memory of the mysterious woman's laughter, Owen set to work. If a doorknob with a lockset put her mind at peace, then so be it.

Maggie wiped the back of her hand across her forehead and placed the empty pail in the sink. As she pumped water, she silently thanked God for sending Owen to fix the dried-out mechanism. Not wanting to get close to the lawman didn't mean she couldn't appreciate his help.

She'd spent the good part of the last half an hour filling bucket after bucket of water. The kettle on the cook stove let out a cloud of steam and gave a shrill whistle. Once this last bucket was warmed, the water would be ready for the twins.

Saturday night baths were a lot of work, but they were all going to church in the morning. The metal tub she and Katie found in the church storeroom was deep and looked brand new. When they moved in, Mrs. Todd told them to make use of anything they found. After weeks on the trail, they were all in need of a good washing.

Hannah and Esther always looked forward to bath time. Both girls sat side by side on chairs next to the tub. They swung their legs back and forth as they waited for the water to heat. Maggie poured the last pail and added the hot water. She stooped to run her fingers through the liquid, stirring the hot and cold streams together. "All right, girls." Maggie straightened and moved next to her nieces to help them undress and climb over the side of the washbasin. "Remember you can't take too long. Katie's next in line."

She gave them a moment to play while she stoked the fire in the cook stove to heat water for Katie's bath.

"It's my turn to have my hair washed first, Aunt Maggie." Esther slapped her hands against the top of the water, causing ripples to spread out to the sides of the tub.

The girls insisted whoever endured the chore of having their hair cleaned first ended up with more time to play. She had tried several times to explain to them it didn't matter who had their hair washed first because their playtime would add up to be the same. The girls weren't convinced.

"All right." Maggie knelt beside the tub. "Scoot over here and let me get your hair wet."

She scooped water in a large bowl and poured it over Esther's hair. Both girls had beautiful blonde hair, like their father. They'd inherited their blue eyes from both parents. Maggie's heart panged at the memory of the family lost to her. Although Sarah was a few years older, their bond had been close. If not for the twins, she would be all alone in the world.

"Will they like us at church?" Hannah poured water from a tin cup over her hand and watched the liquid splash.

"I don't see why they wouldn't." Maggie finished rinsing the soap from Esther's hair and twisted her hair gently to wring out the excess water. "Everyone in town has been very kind to us."

"Are there other children we can play with?" Esther scooted over to the other end of the tub, and Hannah inched her way toward Maggie.

"I have seen some older children in town." The teenage boys who carried boxes in for Mrs. Todd were the only youth she'd met so far. "But I'm sure there will be other children there."

Satisfied with her answer, the girls turned to cleaning and splashing while she washed Hannah's hair. It didn't take long for the water to cool. "All right, time to get out."

She helped them dry off and get dressed while another kettle of water finished heating on the stove.

"Who's ready for a bedtime story?" Mrs. Lamb slipped into the kitchen followed by Katie. Story time with the wise woman became a nightly routine they all looked forward to. The girls loved to hear the Bible stories Mrs. Lamb made so entertaining. Spending time with the little ones put a smile on the older woman's lips and a light in her eyes. Maggie enjoyed the bit of peace and quiet it allowed her.

It was Katie's turn for a bath. Maggie added hot water to the tub. "Do you need any help with your clothes?"

"My right arm is still a bit sore. Can you help me pull the dress over my head?"

"Yes, of course." Maggie undid the long

row of buttons running down the back of the girl's simple frock. "Make sure you have Belinda put some more salve on your legs before you go to bed."

"I will." Katie's submissive reply reminded Maggie of the harsh treatment the child had endured from her aunt and uncle.

She took her time raising the cotton cloth over the girl's head. There was still a bruise the size of a man's hand visible on her right arm. The dark colors were fading away, as were the long red lines crisscrossing the backs of the teenager's legs. It wasn't Maggie's first time to see the markings, but still, she winced at the sight.

Maggie let out a weary sigh as she slid down the wall to join Belinda on the hallway floor outside the kitchen. Everyone had taken a turn in the bath. The girls were in bed fast asleep, and gentle snoring sounds came from Mrs. Lamb's room. Maggie was exhausted but too wound up to go to sleep.

"We might want to rethink this schedule before next Saturday night rolls around." Belinda pressed the back of her head against the wall and closed her eyes.

"I agree." Maggie had already given the issue some thought. "I think the twins can bathe on Friday nights and use a washrag to clean up on Saturday."

"I hope the people of West Ridge appreciate all the effort we put into making ourselves presentable for church tomorrow."

"I imagine it's a common occurrence for most everyone in town." Maggie thought of all the water pumping that must take place on Saturday nights.

"I'm not so sure." Belinda opened her eyes and sat up straight. "I've heard stories about people who live in these hills."

The spooky tone in Belinda's voice sent a shudder down Maggie's back. She sounded so serious and glum.

"What sort of stories?"

"Oh, I'm sure you've heard of how they live by a different set of rules and how people in the hills take care of their own."

"No, I haven't."

"Well, I guess people from New York know more about these things than you all in Boston." Belinda's teasing came as no surprise. New York City was much larger than Boston. "The people in West Ridge aren't exactly what I expected is all I meant to say."

"What did you expect?"

Belinda glanced around the dimly lit hall and whispered, "There's talk about people who choose to live in the hills."

"Really?" Maggie raised her hand to her mouth to cover a yawn. "What do they say about people who live in the hills?"

"Haven't you ever heard the term, 'hill people?' "

It didn't sound familiar. "I don't think so. What does it mean?"

"That is what they call people who live in the hills."

It might be due to being exhausted, but the conversation was starting to sound like nonsense. Maggie was having a hard time understanding what sounded like rambling.

"I've always heard people who live in the hills don't work for a living. They like to shoot up the town on Saturday nights and dress however they please."

"I haven't seen anyone around here who isn't willing to work." The people in West Ridge were some of the hardest-working people Maggie had ever seen. The chicken coop out back was a testament to that fact. If what Mrs. Todd said was true, it had been constructed in less than a day by one man. The people in the community dressed fine, even if it was a bit plain compared to back home. "Other than the hunter's rifle on our way into town, I've never heard one shot fired since we've been here."

"That's what I mean. The people here take

121

care of each other but in a law-abiding fashion." Belinda pushed herself up and stood. "I remember my uncle telling a story once about a man who dared upset the people in a town filled with folks who lived in the hills. The man was never heard from again."

Maggie rose to stand beside Belinda and let out another wide yawn. They would have a hectic morning getting everyone ready for church. "I can't imagine that type of behavior being accepted today. It sounds like something out of the dark ages."

"My father believed the rumors were started by the mountain people themselves because they wanted to keep strangers away."

Keeping strangers away sounded reasonable. Keeping anyone from asking too many questions was what she wanted most.

6

Owen tugged on the cuffs of his long-sleeve shirt, pulling each one until it reached his wrist. His shoes were polished and his hair combed back. His mother would be proud. She said he looked dashing when he dressed up. But still, it was too hot for a suit coat this time of year. His broad shoulders and long arms made it difficult to get shirts to fit right, but Mother was a good seamstress and managed to keep him supplied with going-to-meeting clothes. He made a mental note to write a letter to his folks before the day was over. The mail wagon was due to come by tomorrow afternoon, and he already had a letter ready for his brother.

"All right, buddy." He opened the door and let Buster out into the backyard. "I'll be back in a few hours. Keep an eye on things while I'm gone."

The dog tilted his head as he listened to every word. His tongue hung from his mouth, and he wagged his tail. Too bad dogs weren't allowed in church. Buster was apt to pay more attention than some of the folks.

Sunday mornings were special in West Ridge. The Swenson's Pastry Shop was closed, but Sadie Mae and Anna Grace always doubled their Saturday wares for folks who counted on them for their breakfast. The street swarmed with carts and horses ridden by those who lived on the outskirts of town. Most of the congregation lived within walking distance.

Out on the boardwalk, he took a deep breath and surveyed the busy activity on Main Street. Sunday. It was like no other day of the week. A sense of anticipation permeated the air. The parade of carts and buckboards rolled down the dirt road headed to the new church building at the east end of town.

After some debate, they had decided to move the location of the meeting house to an area with shade trees and level ground, which could be used for outdoor meals as well as a play area for the children. During the week, when school was in session, the building served as the schoolhouse.

The church bells chimed. Time to get going. Owen took a glance toward the old church building just as Katie, Maggie, and her two nieces stepped out onto the boardwalk. They were all dressed for church. He had a good feeling when they'd asked him to pray over the food the other night. It was nice to know they were church-going folks.

The little girls hopped up and down as if competing to see who could go the longest on one foot. Belinda came out from the building, followed by Mrs. Lamb. The older woman wore a bright smile while Belinda's gaze darted from one side of the street to the other.

"Good morning." He tipped the brim of his hat as he started toward them. "May I escort you ladies to church?"

"Good morning, Sheriff." Maggie shot him a slight nod before she bent to pick up one of the girls. It could just be his imagination but when she spoke the word *sheriff,* it sounded as if she'd just swallowed a fly.

Mrs. Lamb straightened her hat and adjusted the string purse hanging from her arm. "We'd be proud to walk to church with you, Sheriff Owen."

Katie reached for the other child, but Belinda stepped in and scooped the little girl into her arms. "I'll carry her. I need something to do with my hands. I'm as nervous as a June bug in a chicken pen."

"There's no need for you to be nervous." He walked beside Mrs. Lamb, with Maggie and Katie leading the way. "Folks around here are looking forward to getting to know all of you better."

"I hope they aren't disappointed." Belinda's sarcasm reminded him of Rudy Brown, but the way she cuddled the little girl in her arms spoke of a warm and loving person.

"Where's your dog?" one of the twins asked.

"Buster stays out behind the jail on Sunday mornings."

"Why do you call him Buster?"

"He was one of two males in a litter of six dogs."

"Outnumbered by girls, just like West Ridge but only in reverse." Belinda seemed to find it a funny coincidence.

"Yep, pretty much."

"But why Buster?" Mrs. Lamb placed her hand on his arm.

He tucked her hand in the crook of his elbow, and a warm smile spread across her face.

"Well, you see, he was the biggest of the litter and, if you ask me, the smartest of the bunch. As they got older, the gate to their pen seemed to open on its own accord just about every night. We put them up at sunset to keep them safe but, come morning, the pups were all over the barn where we kept them. Running free, getting into everything. Finally, my brother and I decided to find out how they were getting out."

The twins had their gazes glued on Owen. Everyone in the group had slowed their steps as they gathered closer to him. He tried not to laugh as he continued.

"Jim and I shut the gate like usual and left the barn, but we came around to the back and sneaked up to the loft where we decided to camp out. We took turns keeping watch. The puppies slept most of the night, but when the old rooster started crowing, it woke them, and they wanted out. Buster went up to the gate and wiggled it back and forth, pressing the top of his head against it until the latch busted free."

"What a smart dog." Mrs. Lamb had to raise her voice to be heard over the sound of the church bells ringing.

"Yes, he is, and that's how he got his name. He was the one busting free every morning."

"We better hurry or we'll be late." Maggie spoke for the first time since they'd started walking. She sounded a bit nervous.

There was no need for her to fret. The

folks in West Ridge would be hospitable no matter what they might think or say in private.

They all picked up the pace. There wasn't much farther to go. The parking area was filled with wagons and horses. Several rigs belonged to part-time parishioners. It seemed everyone wanted to catch a glimpse of the women from the welcome wagon. A few people lingered on the lawn while most were making their way up the steps and into the meeting house.

Owen hung back and allowed the ladies to enter first. Mrs. Lamb led the charge up the steps. Pastor Irvin stood in the doorway halfway in the vestibule and halfway on the porch. It was his practice to greet everyone as they entered the building.

"Welcome." He smiled as he shook Mrs. Lamb's hand.

Belinda slipped past them, giving him a weak smile as she shifted the child in her arms.

Katie accepted the preacher's handshake with a shy nod.

Maggie paraded up to the pastor and took his hand.

"Welcome, Miss." Pastor Irvin's gentle smile had a calming effect on most anyone he spoke with. "We're so happy to have you join us today. Make yourselves at home."

Mrs. Irvin met the ladies inside the foyer nearer to the sanctuary. "I've saved a pew up front for all of you." She motioned for them to follow her.

Owen watched them leave as he took his normal seat at the back of the building, next to the door. Just in case there was trouble during the service. He could make a quiet getaway. Not as though there was ever any trouble in West Ridge.

A blur of smiles, hellos, and how-do-you-dos filled Maggie's vision and hearing as they made their way to the spot Mrs. Irvin had chosen for them. She sat at the end of the pew closest to the outer wall, with Hannah on one side and Esther sitting between her and Katie. The teenager looked lovely in her new blue dress. Mrs. Lamb had convinced the young girl to wear the striking outfit.

Their little group nearly filled the bench. It was nice to be in church. Her heart swelled with joy when the congregation stood to sing the opening hymn. Out of church for so many years, she was pleased to discover she remembered all the words to the songs she once held so dear. As a little girl, she'd sat in the front pew with Mother and Sarah, listening to Father preach. West Ridge's new church building was larger than the one on Main Street. The structure reminded Maggie of the church her father pastored years ago.

When her parents died, she went to live with Sarah and Chester. Although good Christian people, they didn't attend church regularly. After the twins came, there was little time for anything other than caring for the babies and her ailing sister.

The parishioners returned to their seats, and Hannah crawled onto Maggie's lap.

The minister stepped forward. Pastor Irvin was a tall, thin man with graying hair. He had a soft calming voice when he spoke face to face but, from the pulpit, his voice boomed, and his message would be easy to hear. He made a special point of welcoming West Ridge's newest members. He preached about loving thy neighbor. The beautiful message gave Maggie a sense of hope. West Ridge was turning out to be the perfect home for her and the girls.

At the end of the service, the pastor asked if anyone had anything they'd like to share. There was an awkward silence as if everyone were waiting. Maggie hadn't known anyone would be speaking, or she would have gladly prepared something. Of course, she had said thank you so many times, it was well-rehearsed. Her face heated as her mind scrambled for the words to say. She started to hand Hannah over to Katie, but Mrs. Lamb rose from the pew first. A wave of relief washed over Maggie.

"My friends and I want you all to know how much we appreciate the kindness of this community. You have opened your hearts to us, and we will always be in your debt. I, that is, we all hope to be able to repay your acts of kindness one day when we're able." Mrs. Lamb smiled sweetly and slowly returned to her seat.

Some of the people in the pew in front of them turned and smiled. A lady behind Maggie patted her on the shoulder, and those sitting on the other side and farther back clapped.

"We're happy to help and look forward to getting to know all of you better as well." The pastor nodded toward their pew and then looked over the crowd. "We'll be having our monthly Sunday Supper Social this evening and will use the time to officially welcome our town's newest members."

The congregation stood to sing the closing hymn, and then the crowd started to file from the pews. The pianist played quietly as the worshipers headed toward the door.

Maggie's mother had often played the recessional hymn back home. She claimed the faster she played, the faster the people moved. When she was in a hurry to get home, she picked a fast tune. Maggie's heart yearned to see her mother's smiling face.

"We're almost there." Mrs. Irvin stayed by their side as they inched their way toward the door. They were forced to stop every couple of steps as someone new pushed through the throng to introduce themselves and wish them well. Some of them she had seen in town, but it would take some time to match names to faces. Mrs. Lamb smiled and chatted with each person as if she'd known them for years. Belinda only spoke when spoken to and kept her replies short. She and Katie stayed close to Maggie and the twins as they continued toward the door.

They reached the entrance and trotted down the steps. Once they were outside, a cool breeze brushed her cheeks. Owen was right about the summer heat becoming unbearable in the middle of the day. She glanced around at the crowd of people, but there was no sign of the sheriff. He had disappeared before church started. It was safer this way. The less time they spent around him the better.

■ ■ ■ ■

"Is everyone ready?" Mrs. Lamb stood in the hallway with a box while she ushered them toward the door.

"I am." Esther sang out and took Hannah by the hand. Blonde curls danced as she tilted her head side to side. "Are you ready?"

"Me, too." Hannah swung her sister's arm back and forth and laughed.

The girls had taken a long nap and were in good spirits when they woke. The visit to church had been good for them. They met a girl and two boys around their age.

"At least we can wear cooler clothes this afternoon." Belinda shed her fancy church dress the moment they returned home from church.

"I believe we'll be eating outside under the trees where it will be much cooler as well." Maggie knelt to fix Esther's shoe.

The shoes turned out to be a little large for her. Maggie stuffed some cloth inside to help keep them on Esther's feet.

Thankfully they didn't run into the sheriff on their way to the church this time. He was nice, helpful, and wonderful with the children, but she wasn't willing to jeopardize Katie's safety for any reason or person.

A crowd had gathered on the church grounds by the time they reached the hilltop. A long table placed in the shade was covered with a variety of food. Savory smells drifted across the lawn from the plates of chicken, bread, ham, vegetables, and an assortment of desserts. Mrs. Lamb placed their contribution on the food table. The crafty woman had somehow managed to find enough time in the afternoon to make two delicious-looking lemon meringue pies.

They had been warned to bring something to sit on. Belinda carried a patch quilt blanket she had found tucked away in one of the boxes of supplies. They chose a level spot near a small grove of dogwood trees. Katie helped spread out the cloth.

The gathering was informal as people mingled and chatted with one another. When it appeared all who were coming had arrived, the pastor called for everyone's attention. A hush fell over the assembly and he prayed over the food.

The crowd started forward, but Mayor Todd raised the palm of his hand. "We've all tasted each other's dishes. Let's allow our new members to go first."

The men already in place stepped back. Most smiled good-naturedly, but there were a few downhearted looks on some faces as they eyed the food. With the girls by her side, Maggie made her way the length of the table, scooping small samples of food for herself as well as helping the twins find types of food they liked.

It looked as though there was plenty to go around, but as she was learning, the men in West Ridge looked forward to any chance at what they called real food. Fried fish and canned beans were all right but got old after a while.

Katie helped Maggie get the girls settled onto the blanket. Maggie struggled to balance all three of their plates in her hands.

"Here, let me help you with those." A tall man with auburn hair relieved her of her burden.

"Thank you." She took a spot on the blanket between the twins.

Nicely dressed, he appeared to be in his early thirties but what stood out the most to Maggie was his lack of boots. He wore tan military shoes, which were popular among businessmen and politicians back East. Every other man she had seen or spoken to since arriving in West Ridge wore boots, tall leather cowboy boots.

"It's my pleasure." He waited for her to get settled before handing her the plates, one at a time.

Maggie took a moment to sort them out. Hannah didn't like broccoli but loved ham. Esther, on the other hand, adored broccoli but couldn't stomach eating different foods touching each other.

The kind stranger stood by until she had their food sorted. "I'm Dale Sanders. I manage the bank. It's nice to get to meet all of you at last."

Maggie used her hand to shade her eyes from the sun. "It's nice to meet you too, Mr. Sanders."

"Please, call me Dale."

"All right, Dale." A rush of wind tossed her hair across her face. She pulled back the wayward strands and tucked them behind her ear. "I'm Maggie. These two are Hannah and Esther. And the young lady over there is Katie."

"I'm thirsty, Aunt Maggie." Esther used her fork to push the mashed potatoes on her plate away from the creamed corn.

"Oh, I forgot to get us something to drink." Maggie set her plate aside and started to rise.

"Don't get up." Dale waved his hand over them. "I'll get you all something to drink. I'm afraid you'll only find two choices here: water or tea."

"Tea is fine for all of us. Thank you."

When the banker left, Katie began to take a bite of food.

"Hey, we have to pray first." Esther scolded the teenager, who looked both surprised and tickled by the reprimand.

"We already prayed." Hannah came to the older girl's defense. "Don't you remember?"

"Oh, that's right. The preacher prayed for our food." Esther returned to keeping the items on her plate from encroaching on space meant for another.

"Here you go, ladies." Mr. Sanders had four drinks he carried on a tray. "My blanket is right next to yours. I hope you don't mind if I join you."

"Of course, we don't mind." Mrs. Lamb came behind him, carrying her plate and a glass of water. She walked to the other end of their blanket and took the vacant spot between Katie and Esther. "The more the merrier."

Belinda quietly slipped in on the other side of Hannah, leaving the only open space next to Maggie. Mr. Sanders sat beside her with a plate piled high.

"That's a lot of food." Esther's boldness sometimes caused Maggie to squirm. Outgoing and unafraid, the child was her opposite in nature.

"Yes, it does seem like an abundance." He

didn't appear to mind the child's directness.

"But you're not fat."

"Esther!" Maggie groaned inwardly. She would have a talk with the girls about manners later.

Mr. Sanders threw back his head and laughed before responding. "You'll soon learn the single men in West Ridge look forward to the social gatherings when food is on the menu. It's akin to Christmas around here."

"Who made the lemon meringue pie?" Mrs. Irvin strolled through the sea of blankets.

"Mrs. Lamb did." Belinda waved her arm and answered with pride. "She's an amazing cook."

"I'll say so." Mrs. Irvin worked her way back to the food table, giving the diners the answer they seemed to all be waiting for.

Mr. Sanders took a big bite of the pie causing so much interest and grinned as he chewed. "You should consider opening a restaurant, Mrs. Lamb."

The town did need some sort of eatery, especially for the single men. Mrs. Lamb was an excellent cook and had experience cooking for a crowd. It wasn't a bad idea. Maggie made a mental note to discuss it with Mrs. Lamb and Belinda at another time. By the response of the men, they would be interested in having a place where they could eat a good meal.

Maggie glanced around the churchyard. She was beginning to put names to faces. There was the mayor, and his wife, the preacher, and Mrs. Irvin. Over by an old oak tree, Anna Grace and Sadie Mae Swenson sat together with a family Maggie hadn't met. There were more people to meet but that would come in time. She didn't see the sheriff among the crowd. It seemed strange without his presence. Perhaps he couldn't get away from his duties.

Owen sat on the top of the steps in front of the church. Buster lay beside him, chewing on a ham bone. From here, Owen could watch over the picnickers while he ate his meal. He didn't have any spare blankets, other than the one he used on his cot in the backroom of the office. Like many of the single men, he usually joined one of the other families, but tonight he wasn't feeling folksy.

He waited until everyone was served before filling his plate. It was no surprise to him Mrs. Lamb's pie was so well received. He had firsthand knowledge of her cooking skills. Maggie, her nieces, and the rest of the ladies from the welcome wagon sat together on the other side of the lawn. From the church steps, he was able to make out the back of Maggie's head. Her curly dark hair cascaded freely, floating to the side every time she turned to laugh at something funny Dale had to say.

Like him, Dale was a bachelor and looked forward to any type of meeting which involved food. They had a bigger crowd than usual tonight, but it wasn't any surprise as everyone seemed anxious to meet the ladies once their initial suspicions had proven invalid.

The sun was low in the western sky, and the air had cooled considerably. Katydids began to strike up their nightly tune. At times, the repetitive sound made by the insects could be deafening. Tonight, they seemed to be keeping it low.

"Hey, Sheriff. What are you doing over here all by yourself?" Dr. Gentry walked toward him with a glass of tea in each hand. "You looked thirsty, so I brought a drink over for you."

"Thanks, Doc," Owen took the glass while the doctor sat two steps below him. Up in years, the only doctor in West Ridge knew everyone. He had been there to help deliver

Owen and most anyone younger in age.

"Not feeling sociable tonight?"

"I'm feeling fine." He took a long drink, thankful for the liquid to wash down the last of the pot roast he'd been enjoying. "Sometimes I just like to sit back and watch. You ever feel that way?"

"Yes. I suppose it comes with our having jobs serving others."

They sat without speaking for a moment.

The doctor sipped on his tea and surveyed the crowd before turning to Owen. "Have you heard from your folks lately?"

"Yes. I got a letter from Mother the other day."

"How are they doing?" Dr. Gentry glanced toward what was left of his drink and then leaned over to look at Owen. "Are the springs helping your father's joints any?"

"They're doing fine, and yes. The natural hot water does seem to be helping. I forgot, Mother asked me to thank you for sending them to Hot Springs. They seem to like the city and their new neighbors."

"That's good." Dr. Gentry set his empty glass on the step. "I'm glad to hear he's finding some relief. Now, if we can just find you some relief."

"Me?" There wasn't anything wrong with his joints. "What are you talking about? I'm strong and healthy."

"This is true, but I'm afraid there's something else keeping you from your full potential."

Owen had no idea what the doctor was trying to say. He was happy, had a good job, and was well-liked. What more could he want?

Dr. Gentry picked up both his and Owen's empty glasses and stood. "You know, if you ever need someone to talk to, my door's always open."

"Thanks." He was simply being polite. There was no need for him to see a doctor. Owen wanted the community to have full confidence in his ability to keep the peace and uphold the law. He hadn't been handed the job because of his good looks. Far from it. His father had raised him to shoot a gun and hunt. Because of his training, he was one of the best trackers in the area. He'd won several shooting contests over the years at the county fair. He believed he had good instincts about people as well.

Buster came closer and laid his chin on Owen's leg. He petted the dog's head and stared off into the crowd. Fireflies flashed their luminous lights near the dogwood trees at the top of the hill. Soon they would fill the air and it would be time for the closing prayer.

The sound of giggling drew his attention to the trees where Maggie and her family had spread their blanket. Katie and the twins ran with their hands out, trying to catch fireflies. Maggie stood beside Dale, laughing as they watched the children. It made a nice family picture.

7

Maggie marched down the steps of the platform to join Mrs. Lamb and Belinda on the main floor of the auditorium. There was plenty of room as well as a door connected to their living quarters.

"It will take some work, but I think it can be done." Belinda looked up from the slate in her hand. She jotted down a few notes and then looked to their leader. "What do you think, Mrs. Lamb?"

All three of them stood in the center of what had once been the sanctuary of the old church building. They were discussing the possibility of turning it into a restaurant. Katie and the twins sat on the edge of the raised platform, with their legs swinging in unison as they listened to the conversation about turning their new home into a business.

The idea started as a friendly suggestion during last night's church social. By the end of the evening, so many people proposed they start a restaurant, the concept took root and stuck.

"I think it will work just fine." Mrs. Lamb continued to survey the interior of the large room and platform. "We can give back to the community and make our own way. It's the perfect solution for everyone."

"How do we get started?" Maggie was all for them making their own way but had no idea what would be involved in running a restaurant. If not for Mrs. Lamb, it wouldn't even be feasible. More than anything, she wanted a way to support her family without taking charity.

"The old sanctuary would be the dining area, of course." Mrs. Lamb seemed to have a good idea of what would be involved. She stroked her chin and narrowed her eyes. "We will have to make some changes, I suppose. Something to separate the stage area from the eating area."

"Do you mean the platform?" Belinda looked up from her notes.

"Yes. We'll need a bigger stove and a place to prep food and store supplies. There's plenty of room up there on the stage, but it needs to have a wall of sorts to divide it from the area where we would serve the food."

"It sounds like a lot of work." Maggie's head spun with all the details. "But I imagine some of the men would be willing to help with any reconstruction needed."

"What will we call it?" Belinda seemed as sold on the notion of running a restaurant as any of them.

Maggie had no idea what type of job, if any, her new friend had back in New York. Belinda was tight-lipped when it came to discussing her past.

"Call it?" A strange look appeared on Mrs. Lamb's face. "Call what?"

"Our restaurant."

Katie jumped from the edge of the platform, where she and the girls had sat and hurried over to join them. "How about we call it the Welcome Wagon Restaurant?"

A moment of silence stretched among them. The name had a good ring to it, and it identified them as a group. The more she considered it, the more Maggie liked it.

"That's the perfect name for our establishment." Mrs. Lamb's eyes sparkled. She gave the teenager a huge hug and then faced Maggie and Belinda, bubbling with renewed enthusiasm. "We'll need money to get started. There's the food. We'll need bigger pots and pans as well as dishes, cups, and silverware."

Belinda had her attention glued to the slate. She wrote quickly.

"People will need chairs to sit on and tables for their food," Maggie added. There was so much they needed before they could get started. Perhaps this wasn't such a good idea after all.

"I guess we should begin by talking with the manager of the bank." Mrs. Lamb's brow creased thoughtfully. "Mr. Sanders was very friendly last night. I don't see why he wouldn't be willing to help."

Dale did seem like a reasonable person. If the town wanted a restaurant, why wouldn't he help them? Of course, the building wasn't theirs to do with as they wished. She didn't even know who owned it. Pastor Irvin?

"Do you think we should run it past the mayor or Mrs. Todd first?" Maggie didn't want to spoil their excitement, but, at the same time, they shouldn't get their hopes up until they were sure it would be allowed.

"Yes. You have a good point." Mrs. Lamb let out a short sigh. "Why don't you and I pay them a visit and, depending on what they say, we'll take it from there."

"You two can take care of that. I'll stay here with the children and keep adding to this list of things we're going to need." Belinda nodded as she began writing more on the slate.

There were only a few people out and about as Maggie and Mrs. Lamb made their way toward the mayor's office. Some businesses left their doors open to probably try and create a breeze. The heat was near unbearable. She'd been warned the hottest part of the summer in the Ozarks was late July through August. Summer had only just begun.

The door to the jailhouse was closed when they passed. She was glad they wouldn't have to greet Owen. He was so kind, and it was getting hard to keep him at bay. Last night as she tried to fall asleep, she had considered telling him the truth, thinking he might help her. She had to face the fact it wasn't possible. His main duty was to carry out the law, not to help someone get around it.

"Here we are." Mrs. Lamb stopped so suddenly, Maggie almost tripped. They had reached the end of the boardwalk while she'd been woolgathering. The mayor's office was located at the back of the courthouse. "I hope he'll be able to see us."

"We may have to make an appointment." Maggie knocked on the door. "Either way, it's progress."

"Come in," the mayor called out. At least he was in today.

Maggie pushed the door open, and they stepped inside.

"Hello, Mrs. Lamb, Miss Lynn." Mayor Todd stood and crossed the room to greet them. The walls of his office were covered with paintings of the Spring River. There was a large desk near the far wall covered with papers. "Come in and have a seat."

He placed his hands on the back of two chairs before returning to his own. Maggie admired the oak bookcase behind his desk. Books lining the shelves appeared to be arranged by height and size. Mayor Todd waited until they were seated to speak. "This is a pleasant surprise. How can I help you ladies today?"

Silence prevailed. They never discussed who would do the talking.

Maggie cleared her throat and stiffened her shoulders. "We came to discuss starting a restaurant in West Ridge. It seems . . ."

"That's a wonderful idea." He smiled warmly. "Mrs. Todd and I were discussing the very same thing last night. After folks got a sample of your pie, Mrs. Lamb, it was the talk of the town."

"I'm glad they liked it." Mrs. Lamb flushed a pretty shade of pink. "My late husband and I spent quite a few years cooking for a lumber mill company in upstate New York."

"How can I help you get started?"

"We, Maggie, Belinda, and I that is, have spent a great deal of time discussing where and how to have a restaurant, and we think the old church would serve well for the building."

Mayor Todd drummed the fingers of his right hand against the top of his desk. His eyes narrowed and his lips puckered. The man was so deep in thought Maggie wondered if he forgot they were in the room.

After a few moments passed, he began to nod his head. "I see what you mean. It would be the perfect solution to our problem. I'll want to talk it over with Pastor Irvin first, but I don't see why he wouldn't agree to it. The building belongs to the city, but the pastor oversees the maintenance. Let me speak with him and get back to you."

Maggie gave Mrs. Lamb a quick glance. Were they supposed to leave or wait for him to talk to the preacher?

"Of course, I'm sure you're anxious to get started." He seemed to realize the need for clarification. "I'll run over to the parsonage when I'm done with my paperwork here and get back to you later this afternoon."

"Thank you." Mrs. Lamb stood and Maggie followed suit.

The mayor walked them to the door. "Have a good afternoon, ladies. You'll be hearing from me soon."

It was a start. The thought of being self-supporting members of the community put a spring in Maggie's steps as they headed home. The Lord had provided and continued to provide. Her eyes filled with moisture.

"Are you all right?" Mrs. Lamb placed her hand on Maggie's arm.

"Yes." She took a deep breath and blew it out. "God's been so good to me, to all of us. I know I don't deserve it. My heart has been so bitter after all that has happened."

"It's been hard on all of us. You're not alone in feeling confused and upset."

"I wish I were more like you, Mrs. Lamb." Maggie sniffed and forced herself to smile. "You always seem so positive."

"Don't be so sure, dear." The older woman let out a light laugh. "Some of us are better at hiding our feelings. When you get to be my age, you realize when there's nothing you can do about a situation, it's best to leave it in God's hands."

"It's more than that." Maggie searched for the right words.

Mrs. Lamb never complained, no matter how hard things got. The woman was always positive with a kind word to share.

"I can't help but notice how close you are to God. You always see the good in things, no matter how grim the situation."

"I'm humbled you think so highly of me." Mrs. Lamb wrapped her arm around Maggie's shoulders and pulled her close for a moment. "This morning I was reading in the tenth chapter of the book of James. The fourth verse stuck out. Let me see if I can get it right. 'Humble thyself in the sight of the Lord, and He will lift thee up'. I find this verse to be helpful when things in life seem like more than I can bear."

"Thank you." Maggie looped her arm through the older woman's, and they continued toward their new home. The verse was one she knew well from listening to her father teach the Word. "That's just what I needed to hear."

Owen left the barbershop and crossed the street in time to see Mayor Todd walking at a brisk speed, which was unusual for this time of day. Most folks stayed indoors during midafternoon, when the heat rose high enough to draw the breath right out of a person.

"Good afternoon, Mayor."

"Howdy, Owen." He was grinning and called Owen by his first name in public. Something had Thomas Todd in a good mood. "I'm headed next door. I've got some news for Mrs. Lamb. Care to join me?"

"Now you've got my curiosity up. I'll be happy to go with you."

They traveled down the boardwalk without speaking. The mayor's excitement was unmistakable. Whatever it was, it must be really good news for Mrs. Lamb. They reached the old church building, and Mayor Todd knocked on the door, which was opened immediately by Belinda. All the children and women from the welcome wagon were in the sanctuary waiting anxiously. It seemed as if they were expecting to hear whatever it was the mayor had to tell them.

"Well, ladies, Pastor Irvin gives you his blessing and says yes to turning the building into a restaurant."

The little ones cheered, and the women clapped their hands. Maggie hugged Mrs. Lamb. A restaurant was news to Owen. It shouldn't have come as a surprise, what with everyone saying Mrs. Lamb should open a diner. He planned on being one of the first customers the day they opened and almost every night. No more eating out of a can alone in a dark room behind the jail.

"What do you plan to call yourselves?" The mayor sounded as pleased with the prospect as Owen.

"We have the perfect name." Maggie beamed with pride as she placed her hand on the teenage girl's arm. "It was Katie's idea."

"And?" Mayor Todd turned his head and cupped his hand around the ear he had pointed toward Maggie.

"Go ahead, Katie. Tell them."

"Oh, yes. We're calling it the Welcome Wagon Restaurant."

"Perfect. The Welcome Wagon is the perfect name for your new establishment. What can we do to help you get started?"

"First," Mrs. Lamb pointed toward the front of the room, "we need a partition to separate the main floor from the platform, where we plan to do the cooking."

"Now, organizing that project sounds like a job for our sheriff." Mayor Todd slapped Owen on the back.

It wasn't the sheriff's job to play foreman, but who was he to argue with the mayor? Besides, it would give him an excuse to spend more time around Maggie and her family. Katie and the twins had wormed their way into his heart with their laughter and sweet spirits. He believed they shared his feelings, unlike their aunt, who seemed to feel the exact opposite.

"Owen, what say you get a group together to work on designing a plan for the building's reconstruction? I have a feeling several of the men in town will be willing to volunteer time and labor. Especially the bachelors."

"I'll be happy to help." He looked at Maggie.

Her smile twisted into a frown. She didn't seem delighted with the idea of him taking charge.

"That sounds perfect." Mrs. Lamb clasped her hands together and brought them to her lips. "Maggie and I will talk to Mr. Sanders about a loan for the supplies and equipment we need to get started."

"I don't see why he wouldn't agree to it." There was an air of excitement and confidence in the mayor's tone. "If he has any concerns, tell him to come see me."

Of course, Dale would give them the loan. He wasn't about to let them down, not after the way he'd been looking at Maggie at the church social. Owen admonished himself. Dale was a good man and an honest banker. He would never use his power to take advantage of any situation unethically. Maggie was a pretty girl, and Dale had gone to college back East. They had a lot in common.

West Ridge was about to get its first restaurant. So far, the arrival of the women from the welcome wagon had brought their town nothing but improvements. There was no telling what was in store for them next.

The bank was at the east end of town on Main Street, across from the courthouse. The temperature seemed to have dropped a few degrees from earlier in the day. A breeze from the north helped lower the humidity. The short walk took a while to navigate due to people stopping them on the street.

There weren't a lot of women in town, but the few they had were very friendly. Mrs. Lamb seemed to recall all their names, even though she'd only met them on Sunday. Maggie returned their greetings and politely answered their questions, although she was anxious to get to the bank and speak with Dale.

The moment Mrs. Lamb finished giving Mrs. Carter her recipe for sweet potato casserole, Maggie looped her arm through Mrs. Lamb's, and they crossed the street. The bank was the only structure in town made of bricks. It stood to reason one wanted the bank to be strong.

They entered the secure building where a teller stood on a raised platform behind bars in a caged area. He counted out money for a customer while Maggie and Mrs. Lamb waited. To the right of the teller's station was a carpeted section with a desk and chair. A man Maggie recognized from church jotted down figures in a big black book. Behind him was a door with the word *Manager* painted in gold letters.

"Can I help you ladies?" The man behind the bars nodded toward them when he finished with his customer.

"Yes, thank you." Mrs. Lamb stepped forward and took charge. "We would like to see Mr. Sanders."

The teller glanced toward the man sitting at the desk. "Rodney, can you see if Mr. Sanders is available?"

"Just a moment." Rodney raised one finger, finished writing something in his book, and then laid his pencil on the desk. He rose and knocked quietly on the marked door before opening it slightly. Maggie couldn't hear what was said, but Dale Sanders came right out to greet them. He looked quite dashing in his three-piece suit and tie.

"Good afternoon, ladies." Mr. Sanders

smiled brightly as he greeted them. His gaze seemed to linger on Maggie for a moment, and a wave of heat crept up her cheeks. "This is a pleasant surprise."

"Good afternoon to you, too." Mrs. Lamb reached out her hand and took his.

He patted the back of hers and smiled. "How can I help you two ladies today?"

"We have some business we would like to discuss." If Mrs. Lamb's reply surprised him, he didn't show it.

"Well certainly. That's what I'm here for." He stepped aside and motioned for them to enter his chambers. "Come on into my office."

They entered the room and waited.

"Please, sit down." He followed behind them and pointed to two chairs before taking a seat behind his desk.

Dale Sanders's office was nice but simple, much like the town he served. Two filing cabinets stood side by side against one wall. On the other side of the room, shelves were filled with books. The rug looked new and the oak furniture had been polished until it shined. The window behind his desk revealed a lovely view of the ridge from which the town got its name.

"We're thinking of turning the old church building into a restaurant." Mrs. Lamb spoke up the moment she'd settled into her seat. "We have the mayor and the minister's approval but will need some funding to get started."

Mr. Sanders nodded as he tapped his finger against his chin. "I see."

"As you know, West Ridge doesn't have anything other than the pastry shop to offer cooked food to the community." Mrs. Lamb jumped in and continued as if she had rehearsed her words. "I've had several years of experience cooking for large crowds and am pretty good at it, if I do say so myself."

"That you are." Mr. Sanders raised his hand and cut her off.

Maggie's heart sank. Would he deny them without hearing her out? This opportunity was their best chance of making it on their own without depending on the community for support. It seemed like a reasonable request. She didn't want to use the mayor's willingness to back them unless there was no other choice. This was something they needed to do for themselves. They could do it too, if given the chance.

"You don't have to sell me on the idea." Mr. Sanders's laughter startled Maggie, but she relaxed when she realized he agreed with the plan. "After all the good things I've been hearing about your cooking, I meant to make the suggestion myself once I figured out where we could put a restaurant. The old church building is perfect."

Mrs. Lamb raised her hand to her chest. "Oh, thank goodness. For a moment there, I thought you would tell us no."

Dale pulled out a pen and paper. His smile included them both, but his gaze seemed to linger on Maggie long enough to cause the heat to return to her cheeks.

"I'm at your service, ladies. Let's discuss business."

Maggie's spirits were high when they left the bank. A cool gush of wind whipped up from the river and brushed her face. It seemed as though everything was going their way. They'd discussed what they would need to get started and signed papers. It was amazing how easy it had been to get a loan. Of course, they were supplying the community with a unique and desperately needed business.

She and Mrs. Lamb chatted about what needed to be done first as they crossed the street and turned toward home. Sheriff Owen sat on a bench outside the jailhouse, weaving a rawhide rope. Maggie kept a smile on her face, but her guard rose as it always did when she had to deal with the lawman.

The sheriff's dog sniffed the boardwalk on the trail of some unidentified scent. His tail wagged faster, and he took off down the alleyway separating the jail from the old church building they now called home.

"Hello, Sheriff Owen." Mrs. Lamb waved as they drew closer.

"Hello." He set down his work and stood to face them. "How did it go at the bank?"

"Just fine." Mrs. Lamb greeted him with a smile as bright as the sun's reflection on the Spring River. "We're opening a restaurant."

"Well, congratulations!" Enthusiasm warmed his words. He appeared to truly be happy for them. "I can't tell you how glad that makes me. No more cold beans because it's too hot to start a fire in the middle of July. I'm delighted for all of you and the community as well."

"There will be a lot of work to do to get the building ready." Maggie considered the enormous task before they could open their doors for business. "It will be some time before we're up and running."

"When should we get together to plan the design?" His question reminded her of the mayor's comment about having him organize the project.

"Why don't we meet with you tomorrow

morning after breakfast?" Mrs. Lamb looked pleased with the idea of having him help.

Maggie wasn't. Her gaze traveled toward the sky. What if he discovered their secret? She bit her bottom lip and looked at the ground.

"Tomorrow morning will be fine."

Maggie sensed a hint of disappointment in his tone, as if he was aware of her desire to distance herself from him.

"Good. It'll give us time to discuss things tonight." Mrs. Lamb's voice rose and fell in a singsong sort of pattern. She didn't seem aware of the tension in the air. "We'd better be off. Lots of planning to do. See you tomorrow."

Maggie gave him a tight-lipped smile, and then followed Mrs. Lamb. There was sadness in his eyes. When Katie turned eighteen this fall, Maggie could tell him everything. Knowing the truth about her would destroy any chance of their being friends, but at least he would understand that keeping him at a distance had nothing to do with him.

8

The wonderful smell of fresh-baked bread filled Maggie's nostrils. She cut another slice and handed it to Katie, who formed a line of them out on the kitchen table. Belinda spread butter on each one before Mrs. Lamb placed thick portions of meat on every other cut. Preparing lunch for the workers had become a part of their daily routine. After a quick breakfast, they set up the assembly line and got to work. The twins sat on a blanket in the corner, playing with their new toys.

"This morning when I woke up, I didn't hear a sound." Belinda knifed a slab of butter and proceeded to cover a piece of bread. "For a moment, I thought I'd gone deaf during the night."

Katie's hands stilled, her mouth dropped open, and her eyes grew wide with concern.

Maggie fought to hold back a giggle but failed. "I know what you mean. It was unusual not to be woken by the sound of hammering."

"The men ran out of nails last night." Mrs. Lamb piled a thick slice of baked ham on a buttered piece of bread. "They had to wait until Mr. Carter opened his store this morning to purchase more."

"Oh." Belinda brought the palm of her hand to her forehead, imitating the twin's playful gesture. "That explains why it was so quiet."

Over the past two weeks, they had grown accustomed to the constant banging, which started early in the morning, as well as the sound of heavy steps tromping through the soon-to-be dining room. The heart of the building was quickly beginning to look like the eating area in a restaurant. Maggie appreciated the men's hard work and countless hours of free labor.

After they prepared lunch for the work crew, Katie took the two little ones to their room to hear a story and then take a nap.

It was Maggie's turn to do the dishes.

Mrs. Lamb remained at the kitchen table, working on the menu for the restaurant. "I didn't realize it would take so much time to reconstruct the dining area."

"Me either." Belinda placed her empty coffee cup next to the sink and picked up a cloth to dry dishes. "I thought we'd just throw up a wall and find some tables."

There was much more involved. The tables had to be shipped in from Memphis, a large town east of the Ozarks in Tennessee. Mr. Carter's brother had been commissioned to make them.

Most of the other supplies were on order and due next week. Except for the chairs. They were supposed to arrive on tomorrow's mail wagon. One of Rudy Brown's cousins from Batesville was a woodcarver and, because it was a big order, he gave them a good deal.

Batesville was a full day's journey. Maggie remembered the trip well. It was their first stop in Arkansas. Her thoughts and opinions at the beginning of this adventure had changed a great deal. The better she got to know the area, the more she came to appreciate God's handiwork. The Ozarks offered a spectacular array of rustic scenery and were filled with some of the kindest people she'd ever met.

When the dishes were done, Maggie and Belinda joined Mrs. Lamb at the table.

Katie tiptoed into the kitchen. "The girls are asleep."

"Thank you." Maggie tapped the empty chair next to her and Katie took a seat.

The teenager's sweet spirit was a blessing. It was a wonder how well they got along and worked together. Four women living together under one roof. They never fought, and each of her companions had a special gift to add to the group. Mrs. Lamb's wisdom, Belinda's organization, and Katie's willingness to help whenever and wherever needed.

"Mr. Gentry says he'll have our sign ready to put up tomorrow." Mrs. Lamb's announcement pulled Maggie from her musings. It turned out the quiet livery owner was quite a craftsman and an artist.

"Oh, I can't wait to see what it looks like." Katie's eyes shined with joy. It was good to see her express herself without fear or worry.

The sound of hammering stopped, followed by the ringing of a bell. Maggie and Belinda rose from the table as they had every day for the past two weeks.

"It sounds as if they're ready to eat." Belinda gathered the food they had packed for the men and led the way down the hall.

Maggie followed with the pot of hot coffee. They entered the sanctuary where all seven of the workers were lined up at the table, ready to be fed. Sheriff Owen stood at the door, ready to help Belinda with her burden.

"Thank you, ladies." He took the box and set it on the table. "The food smells good."

"I hope you like it." Belinda oversaw the handing out of sandwiches, apples, and cookies. Each worker received two sandwiches, one piece of fruit, and three snickerdoodle cookies.

Mrs. Lamb had helped the twins and Katie make the sweet treats the night before.

"We kept it simple today."

As usual, Owen helped serve the meal to his crew before taking his own.

Maggie filled each tin cup with coffee, and the sheriff handed them out to the men. They worked well as a team. The process moved along quickly, with each man profusely thanking them.

"Hey, Sheriff." Rudy Brown was the last in line. He took his cup and paused. "Have you seen today's paper?"

"Not yet." Owen collected his meal. "I'll have a look at it this evening. Anything interesting?"

"There's an article about folks missing from the wagon train holdup in Missouri."

The lawman's chin shot up, and his brow creased. He cleared his throat as his gaze swung from Rudy to Maggie and back to Rudy.

"Pardon me, Ma'am." Rudy's cheeks

turned bright red. He ducked his head and coughed as he scurried to join a group of men sitting on the floor next to the new wall.

Maggie occupied herself with wiping the table. She didn't want anyone to see her hands shaking. More upsetting than the news article was the reaction of the two men. Did they suspect something? Belinda was at the other end of the table, talking to one of the workers while she collected empty tins and napkins. There was no need for either of them to see the paper. They knew who was missing and why.

After lunch, Owen and the men straightened the new dining room. They collected tools and removed the sawhorses. He was proud of how much they had accomplished over the past two weeks. The kitchen stretched across the platform, where the church choir once stood to sing specials during the Christmas season. A wall with doors at either end had been erected to keep the work area out of sight from the customers eating in the dining area. All they needed now was for the furniture to arrive.

It was kind of the ladies to feed the men lunch each day. The prospect of a good meal brought out several volunteers. Owen enjoyed working alongside Maggie. She greeted each of the workers with a smile. Whether she realized it or not, the men often went out of their way to try and make her laugh. The sound of her laughter reminded him of wind chimes on a breezy day. This last work lunch should have been special. It might have been if he hadn't overreacted to Rudy's comment. It drew more attention to the sensitive subject than a simple nod would have. It wasn't the time or place to drag up painful memories. The women from the welcome wagon were fitting in well with the community and seemed happy with their new project.

Mrs. Lamb had no idea just how busy she was about to become. Her cooking was some of the best he had ever eaten. Opening a restaurant in West Ridge was akin to selling cups of water in the middle of a desert. Folks would come to eat such good food.

"Good afternoon, Owen." Dr. Gentry stood in the doorway, hands on his hips as he surveyed the room. "I thought I'd stop by and see what all the excitement was about."

Owen pivoted to get a firsthand view of the doctor's perspective. With the wall up and finished, the auditorium no longer resembled a church. Most of the scrap lumber and tools had been picked up and removed. They wanted to give the floor in the main room a good cleaning before the furnishings arrived. "Well, what do you think?"

"It looks good." The doctor's gaze swept the room. "I'm anxious to get a taste of some real cooking."

A bachelor, like most men in town, Owen wondered why the doctor never married. Other than the odds being against him, the man was intelligent and not bad-looking. He would have made a good husband and father. Most of the bachelors in West Ridge were that way by choice. Women scared the socks off them. Nothing was scarier to a man set in his ways than the thought of a woman coming along and making him change "for the better."

"How have you been, Sheriff?" Dr. Gentry's gaze was focused on Owen, no doubt searching for whatever it was he believed held Owen back.

"I'm fine." Owen went out of his way to put a bit of enthusiasm in his voice.

"And how are your folks?"

"Good. They send their regards."

"Hey there, Brother." Rob Gentry marched across the room to greet them.

"Did you decide to come do some real work for a change?"

The two siblings were close, although they chose quite different paths in life. Kevin Gentry took care of people for a living while Rob took care of animals. Both men were pillars of the community and well-liked.

"I thought I'd come supervise." Dr. Gentry raised his hands in front of his face and turned them back and forth. "These are too important to risk on physical labor."

"Well, the sheriff here has you beat. We couldn't hope to find a better supervisor than this guy." Rob slapped Owen on the back. "There's nothing the sheriff of West Ridge can't do."

"You make a good point there, Rob." The sincerity in Dr. Gentry's tone wrapped around Owen's heart. "The good folks of West Ridge would be lost without the likes of Owen Somers."

Would they? The people of West Ridge were his friends and neighbors. They were family to him. He never stopped to consider what it would be like in town if he wasn't there. Of course, they'd manage without him. They'd find a way. They'd have to.

9

Maggie slipped her hands into the warm sudsy water and glanced out the kitchen window. There wasn't a cloud in the sky. They were in for another hot sunny day. For the first time in over two weeks, it was quiet out in the new dining area. There wouldn't be any work today. Other than a few finishing touches, the Welcome Wagon Restaurant was ready for business.

"You know what we need?" Mrs. Lamb sat at the kitchen table, stirring milk into her cup of coffee while Maggie and Katie took their turn cleaning dishes. "We all need to take a break, get out, and do something special."

Maggie rinsed off the last dish and handed it to Katie to be dried. The idea of getting away for a while did sound good. They had been so caught up in getting the restaurant ready to open, there had been little time for anything else. With the kitchen clean, they had the rest of the day ahead of them to do something fun. Katie put away the dishes while Maggie emptied the water.

"Why don't we all go to the river?" Belinda sat between the twins, watching them practice writing their letters. The girls yipped with glee, and Belinda turned to Mrs. Lamb. "You weren't feeling well the last time we went."

"Yes, I remember." Mrs. Lamb took a sip from her coffee cup and let out a pleased sigh. "I've heard so much about it. I'd like to see it for myself."

"A visit to the river sounds like a wonderful idea." Maggie wrung out the dishrag and hung it to dry.

The twins cheered louder this time, and Katie smiled.

"Good." Mrs. Lamb rose from her chair and set her cup on the counter. "I spoke with Sheriff Owen earlier this morning while I was out gathering eggs for breakfast. He has agreed to take us."

Maggie's heart sank. She had never come right out and told the women they should avoid the lawman because she'd assumed they could see the danger Owen Somers posed. But the children were excited, and everyone needed some time to relax.

"He tells me he knows a good fishing hole

and a safe place for the girls to splash in the water."

"When are we supposed to leave?" Maggie asked.

"In an hour." Belinda was smiling. So she knew about the idea before they'd mentioned it to Maggie.

Maggie would have said no as soon as Sheriff Owen's name was mentioned. Yes, he was dependable and willing to do just about anything to help them, but his main role was as an officer of the law. He was bound by the law to carry out duties more favorable to the man's rights than those of women or minors. She took the girls to their room to get ready.

Owen showed up right on time. He had a wagon and a team of horses waiting out front. He stood beside the rig and pinched the brim of his hat. Buster sat beside him, wagging his tail.

"Good day, ladies." Owen's broad smile was much too bright for this early. If not for the girls, Maggie might have found a reason to remain behind. It had worked for Mrs. Lamb, but she had to keep an eye on the children and make sure everyone kept the sheriff at arms' length.

Owen helped Katie and the twins into the back of the wagon. Belinda climbed over the side and took a seat next to the children. Buster bounded into the back to join them. The girls made room for him to settle next to them. Maggie and Mrs. Lamb were left with the bench seat. The elderly woman preferred to sit on the outside, where she didn't feel so closed in.

Owen placed his hand on Maggie's elbow and helped her up. She nodded and scooted to the center, fluffing her skirts as he helped Mrs. Lamb aboard. The arrangement was much like their first ride into town, only this time they were happy and would soon be running their own business. It had taken a lot of time and hard work to get this far, and much of that came from Owen's help. It wasn't easy keeping her distance with someone so personable.

They rode down the center of town and turned toward the river, until they came to the new church house. Once the buildings and sounds of people coming and going were behind them, the woods seemed to come alive.

"Look, girls." Mrs. Lamb kept her voice low as she pointed to the side of the road. "A momma deer and her fawn."

Maggie twisted to see the girls' reactions.

"There are two of them." Hannah grabbed hold of the side of the wagon. She stared with her mouth hanging open.

"Twin fawns are common in this part of the country." Owen slowed the team. "White-tailed deer are known for having two and sometimes three babies at a time."

"They are like us, Hannah." Esther scrambled across the back of the wagon to join her sister for a better view.

The shy animals sensed the movement and ran into hiding.

"Look at all the squirrels." Katie turned her head upward toward the tall tree branches where the furry-tailed creatures ran from tree to tree, like acrobats in a circus.

Buster's ears perked up and his tongue hung out as he panted.

"Are they twins too?" Hannah looked toward Owen with wide eyes and a look of awe.

He opened his mouth as if to reply but let out a breath and bit down on his bottom lip for a moment. "I'm not sure, but here in Arkansas, anything is possible."

His answer seemed to satisfy the children as they soon turned their attention back to the forest. Owen glanced at Maggie and winked. His dimpled grin threatened to take her breath away. She gave him a polite smile and turned her attention to the road. He was so charming. It would be easy but dangerous to drop her guard. What if she became too comfortable around him and let her secret slip? What would he do if he found out the truth about Katie?

Maggie shook the thoughts from her mind. She didn't want to entertain such a thing happening. Katie was safe and would remain so if they kept quiet.

"Here we are." He brought the wagon to a stop when they reached an area thick with woods. It wasn't the same place they'd visited with Mr. and Mrs. Todd. On the left side of the road, a narrow path opened. Owen snapped the reins and turned the team. The terrain sloped steadily until they reached the other side of the tree line. A small clearing appeared, and the river meandered a few yards from where he parked the wagon.

Owen helped Mrs. Lamb while Katie and Belinda climbed out and lifted the twins over the side of the wagon. Owen reached up for Maggie. She slid to the edge of the bench and swung around to face him. He took hold of her waist and lifted her off the seat and set her on the ground. She couldn't count the number of times she'd been helped from a wagon, but something about

Owen's touch sent a shiver through her body.

"I hope you all are ready for a cookout." He didn't seem to notice her heated cheeks or unsteady stance.

"We didn't bring a basket of food." Katie gave Mrs. Lamb a look of concern.

They had all learned to depend on Mrs. Lamb when food was an issue.

"There's no need to worry." Owen pulled a fishing rod from the back of the wagon. "You're about to get a real taste of roughing it."

Katie crossed her arms and tilted her head. "Are you sure you'll be able to catch any fish?"

"I hope so. On such short notice, I only had time to dig up one pole. Next time we come to the river, I'll make sure there are plenty to go around."

"Can I watch?" Esther raised her hand in the air and hopped on one foot.

"Me, too." Hannah and Katie echoed in unison.

Everyone laughed.

"Yes, you may." Owen playfully bowed like an actor thanking his audience. He started toward the water, only to halt and face the children.

Gravel flew as Katie and the twins skidded to a stop.

"Anyone can come to the riverbank with me, but you have to be extra quiet." He placed a finger against his lips. "We don't want to scare the fish away before we've had time to catch them."

"I promise." Esther lowered her arm and nodded.

"Me, too." Katie kept her voice low.

"Me, three." Hannah's shout brought looks of doubt from her sister and Katie.

While the sheriff and his helpers went to the water, Maggie and Belinda spread a blanket out under an old oak tree. Mrs. Lamb sat in the shade and opened the large satchel she'd brought with her. She pulled out a ball of bright red yarn and a pair of knitting needles. "This looks like the perfect time to catch up on my latest project."

"What are you working on?" Maggie sat beside Mrs. Lamb, facing the river where she could keep an eye on the children. They were in good hands with Owen, but he was outnumbered.

"I'm making matching sweaters for Katie and the twins."

"That's so sweet of you."

"I know it's hard to believe right now," Mrs. Lamb glanced at the sky, "but I hear it gets pretty cold here in the winter."

"I wouldn't mind a bit of cooler weather." Belinda leaned back against a tree and closed her eyes. "It's so peaceful out here."

Maggie opened her purse and pulled out a book she brought along to read. What with keeping an eye on the activity a few yards below, she didn't expect to get too much reading done.

The sun was high in the sky by the time Owen and his band of silent observers made their way back up the trail to the wagon. Impressed with how quiet the girls had stayed while he fished, he planned to make sure they all had poles of their own next time.

"Look what Sheriff Owen caught." Esther grinned from ear to ear as she skipped alongside him.

Maggie put down the book she held and waved. Mrs. Lamb put her knitting aside and grinned. Belinda moved as if she'd been woken from a nap. They all seemed rested and happy. He was pleased Mrs. Lamb had suggested this venture.

"Let me clean those for you while you get the fire ready." The older woman stood and joined him at the edge of the blanket.

"All right." He handed over the string of five large catfish. "I have no doubt they're in capable hands."

"Let me help you with those," Belinda offered, and she and Mrs. Lamb moved away from their campsite to get the food ready.

"Now what?" Hannah placed her hands on her hips much like he'd seen her aunt do a time or two. "I'm hungry."

"We have to get a fire started, and that calls for sticks. Anyone who plans to eat can either clean fish or gather sticks."

All three girls scattered in search of kindling.

"Stay in sight of the blanket." Maggie put her book away and stood. She dusted off her skirt and then her hands. "How can I help?"

"Right behind you is a peach tree." He looked into her eyes and everything stood still for a moment.

Her brows creased.

Owen flushed at being caught gawking. He tried to swallow, but his mouth had gone dry. Tearing his attention away from her face, he focused instead on the tree behind her. "The fruit available this time of year is one of the reasons why I chose this spot. If you don't mind picking a few, I think the children will enjoy them."

The girls came back with Katie's billowed apron full of sticks.

Owen went to the wagon and handed the girls a small basket. "There's some strawberries out there." He waved in the general direction where he'd seen the plants on a previous visit by himself. Then he reached into his shirt pocket and brought out a piece of flint. As soon as the flames were good and strong, he slipped over to the wagon and pulled a box out from under the bench seat. Taking out a large skillet, he placed it over the fire to heat.

"What else is in the box?" Katie and the twins had returned to the blanket with a basket full of berries.

"I brought some tin plates and forks for eating with." He tapped the side of the box. "And I had time this morning to pick up rolls from the pastry shop."

"It sounds as if you have everything under control." Maggie returned with several peaches. Her smile didn't quite reach her eyes.

Was she making fun of him? He knew the area well, having had more cookouts beside this river than he could count. "Chalk it up to experience."

Mrs. Lamb and Belinda rejoined them, laughing, and chatting as they approached the blanket. He sensed more than heard Maggie's sigh of relief.

"Here you are." The elder of the two women handed the cleaned fish to Owen, and he put the filets in the hot skillet.

While the fish cooked, they snacked on peaches and strawberries.

There was plenty of fish to go around, and everyone got a roll from the bakery.

"The fish was delicious." Hearing Mrs. Lamb's praise pleased him. She was, after all, a professional cook and knew good food.

"Yes. Thank you very much." Maggie's broad smile put a sparkle in her beautiful eyes. The dark-blue hue was like a summer sky just before dawn.

"Katie." Belinda cleared her throat as she gathered dirty plates and forks. Her movements pulled Owen from gazing at Maggie. "Why don't you and I go to the water and clean the dishes?"

"I'll help you." Maggie started to rise, but Belinda motioned for her to stop.

"Katie and I can handle it. The twins have hardly spent any time with you today."

As soon as Belinda left, Esther scooted across the blanket and took her place next to Owen. Hannah moved over to sit on his other side. Their eyelids drooped as each of them yawned.

"Sheriff Owen," Mrs. Lamb pulled out her knitting, "why don't you tell us a story from when you were a boy and camped out at night."

"Well, let me see." Not much of a story-teller, he did have a few funny things happen to him when he was a boy. He leaned back against a tree and rested his hands on his lap. "One night my brother and I came out here, just the two of us. We had fish for dinner and some other food Mom sent along."

"Did you ever sleep in a tent?" Hannah's blue eyes widened with curiosity.

"No." He didn't take the time to explain real cowboys didn't use tents. Those were for city folks. "We slept by the fire."

"Were you scared?" Esther leaned her head on his arm.

"No." He'd had his big brother with him. It was almost as safe as having Father there. "Well, not at first."

"What happened at second?" Hannah stretched out beside him.

Mrs. Lamb let out a chuckle before pulling more string from the ball of red yarn.

"Well, I thought I heard something in the forest."

Hannah's mouth dropped open, and her eyes grew wider.

Esther sat up straight.

Maggie covered her mouth with her hand,

but her eyes crinkled at the corners.

"What was it?" Esther raised her head. She pulled her knees to her chest and wrapped her arms around her legs. "I bet it was a bear or a deer, or maybe even a lion."

"Lion?" Hannah snorted in disbelief but peered toward the trees on either side of them. "There aren't lions here. Are there?"

"Well, we do have mountain lions." They did roam the hills after dark, but he didn't want to scare the little ones. "They're smaller than the lions you're thinking of and only come out after everyone has fallen asleep at night."

"Was it a mountain lion?" Maggie seemed as interested in the story as the twins.

"No, it wasn't."

"What was it, then?" Apparently, he had Mrs. Lamb's attention as well.

"Just a raccoon looking for something to eat."

"Did you chase it away?" Hannah's eyes began to droop again, and she snuggled back into his side.

"No, my brother scared it away."

Belinda and Katie returned from the river and filled the supply box with the clean dishes before making themselves comfortable on the blanket.

"Look at that cloud." Hannah pointed to

the sky. "It looks like a rabbit."

Owen followed her gaze. "It does look like a rabbit."

"That one looks like a tree." Esther joined in the game. Both girls lay on their backs, pointing out shapes between yawns. Hannah fell asleep first.

"There is one that looks like a magic castle," Esther mumbled as she dozed off. "I wonder where the bean stock is."

"They'll sleep for a couple of hours." Maggie put her book away. "We better load the wagon and head back so they can have a proper nap."

Owen carried the little girls to the wagon where there were blankets for them to sleep on. Esther mumbled in her sleep, but Hannah slept like a rock. He and the ladies loaded the wagon and started for town. He had spent many cookouts by the lake, but none as rewarding as this one. The twins warmed his heart. Katie was no longer timid, and they all got along well. Maggie still kept her distance, but even she seemed to enjoy their time together.

10

Owen lowered the newspaper onto his desk. He stared off into space and thought about what he'd just read. Something didn't add up. Pinkerton agents had been called in to investigate the wagon train attack. Several items reported missing were recovered in a cave less than fifty miles from West Ridge. More disturbing than the proximity of the gang's apparent hideout was another new detail. Families separated by the chaos and confusion were trying to locate one another. A man from the caravan claimed his niece was missing. A search was underway for a teenage girl named Katherine.

Katie could be short for Katherine. Yesterday, at the river she hadn't acted like a missing child. She seemed happier than any of them. He recalled how skittish she had been the day the welcome wagon arrived. Her behavior wasn't surprising, considering all they'd been through.

He needed to investigate the matter a bit more, although he didn't want to upset the women. He was sure none of them were kidnappers, but he couldn't look the other way. Might this explain Maggie's reluctance to be around him? He wasn't the brightest or best-looking fellow in town, but there seemed to be something more than his looks or intelligence keeping her from being friendly.

The sound of feet running on the boardwalk stopped just outside the office door. Buster roused from his nap and rose onto all four legs. Rob barreled through the door like a man with a bobcat hot on his tail. He looked so distraught Owen jumped from his seat and reached for his gun belt before realizing his weapon was still in his desk drawer.

"Sheriff, I need to report a stolen horse."

"Calm down." Owen took a deep breath to still his racing heart. He returned to his chair and motioned for Rob to have a seat. "You mean to tell me someone stole Starlight?"

Rob's Tennessee Walker was his pride and joy. The black stallion could outrun any other horse in the county. Rob won first place in the county fair last year with his horse. Who would be brazen enough to take a well-known animal?

"Not Starlight." Rob didn't sit. Instead, he threw his hands up and gawked at Owen as if he'd lost his mind. "One of the horses at the livery stable."

Rob ran the local livery. Most folks had their own horses but, on occasion, it was nice to rent a horse and buggy to take for a drive out along the river. Rob's stable only had three rentals.

"Are you sure it didn't get out on its own?" It wasn't unheard of for an unsettled horse to escape from its corral. The task of rounding up strays had fallen on his shoulders more times than he cared to count.

"Get out?" Rob took two steps toward the stove, pivoted, and took three more toward the desk, gesturing with one hand while he spoke. "I'll have you know, in over fifteen years of running the stables, I've never lost an animal."

There was always a first time, but Owen wasn't about to say that to the already agitated man. He took out a pencil and paper and did his best to stifle a sigh. "When did you last see the horse?"

"Last night when I shut the stables." Calmer now, Rob slid into the seat across from Owen.

"Around what time was it?"

"Now, Sheriff, you and everyone else in

town know I shut the doors at six every night for supper."

Owen shot out the next question to keep the man from returning to pacing the floor. "When did you first notice the horse was missing?"

"This morning when I opened the stable door."

"What time . . . never mind," Owen wrote half past seven on his notepad. "Was the door locked during the night?"

"No."

"Why not?"

"I never lock the doors." Rob's lip curled on one side as he shrugged his shoulder. "Why should I? No one's ever tried to steal one of my horses."

Exactly, and why now? It could be someone messing with him. Some of the teenage boys liked to pull a prank from time to time. Not long ago, all the street signs in town had been turned to point in the wrong direction.

"Describe the horse for me, please."

"It was the tan gelding with the dark mane."

"All right. I'll check around and see what I come up with. Let me know if the horse shows up."

"I will." Rob rose and veered for the exit.

He had his hand on the doorknob but paused. His brows puckered. "See you keep me posted on what you find."

"I will." Owen breathed a sigh of relief once the door closed.

This was the first real theft in town in his four years as acting sheriff. If something went missing, it always showed back up. Like people, animals wanted their freedom. There had been the time when Mrs. Todd's custard cream pie disappeared right off the table at the church potluck. To this day, the pie was still unaccounted for, although gossip had it that the pastry got left at home. No one knew for sure as Mayor Todd and his wife refused to discuss it.

More likely, it was the Wilson boys and some of their friends playing another prank. There was no telling with the teen boys. When they got bored, they tended to get rascally. Owen cleared off his desk and grabbed his hat before pulling the gun belt from the bottom drawer. He'd ride out to the Wilson place and then visit some folks with older boys still living at home and keep an eye out for the missing horse.

Owen tugged the cinch on Jasper's saddle to make sure it was tight. He put one foot in the stirrup and swung his leg over the horse's back. The humidity was high but heavy cloud cover blocked most of the sun's penetrating rays. It was a sure sign they would see a rain shower or two before the day was over.

He rode west with Buster tagging along. When they came to the broken gate at the edge of town, Owen turned Jasper south toward the Wilsons' homestead. Chuck Wilson had three rather rowdy teenage boys known to get into trouble from time to time. Nothing too serious, to date. One year they nailed the school's outhouse door shut. Last winter they stuck a black snake in the schoolteacher's desk. Her screams were heard all across town. The school board hired a new teacher for this upcoming school year. A man who said he wasn't afraid of snakes.

Owen ran the back of his hand across his brow. The farther away he rode from the river, the hotter it got. Finally, he came to the bluffs known for their caves. Cool underground air vented out in spots and the towering cliffs provided shade the rest of the way to the Wilsons' place.

"Howdy, Sheriff." Chuck Wilson sat on his front porch, sipping tea from a mason jar. The farmer was quite a worker but, at this time of the day, it was too hot in the Ozarks for hard labor. "Come on down from there and sit for a spell. What brings you way out here?"

Owen dismounted and tethered Jasper next to the horse trough. Buster rose on his back legs and drank with the horse before following Owen.

"Just out looking for a stray horse." Owen chose his words carefully. There was no sense in getting anyone upset by accusing their kin of possible wrongdoing. Especially way out here where no one was looking.

"Annie," Chuck hollered toward the front window. "Bring out some tea for the sheriff."

Owen removed his hat and mounted the steps to the wide porch. Buster stayed at the bottom of the stairs as he'd been trained. He kept an eye out, with one ear turned toward Owen.

"Sit down." Chuck shoved an old hound dog off the chair next to his and motioned for Owen to fill the empty spot. "Have a seat."

As soon as Owen was seated, the front door opened, and Annie came out with another mason jar.

"Thank you." Owen accepted the cool glass of tea and took a much-needed drink.

Annie gave him a shy nod and disappeared into the house.

"How are the melons looking this year?" Some of the sweetest watermelons came from this part of the Ozarks, and Chuck Wilson had a reputation for growing the best.

"We've got a good crop going." Chuck took a swig from his jar. "The second harvest won't be ready for another month or so."

"Folks in town sure are looking forward to more when they're ripe."

"Me, too. I've hired a crew from Calico Rock to come up and help pick them this year." Chuck set his drink on an old stump used as a table. "I heard about the welcome wagon. How are those new folks getting along?"

"As far as I can tell, they're doing all right." Owen took another long, deep drink.

Annie might not have much to say, but she knew the secret to making sweet tea the way it was meant to be made.

"What kind of stray did you say you are looking for?"

"A tan gelding with a dark mane got out of the stables last night." Owen finished his tea and sat the empty glass next to Chuck's.

"Hey, boys!" Wilson hollered in the direction of the old red barn and then looked toward Owen. "They were out scouting the forests this morning looking for burdock roots for their mama. I imagine they'd have said something during lunch if they'd seen a stray, but I suppose it won't hurt to ask."

All three of the Wilson boys filed out from the barn when their father called them. Tall, broad-shouldered with dark curly hair, it was hard to tell them apart from a distance.

"Hey, it's the sheriff." One of the boys turned to his brothers who both shrugged in response.

Buster's tail wagged as the boys passed him, but he remained seated. The young men mounted the steps and gave Owen a nod as they marched past him to line up in front of their father.

"The sheriff's out looking for a stray horse. Have you boys seen any strange horses around the property today?"

"No, sir." Eyes wide and brows creased, they shook their heads in unison. They looked innocent enough to Owen. They were playful boys but good-hearted.

"What does it look like?" The eldest boy, Calvin, took the role as spokesperson for the trio. "We'll be sure to keep a lookout for it."

"Tan coat with a dark mane." Owen stood. It was a long ride back to town. "If you do that for me, I'd appreciate it."

"All right, boys, you can go."

With their father's dismissal, they scurried down the steps and hurried back to the barn.

Owen held back a laugh and placed his hat on his head. "Thanks, Chuck. I hope to see you all in town soon."

"We'll be there Sunday if the weather holds." Chuck grabbed his and Owen's glasses and rose from his chair. He turned to the front door and paused. "I hope you find your missing horse, Sheriff."

"Thanks." On the way to his horse, Owen slipped Buster a treat.

He had covered most of the south section of the woods, but there was an area of woodland just past the bluffs he wanted to check out. It would put him in the right direction toward town. Tonight was the restaurant's grand opening, and he didn't want to miss out on Mrs. Lamb's cooking or a chance to see Maggie.

He was a fool to keep thinking about her. A beautiful woman like Maggie would never be interested in the likes of him. Although, he wasn't bad looking. According to Mother, he was handsome. No doubt, Maggie had met her share of sophisticated fellas, but she didn't strike him as being a snob. What had he done to make her dislike him so much?

Owen blew out a long breath of air. He needed a vacation. It had been a while since he'd visited his folks. Even the town sheriff was allowed a little time off. A few days down in Hot Springs with his parents would help him clear his head.

"Whoa." He pulled gently on Jasper's reins, looking about.

Buster's low growl let Owen know the danger was gone, but someone had been here. They had ridden into an abandoned campsite. Sections of the tall grass lay flattened. A horse and rider had been through here and not too long ago. Still green, a pattern of crushed foliage showed where someone spent a lot of time. Whiffs of smoke still emanated from the embers of a fire ring.

Owen surveyed the empty forest before dismounting to get a closer look. Buster sniffed around the area, going in circles. Boot prints, the size a man about his height would wear, and the markings left from two, maybe three, horses were all he could find. Whoever had been here cleaned up after themselves well. It could have been kids playing or someone out hunting. It seemed like an odd place to set up camp, though. Owen scouted around a bit more until he came to a line of walnut trees.

He stopped in his tracks and gaped. Goose bumps rose on the back of his neck. From the top of this ridge, there was a perfect view of the town below. It appeared someone had been spying on the folks in West Ridge. He swung around and peered at the empty campsite. Who had been staying here and why?

Maggie took a long look around the dining room. Five tables lined the walls on both sides where pews once stood. Each one had a pair of salt-and-pepper shakers, as well as napkins and silverware ready to be used. She and Belinda spent most of the afternoon getting the room ready. Their grand opening was tonight for the dinner meal. Tomorrow they would be open for all three — breakfast, lunch, and dinner.

The aroma of coffee and tonight's special, beef stew, permeated from the kitchen where Mrs. Lamb reigned. She had her stations set up last night and spent a good part of the day prepping food. The Welcome Wagon Restaurant was ready for customers. Maggie turned to Belinda and gave her friend and fellow waitress the best smile she could muster. "Are you ready?"

"I'm ready as I'll ever be." The petite woman gave a quick curtsy and grinned.

"All right, then." Maggie took a deep breath to settle her nerves. "I'll go unlock the door."

When she stepped into the foyer, the sound of chatter came from outside the building. Surprised, she flipped the open sign and unlocked the door.

"It's about time." Mr. Anderson from the telegraph office joked as he stepped into the foyer. He removed his hat and peeked into the dining room. "It's been a long time since I've had a home-cooked meal."

"We're happy to have you join us." It was restaurant cooking not home, but she got his meaning. She waved her arm toward the dining room. "Welcome to the Welcome Wagon Restaurant."

Mr. Anderson hung his hat on one of the hooks on the wall before he passed into the dining room.

Belinda asked him where he'd like to sit.

Mr. and Mrs. Carter entered the foyer followed by the mayor and his wife.

"Welcome. I'm so glad you could join us."

Mrs. Todd took Maggie's hand. "We're so happy to have a place to eat in town."

"We wouldn't miss it for the world." The mayor's grin spread wide across his face. "The Welcome Wagon Restaurant is a history-making event in West Ridge."

His excitement was contagious, and she could understand why he had been made mayor of the town. The two couples smiled and thanked her as they passed into the diner.

The minister and his wife came next. The blacksmith, Rudy Brown, was with them. She welcomed the trio and then peered out onto the boardwalk. Maggie placed her hand on her neck and gasped. More customers were waiting to file through the door.

"I hope you have lots of hot coffee." Dale, from the Savings and Loan, entered, followed by the two men who worked with him at the bank.

"Don't worry about coffee," Maggie assured their financer. "That's one thing we have plenty of."

After they passed through, she peeked out the window. There were several more men from the community all headed for the restaurant. She recognized most of their faces from around town or church, but she didn't see Owen among them. That seemed strange. She had been so sure he would be there for their opening night.

Happy to be back in town, Owen's attention shifted to the old church building on Main Street. The Welcome Wagon Restaurant swarmed with customers. Horses and buggies filled the street, raising dust as they moved along the road. The small town was bursting with activity. He pulled his mount to a stop in front of his office and tethered the horse before heading for the restaurant. The place looked busier than a fox in a chicken pen.

"Hello, Sheriff." Belinda greeted him with a friendly smile as he stepped into the foyer. "We wondered if you would show."

"I had some business out of town. It kept me longer than I'd planned." He removed his hat, but the hooks on the wall were all taken. He set the Stetson on a table filled with hats. "I guess I'll have to find more hooks for the wall."

"Go on inside." Belinda waved her hand toward the open doorway. "We've slowed down a bit. Maggie and I have switched jobs a couple times already. She's taking her turn waiting on customers."

Owen found an empty table in a back corner. He could have joined just about anyone at one of the other tables, but he had some thinking to do and preferred to be alone while he speculated on what he'd discovered on top of the ridge.

"Are you ready to order, Sheriff?" He expected Maggie, but Katie was the one who came to take his order. "Maggie let me fill in while she puts the girls to bed."

"I'll have some coffee and whatever the special is tonight."

The teenager jotted down some notes on a slip of paper and hurried toward the kitchen. Owen surveyed the room while he waited. There weren't any new faces in the crowd. The only time they had strangers in town was when someone's kin came for a visit. So, who had been camping on the ridge and why? It could have been hunters, but fall season was a more popular time for hunting. The only kids living in that part of the county were the Wilson boys. Chuck wasn't likely to allow his boys to camp out during harvest. Owen was still considering the possibilities when Katie brought his food. He thought over the reason why anyone would want to keep an eye on the town as he ate his meal.

Some time later, Owen glanced at his empty plate. He leaned back and let out a satisfied sigh. The food was good, and he was full. One of the last to show, the diner had cleared out by the time he finished eating.

Across the room, Maggie had returned and relieved Katie. She removed plates and silverware from one table and placed them onto a cart while Belinda followed with a wet rag. After she wiped the table, she straightened the chairs.

"How did your first day go?" He waited until they worked on the table closest to him.

"Good." Maggie brushed off her hands and took a seat across from him. "We had a lot more people show than I expected."

"It's a good thing Mrs. Lamb knows how to cook for a crowd." Belinda joined them, taking the chair across from the window.

"Everyone seemed happy. I never heard any complaints." Maggie paused to cover a yawn with her hand. "A few promised to return soon."

"Don't be surprised if by soon they mean breakfast."

"You weren't kidding about the town needing a restaurant."

"There wouldn't be much of a need for a diner without a bunch of hungry men." Owen pushed his plate away and reached for his coffee.

"Kind of like an empty jailhouse." Belinda's lips turned upward in a brief smile.

It was no secret the holding cells were empty. It must seem odd to the ladies from back East. A town of just under one hundred citizens was quiet for the most part.

"I'm proud to have never had anyone in my jailhouse."

A hint of confusion marred Maggie's brow. "Do you mean to say you've never had to put anyone in jail before?"

"No." The back of his neck heated. He wished he could take back his last comment, but it was too late. "I've never had any reason to."

Belinda's jaw dropped. She leaned forward, placed her elbow on the tabletop, and propped her chin in the palm of her hand. "How long have you been sheriff of West Ridge?"

"Going on about four years." Owen grimaced. Four years without making an arrest might sound incompetent, but that wasn't the case in this situation. He squared his shoulders. They were from the city, where crime ran rampant. Here in the hills, folks were more civilized.

"Have you ever had to fire your gun?" Belinda narrowed her eyes, and she pulled away from the table, letting her arms drop.

"Don't you worry. There's a reason why there aren't any outlaws in town."

"Really?" An impressed smile replaced Belinda's cynical snicker. "You have a reputation, have you?"

She didn't understand. He was good with

a gun, but he wouldn't be baited by a woman from the city where crime was part of the system. Some played by the rules and others tried to work their way around them, looking for an easy payoff. Here in the Ozarks, it was different. People weren't looking out for themselves. Here the law of the land was to treat your neighbor as you would have them treat you.

11

A week later, Maggie stood outside the restaurant, watching the sunset fade with a growing sense of unease. The vibrant red and pink hues painted a swath across the western sky. She couldn't pinpoint what had brought on her melancholy mood. Perhaps it was the fact everything was going so well. Running the restaurant kept her busy, and they no longer depended on the community for their needs. So, why were her thoughts filled with shades of guilt?

The twins would be starting school soon. Sarah would never hear her little girls read their first books or help them spell their names. Maggie and the children were happy, and it seemed so unfair.

She shook away the negative thoughts. She had work to do. This was her first waitressing job, and she enjoyed serving people. Being a waitress brought her in contact with all the customers. They expected to see a smile on her face. Mrs. Lamb did the cooking, Katie watched the girls when they weren't sleeping, and Belinda floated wherever she was needed. They all did their parts well. Over the last few weeks, she had met almost all of the people who called West Ridge their home.

So far, she'd liked everyone she'd met. To be honest, she was growing fond of the community. Dr. Gentry was a wise gentleman with a great sense of humor. It was hard to believe he and Rob were brothers. Still, Rob held a special place in her heart. He was the first person from West Ridge they met the day he picked them up at the way station in Batesville. The two brothers made a point of coming to the restaurant every morning for breakfast.

The mayor and Mrs. Todd were like guardian angels. They stayed in the background for the most part, but whenever a need came along, they were the first to step in to help. Pastor and Mrs. Irvin lifted her spirits and kept her on course.

Mr. Prescott, the schoolteacher, was a nice man, if not a bit eccentric. He didn't come as often as many of the other bachelors, but he did seem to enjoy Mrs. Lamb's roast beef. Dale made a point of coming every other night or so. Most likely he was checking on his investment. There was no need for him to worry. They were staying busy, much busier than she ever dreamed.

Avoiding Owen hadn't been as difficult as she had imagined. First of all, she was too busy at the restaurant for any socializing. Also, he was on a case looking for a stolen horse. The more she got acquainted with him, the more she grew to appreciate he was a multitalented person who took on many different duties. He did each one just as well as the others.

"Good evening, Miss Maggie." Fred Barkley waved as he crossed the street headed for the restaurant.

"Hello." Maggie's break was over. She slipped back into the building and took her place in the foyer. It was her turn to welcome their guests.

Inside the dining area, Belinda took orders.

Katie was watching over the girls in their room.

Maggie thanked the Lord for bringing her and the girls to West Ridge. She couldn't help feeling God brought her here for this specific time to these specific people. She needed them, and they needed her. Well, they needed Mrs. Lamb's cooking, but she had her part to offer. All the wonderful things taking place in her life were thanks to God. How amazing the creator of the universe would care enough to see her needs were met. Events in the past, leading up to the attack on the wagon train, had left her feeling bitter. Not long ago she wondered if God even cared.

The door opened, and Owen stepped into the foyer. He removed his hat and hung it on an empty hook. His shirt was wrinkled and his hair windswept, as if he'd been out riding. Like many other single men in town, it appeared the lawman would be a regular customer.

"Welcome to the Welcome Wagon, Sheriff."

"Thank you." He hesitated at the entrance, peering into the dining room, as if searching for someone. "I'm supposed to meet Dr. Gentry. Has he arrived yet?"

"I haven't seen him." Maggie glanced into the dining room. She could have easily missed the doctor while on her break, but there was no sign of him inside. "No, he isn't here."

"Mind if I wait for him in here?"

"No, of course not." She pointed toward the chair by the window. "Make yourself comfortable."

"I'd rather stand." He moved to allow

room for Rodney Ford from the bank to exit.

The two men acknowledged each other with a nod.

"I've been out riding all day." Owen waited until they were alone again to speak.

She had noticed his absence around town as of late. "Do you always have to travel so much?"

"No, it's very unusual." Owen frowned and blew out a breath. "I'm trying to track down a stray."

She'd heard about the missing horse from the livery stable. The breakfast crowd was very informative. They kept each other up to date better than any paper could.

Owen crossed over to the window and looked outside. "It's pretty low to take an animal that doesn't belong to you."

"Yes, it is."

A sinking feeling settled in the pit of her stomach. Was there a hidden meaning in his words?

The door opened before she could give it more thought. She brushed away any feelings of guilt and turned to greet their new customer.

"Hello, Doc." Owen reached out and shook Dr. Gentry's hand.

"Good evening." The kind older man's

smile included Maggie before he gave his attention to Owen. "I wasn't sure if you'd wait for me."

"It's no problem. I haven't been here long myself."

"I'm sure you gentlemen are hungry." Maggie waved her hand toward the dining room. "Go right in and find a table. Belinda will be with you shortly."

Once she was alone again, she heaved a sigh of relief. Three months until Katie turned eighteen. Maggie prayed she could last another three months. It would be a wonderful day when she no longer had to look over her shoulder or panic at the mention of missing persons.

Satisfied after a full meal and good company, Owen returned to his office. There was a stack of letters on his desk. Most folks picked up their mail at the mercantile, but Fred made a special effort to hand-deliver Owen's messages to his office. If he wasn't in, the mailman left them on his desk. It was just one of the perks of his position. He helped Fred sort the mail and, in return, he didn't have to stand in line at the post office when the mail came in.

Exhausted from their longer than usual ride, Buster finished drinking his water and plopped down on his rug. The missing horse and the unidentified campsite stretched Owen's security perimeter. Today they had scoured the countryside, but there was no sign of the horse or whoever had been making camp on top of the ridge.

He picked up the pile of mail. There was a batch of new wanted posters. He set it aside. He would get to it in a moment. There was a copy of the weekly newspaper. On the front page was a picture of a covered wagon and an article about the attack. The law in Missouri wasn't about to let the crime grow cold. Good for them. Owen put the paper on top of the wanted posters. Next was a letter addressed to him. He recognized his mother's writing.

"Looks like we got a letter from Mom today." He glanced over at Buster.

The dog snored in his sleep and then let out a deep sigh. It might be a good idea to leave Buster home next time he had extra miles to cover. The heat was hard on the animal.

Owen tore open the envelope and pulled out two sheets of paper.

Dear Owen,
   We were so happy to hear from you. It sounds like West Ridge is doing fine. I'm

glad to hear how well everyone is. Your father sends his love. His joints are so much less painful as his arthritis has improved.

Our community welcomed a wagon of women as well. We have close to a dozen ladies and children we have been able to help start anew. One of them has a beautiful singing voice and is a joy to listen to in church.

That reminds me. The sheriff of Hot Springs is looking for a deputy sheriff. He's getting up in age and needs someone with experience to train to take over in a couple of years. I mentioned you to him, and he is interested in meeting you.

Wouldn't that be wonderful? We'd love being able to see your handsome face every day. You would have three deputies working under you, and in Hot Springs, the number of women outweighs the number of men. I think you would be happy here, son. Give it some thought, and prayer, of course.

All our love, Mother and Father

Owen folded the sheets of paper and put them back in the envelope. Leave West Ridge? The thought never occurred to him before. Could he pull up roots and leave

213

everything he had ever known? His talents were wasted here. He was a crack shot and had been trained to track anything that moved. In a bigger city, he would be able to put his skills into practice. No more Mr. Fix It. After all, there wasn't anything holding him here, was there? What had Dr. Gentry said at the church social? Owen needed to reach his full potential. Did he have to move on to make anything of his life?

He set aside the newspaper and went for the wanted posters. The package this week was thin. He looked through them, but none of the names or faces were familiar. They never were, but he liked to keep up to date on whom to look out for.

Owen returned to the letter from his mother. He rubbed his thumb along the front of the envelope, tracing his name and address. He paused his finger when he came to the town. West Ridge. This would require some thought and much time in prayer. He tucked the news from his parents into the drawer where he kept his personal papers. What it boiled down to was whether he was happy to remain where he wasn't needed and there was no future for him, or should he move on to greener pastures.

12

"I think we should consider adding biscuits and gravy to the breakfast menu." Maggie and Mrs. Lamb sat at the kitchen table discussing what they needed to order for the restaurant. "I've had more than a few requests."

"That's a wonderful suggestion." Mrs. Lamb added something to her list. "Sausage gravy is easy to make and to keep warm. We always have more than enough biscuits."

Maggie raised her head at the sound of footsteps in the hall. The twins were taking a nap in Mrs. Lamb's room, and Katie was at the pastry shop.

Belinda marched into the kitchen, smiling. "You won't believe what just happened."

"Well, will you tell us or make us guess?" Mrs. Lamb smiled at Belinda's dramatic pause.

"I've been invited to join the Women's

Church Committee."

"That's wonderful." Maggie jumped from the table and gave her friend a quick hug. "I'm so happy for you."

Belinda had been reluctant to attend church when they'd first arrived, but since they started the restaurant, the somewhat-reclusive woman had made new friends and had begun to open up more.

"I'm not so sure how I feel about it, but I said yes." Belinda's cheeks reddened.

"Come sit down." Mrs. Lamb pulled the chair beside her away from the table and patted the seat. "Tell us all about it."

"Well, Mrs. Todd stopped me when I came out from the pastry shop." Belinda placed a bag on the table and pulled out three doughnuts. "I almost forgot. I picked up something for us to snack on. There are three more for the twins when they get up from their nap. And for Katie."

"So, tell us what Mrs. Todd had to say." Mrs. Lamb placed one of the doughnuts on a napkin.

"She said she wanted to ask me a question. Then she told me how the church has ladies representing different businesses in town. They get together and discuss ways to help the community. At their last meeting, they took a vote and decided they would like for me to join as a representative from the restaurant."

"You're perfect for the job. I'm so glad they asked you."

"Aunt Maggie." Esther walked into the kitchen, rubbing sleep from her eyes. "I'm awake."

Maggie glanced down at the watch pinned to her dress. "Good. It's almost time for us to go. Let's get Hannah and get ready."

She and the twins had an appointment at the schoolhouse to meet with the teacher, Mr. Prescott. With school starting in less than a month, he wanted to meet with them and give suggestions to help them be ready for the school year. After a few minutes, Maggie and the twins set out to their appointment.

The girls skipped beside Maggie as they held onto her hands. It was hot out, a sticky hot she'd come to associate with the Ozarks. She was thankful they were headed toward the river. As they drew closer to the water, a slight breeze caressed her cheeks and forehead.

The new church building served as the schoolhouse during the week when school was in session. Mr. Prescott was standing at the top of the steps when they reached the property.

"Hello," he called and waved. "Good afternoon, ladies."

The tall, thin man waited until they reached the last step to move aside and usher them into the building.

"We only have eleven students this year and won't require much space." Mr. Prescott motioned for them to follow him to the front of the room. "They will start building a schoolhouse this fall. It will be next to the church. Until then we will have class in one of the Sunday school rooms. You can see why this location is perfect. It's more centralized for students living out of town, and there's a breeze from the Spring River when the temperature gets hot."

Maggie took a seat on one of the back pews while the teacher quizzed the girls on their numbers, the alphabet, and colors. She was quite sure they would both do well. They had been working on all three for some time and were making progress.

"Very good." Mr. Prescott smiled when he was finished. "You girls may go play on the swings. They're right outside this window, so I'll be keeping an eye on you while I speak with your aunt."

"Yes, sir," they answered in unison. They looked so somber that Maggie had to fight to keep from giggling.

"Miss Maggie." The schoolmaster came to sit beside her. "I'm impressed with how well the girls did. They will fit in well with their class. There are two other children in their grade, a boy and a girl."

"The twins are looking forward to making new friends."

"Yes. They seem to be on level both socially and academically." He glanced toward the window.

Maggie followed his gaze. The girls were singing while they swung.

"I believe you're from the East Coast. May I inquire as to where?"

"The girls and I are from Boston."

"Oh, a Bostonian." His eyes sparkled and red blotches spread across his cheeks. "I come from Newark and enjoy talking with anyone from home. I want to assure you I have the proper credentials to teach. I'm the youngest son of a family of three boys and two girls.

"But you're here to talk about school. The twins are the last two students for me to meet with. I expect us to have a fine class this year. Most of the older kids graduated last year, so I have mainly beginners and some middle school-age children. It will allow me to concentrate on helping the younger students with the basics."

"That's good to hear." She would miss the girls during the day, but it was nice to know they would be with children close to their own age.

"How are you adjusting to life in the Ozarks?"

"Just fine. We're busy with the restaurant, of course."

"Oh, yes, thank goodness for the Welcome Wagon Restaurant. I love the food there. Mrs. Lamb is a fine cook. I've been to several dining establishments back East, and if she would like to discuss some of the dishes I've found to be exceptional, she only needs to ask."

"Thank you. I'll let her know." Maggie glanced out the window.

The girls were still sitting on the swings but were dragging their feet through the dirt rather than swinging.

She stood to leave. "I better get the girls back home and help prepare for the dinner crowd."

"Well, then, it was nice to meet you. Please don't hesitate to ask any questions you may have. I'm happy to help." The schoolmaster walked her to the door. "If Mrs. Lamb needs some menu ideas, I can always write home to Mother. She'd be happy to pass on some of her cooking secrets."

He sounded a bit homesick. She would put in a good word with Mrs. Lamb and see if they could accommodate his desire for one of his mother's recipes.

"Thank you. I'll let her know." Maggie called for the girls when she reached the bottom step outside.

They both jumped from the swings and ran over to her side. All three of them waved good-bye to the teacher as they started down the hill. She was learning her way around town and was comfortable with the setting.

As they neared the jailhouse, Owen was outside the building, preparing to enter his office. Maggie tried to slow their steps to avoid speaking with him, but the girls pulled on her arms, calling out his name. "Sheriff Owen."

He waited for them to reach him.

"Guess where we went?" Esther loved to play guessing games or any kind of game, for that matter.

"Let me guess." He glanced at Maggie and tipped his hat before turning back to the girls. "I know, you've just come back from seeing the Great Wall of China."

"No." Hannah shook her head and put

her hands on her hips. "We met our teacher."

"Oh, and who is your teacher?"

"Mr. Prescott." Esther tilted her head to the side and squinted. "Didn't you already know that? Isn't the sheriff supposed to know everything?"

"You would think so, wouldn't you?" He scratched the back of his head and wriggled his brows before turning serious. "It sounds as though you two will enjoy school."

"I will," Hannah said.

"Me, too," Esther echoed.

"Girls, it's time to tell the sheriff goodbye. I need to get back to work, and you both have some letters to practice."

The look in his eyes drew her in for a moment, but she stiffened her shoulders. "Good day, Sheriff."

Owen hung his hat on the hook and glanced around his office. It had been a while since he'd done any cleaning. He grabbed the broom from the corner and started sweeping the floor. It wasn't as if anyone would stop by and inspect the place, but as Mother always said, "a stitch in time saved nine." It was too bad she never had any daughters. The woman had a lot of knowledge to pass on to a girl. He and his older brother were all boy and constantly getting into scrapes.

Buster sat by his food bowl and watched.

Owen's thoughts filled with images of Maggie, and a knot formed in the pit of his stomach. It was good to see the twins settling in so well. There were at least two other children their age who'd be starting their first year of school too. Hannah and Esther would fit right in. If only it was as easy to figure out their aunt. She hadn't said one word to him. Well, there was the polite, "Good day, Sheriff," but other than that, he might as well have been invisible.

Maggie fascinated him, plain and simple. She appealed to him in a way no other woman had before. He looked forward to running into her on the boardwalk or being on-call to help when anything went wrong at the restaurant. Nothing would ever come of it, no matter how much the blue-eyed beauty appealed to him. For some reason, she despised him.

The door flew open.

Buster barked and moved back to the rug behind Owen's desk.

"Sheriff." Jessup Carter came barreling into the room like a building was on fire.

Owen stilled the broom and eyed the owner of the town's lone mercantile. The man's calm and quiet demeanor was all but gone. His mouth gaped open, and he breathed heavily while running an unsteady hand over his balding head.

"What is it, Jessup?" Owen leaned the broom against the wall and crossed the room. "What's wrong?"

At the sound of his name, Jessup turned his intense gaze from the empty sheriff's desk to look at Owen. "Oh, there you are. Sheriff, a gun has gone missing from my barn."

Jessup had a small farm less than a mile from town. His wife raised chickens and sold the eggs at the store. Last time he'd paid the family a visit, there had been three horses and a milk cow in the corral.

Owen eased over to his chair and took a seat. "Why do you keep a gun in your barn?"

"I don't carry one with me wherever I go." Jessup shrugged one shoulder and raised the palms of his hands. "If I happen to run into a copperhead, I want a gun nearby. I've come across a few of those ornery critters out behind the barn over the years."

"You know, you should let some of Bertha's chickens run wild out there. They'll cut down on snakes."

"I know that." Jessup's cheeks turned a light shade of pink and his eyes bulged. "Everyone knows that. In fact, I think I'm the one who told you that."

Owen grabbed a pencil and tapped it against his chin. "Come to think of it, I think you're right. You did tell me about chickens cutting down on snakes. It was a few years back when they found a rattler's nest out behind the livery stable."

"Right." Jessup pulled out a chair and sat. "But that's not what I'm here for. Someone stole my gun."

Another stolen piece of property. There was the horse still unaccounted for and now a gun. Only a gun couldn't move on its own accord. "Are you sure you didn't misplace it?"

"No. I never use it." Jessup shook his head, leaned forward, and placed his hands on the desktop. "It's been hanging on the wall for over two years until today."

"When did you last see your weapon?"

"Last night when I checked on Jinny. She's due to calve soon."

"Any special markings?"

"You know Jinny. She's got a black ring around her right eye. One of the best milk cows I've ever had."

Owen looked up from his notes. "On the missing gun. Is there something I can go by to identify the weapon?"

"There sure is. My name's carved into the

handle."

"Anything else missing from the barn?"

"No, not that I could see." Jessup let out a deep sigh and rose from his seat.

Owen stood as well. He came around to Jessup's side and walked him to the door. A sick sensation swirled through Owen's stomach. The store owner waited on customers all day, and he loved to talk.

"Jessup, can you do me a favor?" They stopped, and Owen placed a hand on his friend's back. "Let's keep this quiet for a couple of days. I have an idea but need the element of surprise to carry out my plan."

"You know who took my gun?"

"Not exactly, but I think I know where to start looking." Whoever made camp up on the ridge was his first guess. "But I need this to stay between the two of us until I can check it out."

"All right, Sheriff." Jessup scrubbed the palm of his hand over his face. "I'll do whatever you say so long as I get my gun back. It was a gift from my pa when I was a boy."

Owen opened the door. "You can count on me doing everything possible."

Once he was alone again, he let out a weary sigh. If news of this got out, things would get out of hand fast. The two robberies sounded similar. He didn't believe in co-incidences. There was a thief among them. He had to be careful about how he handled the situation. Things hadn't started to go missing until the welcome wagon arrived. Rumors might spread one of the women must be a thief. Accusations caused hard feelings, and people were likely to shy away from the restaurant.

He dug through his files until he found the notes that he'd taken the day the women arrived. He considered crossing off Mrs. Lamb and Maggie's names, but, at this point, everyone was a suspect.

Owen started with Belinda. As difficult as it was to believe her possible of committing the crimes, she was the hardest to figure. Her sarcastic humor didn't mix well with the general population of West Ridge. Could it be she wasn't happy here and was plotting a way to get out of town? No one was holding her here. They were all free to do as they pleased.

Next on the list was Katie. A child on the verge of becoming an adult. He doubted she knew how to shoot a firearm. Folks around here learned to ride and shoot when they were young, but she was a city girl. What would she want with a horse and a gun? Belinda was his best prospect. He needed to talk to all of them and find out where they were last night. He didn't actually expect to find any of them guilty unless they had an accomplice camped out on the ridge. Even that didn't make any sense. He would know if any of them had been slipping out of town. Still, it was possible to hide a gun but not a horse.

13

Maggie sat alone at the kitchen table gazing out the window. Shafts of bright sunlight lit the quiet room. A red bird landed on the ledge outside. Maggie held her breath. The lovely creature tilted its head from side to side inching closer to the pane before darting off. If only the twins were here instead of taking a late afternoon nap. The girls and Mrs. Lamb would have loved the spectacular sight. Mrs. Lamb was in her room reading. The restaurant closed early and wouldn't open again until tomorrow morning. They were taking the evening off to enjoy the town's anniversary celebration. There would be fireworks and homemade ice cream on the church grounds. With Katie and Belinda helping the Women's Church Committee decorate for the celebration, the house was quiet.

Under normal circumstances, she would have taken advantage of a few moments of peace, but today the silence left her feeling empty and alone. Her thoughts strayed to her sister and the twins. Sarah had never fully recovered after giving birth to the girls. Their lives should have been so different. Maggie loved her nieces and would do anything for them, but the one thing they needed the most she couldn't give them, their mother. Sarah would have been a good mother. She would have devoted her whole life to caring for them. Unlike Maggie, who worked all day and counted on others like Katie, Mrs. Lamb, and Belinda to help with the girls.

Stop feeling sorry for yourself. Mother said when one was feeling sad it was time to start cleaning. There was no better feeling than living in a clean house. Maggie went to the sink and, as quietly as possible, filled a pail with water and added soap shavings. Once she had a good amount of sudsy water, she carried the cleaning supplies out to the dining room.

It might not help, but cleaning wouldn't hurt. She dipped a cloth into the water and wrung it out before starting on the table nearest the entrance of the restaurant. Once the tabletop was clean, she wiped the legs and then each chair.

On one of the chairs lay a newspaper left

by a customer. Maggie picked up the paper. The article on the front page caught her attention. It was about the attack on the wagon train. Her heart raced as she read the story. There were survivors from the attack as well as other family members back East looking for missing relatives.

Maggie gasped and covered her mouth with her hand. Mr. Maxwell was looking for Katie or Katherine, as he had called her. The man claimed to be her guardian. A court would have to decide that. It was a man's world, and if it came to legal action, Katie didn't stand much of a chance. A crippling fear threatened to shake her to the core. If the truth got out, she could lose everything, the twins, her job, her freedom. She shoved those negative thoughts away and returned to scrubbing. The room didn't need cleaning, but she pushed on, anything to keep her mind from worry.

She was working on the third table when a knock came at the door. *What use was having a closed sign if no one paid it any mind?* Maggie rose from where she knelt. With a heavy sigh, she put aside the damp cloth and went to see who was at the door.

The shadow of a tall man with broad shoulders filled the window. Maggie's heart skipped a beat. *What is Owen doing here?*

Her thoughts flew to the newspaper article. She took a deep breath and her pounding heart began to slow to normal. She opened the door and moved aside to allow Owen into the room. "Hello, Sheriff."

He removed his hat and hung it on a hook. "Sorry to disturb you."

"You aren't disturbing anyone. It's pretty quiet around here for a change." As much as she feared getting too close, he had done so much for them it would be rude to turn him away. He didn't look as if he was here to arrest anyone. "Come on in. I was just cleaning the tables and chairs."

He stepped into the dining room. Hands on his hips he surveyed the area. His brows creased and he let out a low whistle. "You all sure do keep the place clean."

"I'm happy to have an excuse to stop." She took a long look at the room. He was right. The restaurant was already spotless.

"Well, good then." His hazel eyes deepened, and his dimples flashed alongside his grin. "You all seem to be getting along well. The word around town is the restaurant is the best thing to happen to West Ridge since as far back as anyone can remember."

"I'm glad to hear everyone is pleased." Her mind blanked for a moment then raced into action. She had no idea what he was doing here, but a show of hospitality would hide her uneasiness. "Have a seat. I think we have some coffee left. Would you like some or maybe a glass of water?"

"Coffee would be good, if it's not too much trouble."

"Certainly." Maggie took a deep breath and forced a smile to calm the ball of nervousness floating in her stomach. "I'll be right back."

As soon as she was out of the sheriff's sight, Maggie closed her eyes and willed her muscles to relax. One . . . two . . . three . . . she counted to ten and then opened her eyes before mounting the steps to the kitchen. Mrs. Lamb had left the room clean and ready for the next round of customers. Maggie touched the side of the pot and pulled her hand away. It was still hot. She pulled two cups from the shelf and set them on the counter. With a cloth wrapped around her hand, she took hold of the handle of the coffeepot while she filled the cups.

Owen took a seat at the table nearest the foyer and waited. Other than the sound of Maggie in the kitchen, the restaurant was quiet. Everyone in town was taking it easy to prepare for the late-night activities. The town's anniversary party was one of the biggest events of the year. The sense of wonder it brought to him as a boy still lingered. He looked forward to sharing it with Maggie and her nieces.

Maggie returned with a cup in each hand. He started to stand to help her, but she nodded for him to stay put as she set one cup in front of him.

"Thank you." He couldn't stop the smile spreading across his face when she took a seat next to him. They were alone, which was usually her cue to find something pressing to do elsewhere. He quietly cleared his throat and kept his voice low. "I guess the twins are excited about the fireworks tonight."

"Yes, and the ice cream. They can hardly wait. I finally managed to get them down for a nap." Maggie glanced toward the door leading to their living quarters before taking a sip of coffee. "They'll be sorry they missed you. I'm impressed with how good you are with children."

"Children are great, especially Esther and Hannah. It's amazing how well they have adjusted to everything." The twins were as comfortable with Maggie as if she were their mother and not their aunt.

"Yes, they have adapted well." Her gaze

dropped to her hands for a moment. "My sister, Sarah, had a hard time after the girls were born. She never fully recovered and seemed to get worse with each passing month. Last winter the doctor told us she didn't have long to live, but Chester refused to accept it."

Maggie shook her head and bit down on her bottom lip. A hint of sadness marred her brow as she looked off into the distance. He could kick himself for dragging up painful memories. He longed to comfort her. Instead, he clasped his hands tightly together for fear he would reach out to her and send her running.

"She was so frail." Maggie blew out a heavy breath. "In a way, I'm the only mother the girls have ever known. All they will remember of their parents are the stories I tell them."

"Your family was headed to California but not to dig for gold?"

"Yes, we were. Chester read about the air out west having healing properties. So many people searching for riches while all Chester wanted was a miracle. We would have left sooner, but it took two years for him to save up enough money for the trip."

His spirit roused at the thought of how hard they worked only to have it end in a senseless attack. The injustice of it set his blood on fire. A sensation he never experienced before exploded in his chest. Fury? Rage? Whatever it was, the immensity of it shocked him.

"Sarah passed the night before the attack. Chester was inconsolable. He rode away and didn't return until daybreak, not long after the bandits had attacked. The wagons were still burning. There was fire in Chester's eyes. I'd never seen anyone look so stricken. He took off with the posse."

"I read in the papers they lost the bandits' trail when they reached the Mississippi River."

"That's right." Maggie was quiet for a long moment. When she spoke again, her brow creased and her chin trembled. "Chester's horse was worn from so much riding, and the poor thing collapsed. He was crushed under the horse and died before the men returned to the camp."

Compassion strummed through Owen's veins. His heart broke at the thought of all the pain she had endured. He reached out to take her hand in his.

"Aunt Maggie." One of the twins called from the back of the building.

She jumped to her feet. "I need to go take care of the girls."

"That's fine." Owen rose from the table and watched her hurry across the room. "I'll let myself out."

He grabbed his hat and stepped out onto the boardwalk. Buster came running from the alley. Owen's mind was troubled as he stroked the dog's head. Here he'd been feeling sorry for himself because she didn't seem to like him, and all the while, the poor woman had been in mourning. If only he could find a way to comfort her. He'd know what to do if it were one of his friends. Take him down to the river and spend the day fishing. He yearned to help and protect her from the pain, but he had no idea how.

Neither Belinda nor Katie was around. He'd have to talk to them later. Instead, he went to Jasper's stall and saddled his horse. There were a few good hours of daylight left for him to canvass the woods and take another look around the abandoned campsite. The air was hot and damp. Buster trudged alongside Jasper's heavy steps. Owen let out a sigh of relief when they reached the cavern road. The shade and cooler air were a blessing.

At the campsite, he discovered the fire had gone cold and there were no piles of kindling nearby. It didn't appear anyone planned to return. This time there were two sets of horse prints. Did the mysterious camper have a partner? Owen followed the prints. They led him to the broken-down gate and then disappeared. The layers of fallen leaves were thick here, and the wind had been blowing hard most of the afternoon.

The sun was dipping low in the eastern sky by the time he got back to town. Owen brushed down Jasper before going to his office. He took a seat at his desk. They would need him at the church grounds for tonight's activities but first, he needed a moment to gather his thoughts. Someone had been keeping an eye on the town. He was sure of it, but what could they want? West Ridge was a long way to travel from anywhere if all you wanted was a horse and a gun.

14

Maggie surveyed the large crowd of spectators on the church grounds. The air was filled with excitement. Several of the men churned buckets of ice cream while most of the women and children sang hymns. Those assigned to the fireworks committee were busy preparing for the main event. They had had the same type of celebration last month for the 4th of July, but it seemed to her more people were attending the town's anniversary celebration.

"Ice cream's ready." Rudy the blacksmith waved his hat in the air. "Come and get it. It won't last long in this heat."

Children of all ages and some of the men scrambled to be first.

Mayor Todd stood at the front of the line and raised his hand. "Just a moment, folks. Let's have Pastor Irvin say a few words before we eat."

"Thank you, Mayor." The pastor removed

his hat and held it in front of his body as he bowed his head. "Heavenly Father, we thank You for this fine community and all the families represented here today. We ask that You continue to keep Your hand of blessings on us as we strive to follow Your leading. Amen."

Someone yelled amen as others clapped.

Mrs. Irvin and Anna Grace Swenson handed out bowls to each person when they reached the front of the line. The twins were looking forward to the rare treat. Standing on either side of Maggie, they made their way to the table and each of them received a bowl filled with vanilla ice cream from Mrs. Irvin and a spoon from Anna Grace.

"Thank you." They spoke in unison and put a smile on the servers' faces.

People gathered in clusters to socialize while they ate and waited for it to get dark enough for the fireworks. Maggie's little family migrated to an old oak tree at the top of the hill. Maggie looked around the churchyard. These were her friends and neighbors. She'd come to know most of them by name and was beginning to learn bits of their life stories. A tug on her sleeve drew her attention toward Esther, who stood by her side.

"I have to go to the outhouse." Her brows

were creased in a single line and her lips stretched tight.

Maggie glanced around for a familiar face. Katie stood nearby, biting on her bottom lip as she gazed at the crowd. Anna Grace Swenson and Mrs. Lamb joined her and the teen visibly relaxed.

"Katie?" she called out to get her attention as she led the twins to where she and the two older women stood. "Do you mind keeping an eye on Hannah while I take Esther to the outhouse?"

Katie reached out and took Hannah's hand. "I don't mind."

"Why, hello there." Anna Grace leaned forward and smiled. "You must be Hannah."

"How did you know?" Hannah's mouth dropped open as her brow furrowed in confusion. "New people can't ever tell us apart."

A grin spread across Anna Grace's face. "Just a good guess."

Katie giggled and tugged gently on the little girl's ponytail.

"We'll be right back." Maggie waved as she hurried Esther toward the outhouse. She prayed there wouldn't be a line.

There was a line, but it seemed to be moving at a good speed. Two outhouses stood back-to-back behind the church building. The girls' line was longer than the boys'. A string of lanterns marked the path, but there was still enough twilight to see clearly. The lamps gave the area a whimsical feel but did nothing for the smell.

When she and Esther returned to the old oak tree, their little group had grown. Belinda and Katie were playing a guessing game with Hannah. Anna Grace's sister, Sadie Mae, had joined them. The Swenson sisters were swapping recipes with Mrs. Lamb. Owen and Buster were there as well. A sinking sensation filled her stomach. Their gazes met and held. His hazel eyes were so piercing. Sometimes it was as if he could see her thoughts. Had he discovered her secret?

"We were about to send out a search party for the two of you," Mrs. Lamb teased.

"There was a long line." Maggie glanced at Esther and gave her a quick hug. "But we made it."

"It looks as if you're both just in time for the show." Owen nodded toward the men preparing to set off the fireworks. The sky had grown dark, but there was enough light from the stars and lanterns for her to see the outline of his face. He was at least a foot taller than her, but she could still make out his strong jawline and high cheekbones.

"All right, everyone," Mayor Todd shouted from the area designated for shooting off fireworks. "Get ready to watch but stay back."

"I can't see." Panic filled Esther's voice as she jumped up and down.

"Here, let me help you." Owen reached down and scooped her up. He placed her on one broad shoulder.

"Me too." Hannah raised her arms and jumped just as her sister had. Her eyes were wide with hope, while her mouth drooped in fear.

Owen laughed as he easily picked Hannah up and placed her on his other shoulder.

Buster looked up at his master, his tail wagging until, as if accepting his fate, the dog turned and sat at the feet of the man adored by so many.

Maggie's heart filled with memories and a sense of wonder. Owen held the girls, one on each shoulder, just as their father once had. Smiles spread across all three of their faces as they watched the spectacular burst of fireworks fill the night sky.

Owen opened the door to the jailhouse and let Buster enter first. "What did you think of the fireworks?"

The dog tilted his head to the right and panted.

Had he expected him to answer? No, not really, but he had been speaking aloud to the animal more often than usual. He filled the dog's water dish and took a seat at his desk. It was late, and the crowd from the anniversary celebration had dispersed hours ago. He had hung around the church to help the cleanup crew.

Owen leaned his head back and closed his eyes. It was time to head to bed, but his mind was too wound up to sleep. The letter from his mother was heavy on his mind. If only there were a faster way to communicate with his parents without his thoughts and questions being sent all over the telegraph lines. He would like to have someone to talk to. Someone who would answer his questions without expecting a treat.

There was always Dr. Gentry. He trusted the man like an uncle or even a father. Should he tell the doctor about his prospect of a job in Hot Springs? It would help to get another person's thoughts on the matter, but he didn't want word getting back to the mayor, not until he knew for sure what he planned to do.

There was a gentle rap at the door before it opened.

"Good evening, Owen." Mayor Todd entered the room. "I just thought I'd stop by and thank you for all the hard work you did for the celebration tonight."

"No problem." Owen sat up straight. "Just doing my job."

"Speaking of your job, have you had any leads on finding Rob's horse?"

So that's what this late-night visit was about. Rob must be after Thomas to set a fire under Owen. He raked his fingers through his hair and stifled a frustrated sigh. "No. I've covered a lot of ground and spoken with just about everyone in the county, but no one has seen it."

"It's as though it just disappeared."

What did he mean? Of course, it didn't just disappear. It was bad enough Rob had been giving him grief almost every day when he came back empty-handed. Owen took a deep breath to still his temper. He wasn't usually one to get upset, but it was late, and he had a lot on his mind.

"If it's still in the county, I'll find it. I've spoken with lawmen from surrounding towns, and they're on the lookout. Trust me. I'm doing everything possible to find Rob's horse."

"I'm sure you are. I didn't come here to give you a hard time." The mayor backed toward the door. "With Carver's gun missing, folks are getting concerned."

Owen stood. "I asked him to keep quiet about the gun and give me time."

"It's all over town. You know how word spreads."

"Yes, I do." And it frustrated him to no end.

"Well, then, good night." The mayor retreated with a weak smile and shut the door.

Owen groaned aloud. Buster came to stand next to him.

Too late to do anything more tonight, Owen petted the dog's head and blew out the big lantern on his desk. He rose from his chair and carried the smaller oil lamp to his room. Buster followed. They both could do with a good night's sleep. He hung his gun belt on the wall before pulling off his boots and trousers.

The dog curled up on the rug beside the bed and soon started to snore.

Owen laid his head on his pillow and let out a weary sigh. He was ready for a long night's sleep.

15

Maggie jolted awake. *What was that?* She sat up and looked around the room. All three girls were asleep. It sounded as if something or someone was outside. She tossed back the covers and got out of bed, careful not to wake Esther. Without making any noise, she tiptoed over to the window where she pulled a section of the curtain back. The door to the outhouse was open, but she couldn't tell if anyone was out there.

Katie and Hannah were sleeping peacefully in the bed they shared. Esther murmured in her sleep and turned over. Satisfied the girls were fine, she stepped out into the hall.

Perhaps the sound came from Mrs. Lamb's room and not from outside. She started toward the elderly woman's bedroom when voices from the other end of the hall caught her attention. Maggie froze and held her breath.

"What are you doing here?" Belinda hissed.

"Don't tell me you haven't missed me," a man teased.

Maggie recognized the voice of Belinda's one-time partner. What was Brent Cooper doing here? The short, stocky man had disappeared from the wagon train the night before the attack. Most of the men had been out looking for him when the bandits showed up.

"I've come to get you." He spoke quietly but still loud enough for Maggie to hear. She glanced toward the bedroom door, praying he didn't wake the girls. "I've got two horses tied up out behind an old broken-down gate at the edge of town."

"What do you mean, you've come to get me?" Belinda sounded confused and angry. "Where did you disappear to, Brent? I thought you were dead or took off without me."

"No. I'd never run off on you, darling." His voice dripped with feigned charm. "I just met up with some old friends of mine."

"Where have you been since then?" Belinda's shock-filled voice stunned Maggie. "What happened to you?"

"Let's not worry about that now." When charming her failed, Brent's words took on an authoritative tone. "We need to get going."

"Go where?"

"It doesn't matter where we go so long as we're together."

What had Belinda ever seen in him? His nonchalant attitude was irritating to say the least. She should have stayed in bed, but Belinda might need her help.

"Do you have any money?"

"Money?" Belinda's gasp was audible. "No, I don't have any money."

"Get your things and meet me in half an hour. And try to get your hands on some money or something valuable we can sell later."

It didn't sound as though he would take no for an answer. Maggie hated to leave the girls, but she had to do something. If she went through the restaurant, she could make a run for the jailhouse and wake Owen.

"No, Brent. I'm not going with you."

Maggie's nose itched. Before she could stop herself, she sneezed. Her heart raced. She considered inching her way down the hall to the door to the diner, but any wrong move might make matters worse.

"What was that?"

"Nothing. It must have been Mrs. Lamb's cat."

"Who's Mrs. Lamb?"

"No one you'd know."

"Hurry up." His words were harsh and low, reminding Maggie of an angry animal. The level of impatience building in his voice sent a shiver through Maggie's body. By the sound of it, he was unpredictable and perhaps capable of almost anything.

"All right," Belinda lowered her voice as she spoke. "I'll see you soon."

"No, I'm coming with you."

The door flew open before Maggie could react. Brent shoved Belinda into the hall in front of him and shut the door behind them. Maggie covered her mouth with her hand. The man's steely-eyed gaze centered on her face. She shuddered. Brent grabbed her arm and wrenched it behind her back. She twisted her shoulders, trying to get away, but his hold on her sent pain shooting up her arm to her neck.

"Be still," Brent ordered through clenched teeth as he pulled out a gun. He waved it in the air close to her face.

A name had been carved on the handle. Jessup Carver. Maggie's heart started racing.

"Brent, let her go," Belinda demanded

with frustration and fear in her eyes.

"No, she'll run to the sheriff."

"I'll run to the sheriff if you don't let her go."

Brent backed toward the door, pulling Maggie with him. She didn't dare make a sound for fear it would wake the children. Belinda followed them out into the alley.

"You go for the law, Belinda, and she's dead."

"Maggie." Belinda's eyes filled with tears.

"Get Owen." She mouthed the words for Belinda to see. They needed Owen. He was the only one who could get her out of this situation.

Brent gave her a strong yank and marched her down the alley. When they reached the side road, he let loose of her arm but made a point of letting her see the gun. He held her by the elbow as he continued west. The moon was full and bright, lighting their way once they left the outskirts of town.

"Why are you doing this?" She managed to ask between gasps for air. The pace he kept was faster than even her long legs were used to.

"I need help getting out of these blasted mountains. I thought I could count on Belinda. When the law finds out my part in the attack, I want to be miles from here."

His part in the attack? On the wagons? Anger and fear surged through Maggie's veins. She had to keep a clear head. The broken gate wasn't much farther, and if Owen didn't get here soon, she might never see him or her family again.

"Go away," Owen mumbled at the rapping sound coming from the back door. It sounded like a hammer banging against an anvil. Roused from his sleep, he shouted toward the door, "Do you have to bang so loud?"

The noise persisted, and Owen gave up trying to get back to sleep. He sat up in bed. Someone was knocking on the back door. Who would use the back door instead of the front?

Maggie.

Fear wrapped around his heart. Something must be wrong. Buster approached the door, his tail wagging.

Owen jumped out of bed and pulled on his trousers. "I'll be right there."

His boots would have to wait. He crossed the room in his socks and a fork that had somehow fallen onto the floor during the night stabbed his instep. Limping while still buttoning his shirt, he swung the door open.

Belinda wore a cloak over what he presumed to be her nightgown. She looked small standing there wringing her hands in the bright moonlight. Her hair was disheveled, and her feet were bare.

"What's wrong?" Owen reached for his gun belt hanging on a hook beside the door. He prayed none of the little girls were ill. They all looked healthy at the anniversary celebration a few hours ago.

"Brent's in town." She gasped for breath as if she'd been running.

Owen wrapped the belt around his waist. He tried to shake away the cobwebs in his sleep-deprived brain and make sense of her words. "Who's Brent?"

"He was on the wagon train with us."

Once Owen finished fastening the belt, he grabbed his hat. When he stepped outside, a sharp rock poked his big toe. How could he have forgotten to put on his boots? He raised a finger, left the door open, and sat on a chair to pull on his boots.

"We were traveling together." Belinda continued to wring her hands together as she took quick glances toward the restaurant. "We all thought he was dead when he disappeared the night before the attack. He's back, and he wants me to leave with him."

"That's not a crime." Fully dressed, he

joined her out on the back step.

"You don't understand," Belinda huffed as if irritated with him for having no idea what she was talking about. "He has Jessup Carter's gun, and he took Maggie with him."

Owen's heart plummeted. He returned to his room long enough to grab his rifle. "Where are they?"

"He said something about meeting me by the rock gate at the edge of town." Her voice broke with concern. "When I told him no, he took Maggie. He said he'd kill her if I told anyone."

"You stay here." Owen sprinted toward Jasper's stall with Buster on his heels.

"But maybe I can help you." Belinda pleaded as she followed. "I know Brent better than anyone."

"Just do as I say," Owen ordered through clenched teeth. He set the rifle aside until he had the horse saddled. After he tightened the cinch, Owen shoved the rifle into the scabbard. He grabbed the reins and swung into the saddle. "I'll be back with Maggie. You stay here and keep watch over the children."

"Be careful."

Determination set a fire in the pit of his stomach. "I'll bring her back safe."

The road was empty and the sky still dark at this hour of the morning. The tension in his gut tightened. At the edge of town, he turned Jasper toward the gate wall. Buster ran alongside them.

"Lord, please keep Maggie safe." God would keep her from harm. Owen had to believe that to think straight.

Every step the horse took brought him closer to finding her. She was a strong woman. The first day the welcome wagon rolled into town, he'd been prepared to coddle a bunch of frail females. Instead, he'd been met with a group of tough, determined, and surprisingly independent women. The bravest of them all, Maggie would be fine. She had to be.

"Lord, please keep her safe."

At the edge of town, he rounded the bend and proceeded toward the broken gate. When he reached the fragmented landmark, he slid from his horse and hunkered down behind a rock. It was hard to make out features from this distance. He could hear Maggie's sweet voice and the voice of a man he didn't recognize. Tethered to a nearby tree were two horses. One fit the description of the mare taken from Rob's livery stable.

"How could you?" Maggie's voice broke

as she yelled. "Belinda never would have agreed to go with you if she'd known what kind of person you really are."

Owen drew his gun. He listened carefully as he inched forward, taking stealth-like steps. He was an expert shot but didn't want to take any chances of Maggie getting hurt.

"Aw, keep quiet," the man's distinctive, deep voice snarled. "You don't know what you're talking about. I didn't mean for anyone to get hurt."

"Hurt?" Shocked silence filled the air. "Brent, people died."

"I know. I know." The man holding Maggie captive sighed. "That's why I stayed away for so long. I felt terrible."

The man's words made the hair stand up on the back of Owen's neck as he listened to the shocking confession.

"They said they might have to burn a wagon or two to make it look like a gang of bandits were behind the attack. They never said anything about hurting anyone."

So, he was part of the attack on the settlers. His own people. The muscles in Owen's gun arm tightened. He had to keep his head clear for Maggie's sake, but he wasn't letting this man get away.

"How did you meet up with them in the first place?" Maggie spoke in disbelief.

"They couldn't have been part of the caravan. Everyone was accounted for after the raid except for you and one other person."

"No, they weren't on the wagon train. I ran into some old friends while out hunting for fresh meat. They were at a campsite and had a game of poker going. I joined in, of course. When they found out the caravan had to stay put for a while, they asked me to create a diversion to get the men out of camp while they collected some loot."

"You didn't see anything wrong with them robbing innocent women and children while their menfolk were trying to find you?"

"It sounds so bad when you put it like that."

"Oh." Her voice rang with exasperation. "I don't know what Belinda ever saw in you."

"Shut up before you make me mad." At the sound of heavy footsteps pacing, Owen pressed his back against the wall to stay in the shadows. "You and these hill people have gotten Belinda all mixed up."

"Let me go." The panic in Maggie's voice moved Owen into action.

He sprung out from behind the section of the gate. "Hold it right there."

Brent pulled Maggie in front of himself and fired his gun. Owen dropped and rolled behind a boulder, counting shots as the outlaw continued to shoot. After the sixth shot, the empty mechanism clicked.

Owen came out from behind the massive stone with his gun aimed.

Brent shoved Maggie to the ground and took off running.

Owen fired a warning shot over his head. The outlaw continued to flee, so he fired again, but the man was out of range. He dashed over to Jasper and pulled his rifle from the scabbard.

Maggie sat up. She held her right arm close to her body. Barefoot and wearing only a nightgown, there was a look of terror in her eyes.

"Are you all right?" He took hold of her left elbow, helped her to her feet, and placed his hands on her shoulders.

Their gazes locked. Owen was overcome with relief to see her alive.

"I'm fine." She nodded, although a look of pain filled her eyes. "You need to stop him."

"Stay," he ordered Buster and then motioned for Maggie to stay down as he ran after the man who had caused so much harm and heartache.

The outlaw was headed for the horses. When he reached them, he grabbed the reins of the missing livery mare and struggled to get his boot into the stirrup.

Owen raised his rifle, the man in his sights. "Hold it right there."

The skittish horse staggered, and Brent slid sideways, landing on his back. Owen pulled his gaze from the rifle sight and squinted at the dark figure nearly fifty yards away. The man took hold of the stirrup and tried to pull himself up. The horse whinnied, reared, and took off with the other horse on its heels.

Owen held onto his rifle with one hand and ran hard to reach the outlaw before he'd have time to reload his gun.

Brent crawled as he took cover behind a large boulder.

Instead of standing out in the open, Owen made his way around the scattered pieces of the old broken-down gate and boulders. Taking slow and steady steps, he moved until he came to a point where he could see the outlaw fumbling to pull bullets from his gun belt. Just as Brent snapped the cylinder into place, Owen descended upon him. "Drop the gun."

The man began to raise his weapon but hesitated at the metallic sound made by Owen's lever-action rifle.

Defeated, the stranger dropped his gun

and rose slowly to his feet. His steely-eyed glare was wasted on Owen.

"Turn around, mister." Owen pulled a length of rope from his back pocket and used it to bind the man's wrists together.

"Hey, that's too tight."

"Stop your bellyaching." Owen picked up Jessup's gun and put it in his belt. "Just be glad I don't shoot you and leave you for dead."

"I should have put you down when I had the chance."

"When was that?" Owen snorted.

The man never had him in his sights.

"The first day you came poking around my campsite."

"Start walking."

The man did as he was ordered. Owen marched him back to the road at gunpoint. Maggie stood beside the gate, rubbing her arm. The urge to sweep those dark curls away from her face and kiss her was strong. He resisted, though. It wasn't proper and, besides, it would most likely earn him a slap in the face. This wasn't a time for him to give in to his emotions. Especially when they were unwanted.

"Are you sure you're all right?"

She still seemed to favor her right arm. He'd have Dr. Gentry look at it when they got back to town. Maggie nodded silently and walked alongside him, with her head down. His mount trailed behind them. It was a short walk, but he was anxious to get her back to the restaurant and home to her family. She wiped tears from her cheeks, and he longed to wrap his arms around her shoulders and hug her close, an action she was sure to spurn. As much as it pained him, the smart thing to do would be to keep his distance and guard his heart.

Maggie wrapped her arms around her waist and started to sob.

Owen froze in his tracks. He draped his free arm over her shoulders and pulled her close to his side. She responded by leaning into him.

They all stopped walking, and she pressed her face into his chest. He rubbed his hand over her back and held her tight. Her shoulders shook. He raised his face to the sky. *Lord,* he pleaded. If there was anything in the world he could do to take the pain from Maggie, he would. His heart ached for her, but it was nothing compared to the pain she bore. He lowered his gaze and softly rested his chin on top of her head. His prisoner let out a disgruntled groan.

Buster growled and snapped at his feet.

"Hey, get your dog off of me."

Owen ignored him. There would be a treat for Buster when they got back to town and a cold cot for the prisoner.

16

Maggie set her plate in the sink. A sharp pain shot up her right arm and she gasped. It hurt when she moved too fast or tried to lift anything. Dr. Gentry gave her a sling to wear last night. He didn't think the bone was broken and told her to take it easy for a few days.

"I feel so ashamed." Belinda sat with her elbows resting on the kitchen table, quietly sobbing. She shook her head before covering her face with her hands.

"You're not to blame, dear." Seated beside her, Mrs. Lamb rubbed her hand across the distraught woman's back and shoulders.

Maggie stood beside the kitchen window. She could see the alleyway separating the restaurant from the sheriff's office as well as a section of Main Street. Somewhere in the distance, a rooster greeted the day, bragging proudly to be the first to stir. Not true. She and Belinda had been up since before the sun rose. It was still early, and there weren't many people out and about. They all agreed it was best to remain closed today. Word would spread fast enough as to why. Katie and the twins were sleeping in their room but would be rising soon.

The back door to the jailhouse opened and Buster dashed out into the yard. Owen must be up. Maggie's stomach twisted. Much of the night's events were a blur. She could recall them in segments. Fearing for her life, discovering who, in part, was responsible for destroying the lives of so many, and ending up in Owen's arms. His strong, warm, comforting arms. He had held her tight until she had no more tears to cry.

She returned to the table and rested her left hand on the tabletop in front of her. It was hard to keep her emotions in check. Logic told her it wasn't Belinda's fault. She had had no part in the horrific crime. At the same time, though, how could her new friend have been traveling with such a scoundrel? He must have been very charming and convincing to hide his true nature from such an astute person as the girl from New York City.

Belinda looked up and rubbed the palm of her right hand over her eyes. "I knew he wasn't an angel, but I never thought he could be so evil."

"We know. You're not to blame." Mrs. Lamb's soothing words brought comfort to Maggie, if not Belinda.

"What will people say?" Belinda took the handkerchief Mrs. Lamb handed her. "What if they run us out of town? They might, you know, when they find out how close I was to Brent."

"We're your friends, and you can count on us to stand by your side."

Maggie rose again and moved over to the stove this time. The pan of hot water started to steam. She stifled a yawn as she checked to see if the fire was burning hot enough to cook their breakfast. Mrs. Lamb usually cooked for them, but Belinda needed her more this morning.

Thankfully, no one had been hurt, and Brent was behind bars. Neither she nor Belinda had been able to get back to sleep after the sheriff left last night. Belinda wanted to hear how Owen surprised Brent and rescued her. Brent had been no match for Owen.

Maggie had had to retell the story when Mrs. Lamb came into the kitchen to find them up before her. Upon hearing all which had unfolded, the motherly woman took Belinda under her wing and proceeded to minister to her grieving spirit.

Maggie didn't know how she could muster the strength to appear happy when the children came into the kitchen for breakfast. The memory of Brent's confession filled her with anger. She forced herself to take a deep breath. She wasn't a short-tempered person, but learning the truth brought back the pain she'd suffered at the loss of her family.

Down the hall, a door opened and slammed shut. Laughter and happy voices defied the heavy atmosphere in the kitchen. By the sound of it, all three girls were awake. They didn't know what had taken place last night. Their morning routine consisted of the adults preparing breakfast while Katie helped the girls dress, and then took them to the privy.

What would the people of West Ridge say? Maggie chewed on the edge of her mouth while she scooped oatmeal from the sack and added the grain to the pot. She grabbed a spoon with her left hand and began to stir. What would Owen do? Somewhere along the line, his opinion had become important to her. Would he think they were all in cahoots with the outlaws?

Another burst of laughter was followed by happy chatter. The girls were back inside and would be hungry. Maggie glanced toward the table. Belinda pocketed her hankie and rose from the chair. She gave Mrs. Lamb a teary-eyed nod. "I'll be in my bedroom if anyone needs me."

Owen whistled while he dressed. Brent Cooper's confession meant the ladies next door were no longer under suspicion. Upholding the law meant not playing favorites, and now he could toss his list of possible suspects. The memory of Maggie's grief silenced the song on his lips and fueled his determination to see Mr. Cooper was held responsible for his actions.

The prisoner slept. Owen glanced at the clock on the wall. Ten minutes to eight. Time to run an important errand. For the first time in four years, he locked the door to the jailhouse behind him. There was purpose in his steps as he made his way to the telegraph office. He wanted to be there as soon as Mitchell opened the doors. He had spent most of the morning contemplating what he would say in his message.

The telegraph office sat on the corner of Main and First Street. Inside, the telegrapher sat at his desk sorting a stack of papers. Owen cleared his throat and Mitchell Anderson looked up from his work. If he was surprised to see Owen this early in the day, he didn't show it.

"Morning, Sheriff."

"Good morning." He took the time to return the greeting, despite wanting to get right to the matter at hand. "How are you doing today?"

"Couldn't be better. How about you?"

"Good. I have a message to send."

"Fine. There's some paper and a pencil over there." Mitchell motioned toward the pad of paper resting on the countertop. The telegraph office was neat and organized, with supplies placed on a tall stand for customers to send and retrieve telegrams.

"Thanks." Owen nodded before picking up a pencil. He paused a moment to put his words together as he debated whether to send the telegram to the town sheriff or the county marshal.

He wrote out the message and decided to send it to the town's sheriff. This was perhaps the most important telegram he had ever written. When he finished, he tore off the top slip of paper and handed the missive to the telegrapher.

Mitchell Anderson took the note and pushed his glasses higher on his nose. Without asking for any clarification, his brow creased and his eyes grew wide. "I'll get right on it."

"I'd appreciate you letting me know as soon as you get a reply."

"Sure thing, Sheriff." Mitchell returned to his seat and started typing out the message for Sheriff Wright in Wet Creek, Missouri. Patterns of clicks and pauses rang out from the telegraph machine as Mitchell's practiced fingers went to work. A deacon at the church, Mitchell was good at his job. He'd been sending and receiving messages for the community ever since the telegraph line had been installed six years ago.

Out on the street, Owen made his way toward his office. The last thing he expected to see was Maggie sitting on the bench in front of the jailhouse. She scooted over, leaving room for him to join her. He removed his hat and sat beside her.

"The door's locked." Her head spun toward his and the humbleness in her eyes stamped a mark on his heart.

Owen struggled to keep his expression aloof. He'd never seen her look so vulnerable.

"I had to send off a telegraph." Owen fingered the brim of his hat and cleared his throat. "I needed to let the law up north know about Brent and his involvement in the attack."

"I'm sure they'll be interested."

"I expect they'll send someone to escort Brent to Shannon County." He didn't need to tell her that was where the attack took place. She knew. This break in the case was a good lead. Although Belinda's friend hadn't been in on the physical attack, he had taken part in the planning and had created a diversion to weaken the defenseless group of settlers.

"I wonder where his friends are hiding out."

"I'd like to know the answer to that one as well." Caravan travelers weren't safe as long as this group of bandits ran free. "I hope to convince him to talk on the grounds it may get him leniency."

He couldn't make any promises. It wasn't his call, but he would suggest to the prisoner helping solve the case wouldn't hurt his position. The prisoner. This was his first time to lock anyone up in one of the cells. For four years he'd cleaned and maintained the jailhouse for such a time as this. His first arrest turned out to be an important one. It was too soon for a reply to his telegram, but Owen expected one before the day was done. Until then, he had a real prisoner to watch over.

"Hopefully, he'll give you the names." Maggie jumped from the bench. "I just wanted to thank you."

He quickly joined her. "For what?"

"For being there for us." Maggie's eyes filled with tears and her lips quivered. "You saved my life."

He peered into her beautiful blue eyes. A warmth glowed in their depths, filling him with hope. The pink of her lips beckoned. It took him several seconds to drag his gaze away. He blinked and refocused on the woman in front of him. "That's what I'm here for."

"I need to get back to the girls." She gave him a hint of a nod before darting toward the Welcome Wagon Restaurant.

He watched her until she was no longer in sight. There wasn't anything he wouldn't do for that woman. Owen pushed aside his confusion and mixed emotions and entered the jailhouse.

He didn't have to wait long to get an answer from the law in Missouri. Mitchell sent a runner to the office when the reply came over the line. Owen paid the boy a tip before opening the telegram. Two officers were on their way and expected to arrive by nightfall the next day. The response was fast, but not surprising. The crime had made national news. It had given the state just north of theirs a black eye.

"What are you grinning about?"

The question startled Owen. Having a person in one of the cells would take some getting used to. Brent had a perfect view of him at his desk. He'd have to rethink the arrangement of his office after the prisoner was gone.

"Well, what did they say?" Brent had already been told Owen was waiting for instructions on what to do with him.

"They'll be here tomorrow to pick you up."

"You know, I didn't have any part in the robbery."

"You helped set it up and, therefore, made it possible for the attack to take place."

Brent stepped back from the bars and paced the narrow cell back and forth, muttering under his breath.

Buster growled from his resting spot beside Owen.

Brent stopped in his tracks. He placed his hands on the iron barricade. "What proof do you have?"

"Your word." Owen forced himself to take a deep breath and relax. He didn't like losing his temper, but the prisoner's insolence was getting on his last nerve. "Remember, I heard you confess the whole thing last night to Maggie."

"Oh, yeah, that." He dropped his arms and started to turn his back when his eyes lit up. He rose one finger in the air. "Isn't that just hearsay?"

"No. The fact I heard you say it does not make it hearsay."

"Are you sure?"

Owen rolled his eyes. "The other members of the gang have stronger charges against them." He tossed his pencil on the table and leaned back. "There might be a way you can help yourself."

Brent pressed his face against the wrought iron bars. "I'm all ears, Sheriff. Tell me what I have to do."

"Now, you know I can't speak for the folks in Missouri, but I don't think it would hurt your case if you gave them the names of your friends and a way to find them."

"Why don't I just go out and dig a hole for you to bury me in?"

"Suit yourself." He hadn't expected it to be easy, but it didn't hurt to try. Owen rose from his chair and motioned for Buster to follow. They stepped out onto the porch, and he took a seat on the bench.

Buster took off for the alley where he liked to play.

One more night with his first prisoner and then the man was Missouri's problem. It was a relief to be out of hearing distance from the outlaw. The man was once Belinda's business partner. She had changed since the first day when the welcome wagon arrived. They were all a bit different now, or maybe his perception of them had changed. Enthusiasm replaced Belinda's sarcasm, and Katie was a happy teenager. Mrs. Lamb was loved by the community. If her nephews ever did come for her, they would have a whole town to compete against. It was easy to tell the twins apart. Two very different personalities. He had grown to love them both.

Then there was Maggie. He closed his eyes for a moment as he swallowed back a lump in his throat. He couldn't put his feelings for her in words. Infatuation? Fascination? Love? He had never felt this way for anyone before. Once again, the building next door drew his gaze and prompted an ache in his chest. Maggie was safe, and for that he was thankful.

17

It was hard to believe a week had passed since the arrest of Brent Cooper. A copy of the newspaper was waiting on Owen's desk when he returned from making the morning rounds. The big news on the front page was the capture of the man who played a part in the wagon train attack. Owen's name was mentioned as the arresting officer.

The praise he'd received around town made him a bit uncomfortable. He'd just been doing his job. The article made no mention of Maggie's abduction or Belinda's connection to the outlaw. It was better this way. Safer for them. Since the paper came out of Springfield, Missouri, most of the news didn't apply to the folks in West Ridge.

When the Missouri detective, along with a Pinkerton agent, came for Brent, they hadn't waited around long. After getting statements from the welcome wagon ladies, they took their man back to Missouri, where he would face a multitude of charges.

Owen set the paper aside and finished getting ready for church. He had already let Buster out back and only had to adjust his tie before heading out the doorway. There were a few people headed up the hill, but the walkway in front of the restaurant was empty. He hoped all of them would be in church today.

According to Mrs. Lamb, Belinda wasn't taking things well. She explained Belinda was mortified her friend played such a big role in the attack. Both Mrs. Lamb and Maggie tried to keep the distraught woman busy so she wouldn't dwell on the situation.

Owen hoped staying busy included going to the church service. More than anything, Belinda needed to hear God's Word. Nothing could mend a broken spirit better than time spent with the Great Healer.

If she was concerned about what people in town thought, there was no need for her to worry. Once the stolen horse and gun were returned, the excitement in town settled down, and everything quickly returned to normal. No one believed she was to blame.

The church bells chimed. He had to hurry or he'd be late. Halfway up the hill, he ran into Dr. Gentry.

The doctor had a sprightly step for a man his age. "Good morning, Owen."

"Howdy, Doc." It was surprising to see the doctor among the Sunday stragglers. The head usher, he was usually one of the first to arrive for church. "How are you this morning?"

"I'm doing all right." He covered a yawn with the back of his hand. "A little behind schedule today. Benny Wilson broke his arm last night. I was late getting back to town."

"How did he manage to do a thing like that?" Boys would be boys, of course, but few were more adventuresome than Chuck Wilson's youngsters.

"He fell from one of the rafters in the barn." The doctor trotted up the steps and stood outside the door of the building. "I remember you breaking a bone once. Which one was it now, your foot or your shoulder?"

"My foot. Jim is the one who broke his shoulder."

When he was ten, he and some friends were playing in the river near the falls. Barefoot, they were knee-deep in the water, looking for crawdads. They tended to hide in dark, cool areas, such as under rocks. While trying to catch one, a loose boulder under the water slipped and landed on his foot. His big brother had been the one who managed to free his foot and carry him home before running to fetch the doctor.

"Well, if it ever gives you any trouble, you can always pay your folks a visit in Hot Springs and take advantage of the healing waters."

"I'll keep that in mind." Owen filed away yet another reason for moving to Hot Springs to consider later.

Folks were still finding their seats when Owen followed the doctor into the church. He always sat on the back pew on the left, but Dr. Gentry motioned for Owen to follow him. There was space for both of them where the Gentry brothers sat.

He took a quick glance around the room. Maggie was nowhere in sight. None of the ladies from the welcome wagon were in church this morning. Maybe he should run down there and make sure they were okay.

"Good to see you this morning, Sheriff." Pastor Irvin reached out and shook his hand.

"Thank you." Owen nodded. "It's always nice to be here."

The pianist started to play, and everyone took their seats. There was no escaping without interrupting the service. He'd stop by the restaurant after church.

■ ■ ■ ■

Maggie was the last one to slide into the pew, putting her on the inside aisle. She could see everyone in the church building from here. It had taken some convincing, but they'd convinced Belinda to attend church with them. They ended up being late and slipped in during the opening song. As if waiting for them to arrive, there was an empty pew in the back.

Scanning the room, Maggie made eye contact with Owen seated one row ahead of them on the other side of the aisle. He sat between Dr. Gentry and the doctor's brother, Rob.

Owen leaned back slightly and raised one brow in her direction.

She immediately lowered her gaze and began straightening Hannah's dress. Did he think she was purposely seeking him out?

Her niece stared at her in confusion and pushed her hand away.

After a few moments, Maggie took a sideways glance in Owen's direction. He had his face turned as he said something to Rob Gentry. Had it only been a week since he'd rescued her from Brent? She appreciated his support when she fell apart, but it was hard to get past the memory of his arms around her. The images filled her dreams at night.

Belinda cleared her throat, and Maggie looked up. Everyone started to stand to sing another hymn. She rose from the pew and joined in the singing about a day coming when there would be no more heartache and no more tears. While everyone faced forward, she shot another quick glance in Owen's direction. He was tall, at least two or three inches taller than the men on either side of him. The man sang without looking at a hymnal as if he knew the words by heart. She pulled her songbook to her chest, looked toward the altar, and joined in the singing. Joy filled her soul. It was good to be in church.

Her father had been a spiritual man. As a pastor, he taught Maggie the importance of church and time spent reading God's Word. After her parents died, everything changed. Her brother-in-law, Chester, believed in God, but church was a waste of time to him. Other than special occasions, they didn't attend. At first, it had seemed foreign to Maggie but as the weeks passed without going to church, it became less and less of an issue until finally, she never thought of attending. But now, she was happy to be back in church. Pastor Irvin stood to pray, and Maggie bowed her head. *Thank You, Lord, for helping me find my way home.*

After the closing song, they slipped out as quietly as they entered. Maggie understood Belinda's need to leave as soon as church ended. They were halfway down the hill when Owen caught up with them.

"I wasn't sure if you all would make it this morning."

"We were running late." Maggie didn't mention it took them most of the morning to convince Belinda no one blamed her for what happened.

"Where's Buster?" Esther skipped alongside the sheriff's longer strides.

"He's out behind the jail. It's his favorite place to play."

"I like Buster." Hannah sang the words as if she was singing in an opera.

"Me, too," Esther chimed in.

Owen's shocked look nearly made Maggie laugh out loud. His eyes grew wide and his lips thinned while he nodded along to their song. He started to hum and wave his hands like an orchestra leader while the girls continued to make up words to their silly song. Everyone, including Belinda, was laughing by the time they reached the jailhouse.

"Good-bye." The twins sang as the lawman slipped inside his office.

Maggie wiped tears of laughter from her eyes. Her cheeks hurt from smiling so hard. Their need to maintain distance from the lawman would be much easier if he weren't so much fun to be around.

18

Maggie sat at her favorite table in the back corner of the restaurant. The three-hour break between lunch and dinner gave them time to clean up, prep for the next shift, and relax. She was relaxing. The twins were at school, and Katie was across the street visiting the Swenson sisters.

So much had happened in the nearly three months since they'd arrived in West Ridge. There was so much to share, she had an urge to write a letter, but there was no one to write to. Everyone she loved lived in West Ridge. She had kept a diary over the years, but it had burned with the wagon. So many memories lost. She brushed her cheek with the palm of her hand.

Maggie glanced toward the vestibule. She couldn't see the road from where she sat, but she could envision Swenson's Pastry Shop across the street. Katie continued to help Anna Grace and Sadie Mae make loaves of bread and cakes every day but Sunday. Sadie Mae and Anna Grace were like a pair of doting grandmothers spoiling the child with love and praise. Their attention seemed to be just the healing balm Katie needed.

"There you are." Mrs. Lamb waved from the other end of the room. She made her way across the auditorium, weaving around chairs and tables. It was a long walk and Maggie considered meeting her halfway, but the older woman was as independent as anyone and wouldn't appreciate being coddled.

"Did you need me for something?" They started prepping for the dinner crowd half an hour before they opened. There were times when the menu called for more work, at which time Mrs. Lamb would have them start earlier.

"No." She pulled out the chair next to Maggie and took a seat. "I just wanted to see how you're doing."

"I'm fine." She appreciated her friend's concern, but there was nothing wrong with her. "I'm just sitting here thinking."

"I worry about you sometimes." Mrs. Lamb placed her hand on Maggie's arm. Her eyes narrowed with sincerity. "You work so hard without taking any sort of break."

"I'm taking a break right now." Maggie held out the palms of her hands and looked to her right and then to her left as she shrugged her shoulders.

"You need to get out more." A long silence stretched between them. Mrs. Lamb was right. Other than attending church, she spent all her time at the Welcome Wagon Restaurant. "Do something fun and get to know our neighbors better."

"All right." Maggie stood. It wasn't as hot out today as it had been, and she could use the exercise. "Let's go for a walk."

"A walk sounds wonderful." Mrs. Lamb clasped her hands together the way she did when she was pleased about something. "Why don't you go do that? I have some thank you letters to write, but you take your time. Get some fresh air and smell the flowers."

Maggie stood there dumbfounded. She'd just been talked into taking a walk by herself. Where was she supposed to go? Mrs. Lamb wiggled her fingers and pointed toward the door.

Resigned to taking a fun break on her own, outside, all alone, Maggie stepped out the doorway. The air humidity was low. There was a gentle breeze coming from the direction of the river. She smiled and started to take a deep breath when the sound of birds squawking angrily startled her. A blue jay swooped down and screeched as it dived for her face.

Maggie placed her hands over her head and squeezed her eyes shut. Strong arms caught her around the waist and pulled her away from the doorway. A dog's barking faded as it ran off after something. When she opened her eyes, she found herself staring at the badge on Owen's vest.

"Are you all right?" The husky quality in his voice made her swoon much as she had the day down by the river when he helped her from the wagon. She pressed the palms of her hands against his chest and pushed away.

"I'm fine, thank you." She concentrated on fixing her hair as she tried to collect herself. "I don't know why that bird is so angry with me."

"It wasn't you." He assured her with confidence, as if he could read a bird's mind. "It was Mrs. Lamb's cat. He ran right up the side of the tree, chasing the bird not long before you stepped outside. The bird dove at the cat, and it took off. I guess the blue jay thought you were reinforcements and was ready for a second round."

She tried to make sense of his words, but

she couldn't help being distracted by the man standing in front of her. Why did he have to be so handsome? And tall? And kind? *Focus on the badge.*

"Are you sure you're all right?" The concern in his voice wrapped around her like a warm blanket on a cold day.

"Yes, I'm fine." She took a calming breath to still her racing heart. Racing from what, the bird attack, or the sheriff? She squared her shoulders. "I was going for a walk and had no idea I'd marched onto a battlefield."

"Mind if I join you?" There was a twinkle in his hazel eyes as well as a look of doubt.

"Of course, I don't mind." She did, but she wasn't about to say so after all he'd done for her and the others. The more time she spent with him, the harder it was for her to keep up her guard.

"Where do you plan to go on your walk?" Owen clapped his hands, and Buster strutted back to them with his head held high. The vigilant dog had chased away a vicious cat and a rogue bird all in one day.

"Anywhere, nowhere. I hadn't thought that out yet."

He was glad he'd caught up with her before she took off. For the most part, the town was safe, but this time of year, one had to keep an eye out if they strayed too close to an unoccupied wooded area. Snakes came out when the weather was hot, and there had been a couple mountain lion sightings recently. He'd have to educate these city folks on what to look for in the wild.

"There's a nice spot behind the mercantile. It has a bench where you can see the waterfall that feeds this branch of the river." It would be a nice place to take the twins on a picnic one day as well. "Would you like to go there?"

"It sounds lovely." She sounded genuinely interested. Up until recently, she'd made it clear she wasn't interested in him as anything more than a neighbor and handyman. Things had changed since Brent paid them a visit.

He started to offer her his arm but decided it was best to keep a small distance between them. No sense in scaring her off. Sometimes she reminded him of a skittish new foal. A gentle hand was the best way to keep her from running away.

They strolled together in comfortable silence. The path next to Carter's store wound along the side of the hill. After less than a quarter of a mile, the sound of water crashing on rocks below filled the air. A line of tall timbers blocked the view, but, on the other side, there was a beautiful sight. A bench had been constructed there years ago and the area had been nicknamed Lover's Bluff. He didn't think she would appreciate that bit of history.

"How's your arm?" He motioned for her to have a seat before he joined her.

"It's much better. Still a bit sore at times, but nothing I can't handle."

They sat in silence, watching the water cascade over the falls. He welcomed the cool breeze and droplets of cold water carried by the wind. This was one of the prettiest parts of the Spring River. Too bad he wasn't the sort of man who knew how to court a woman with pretty words.

"I had no idea this was even here." Her eyes widened slightly as a smile played on the edges of her lips.

"More people come out here in the spring and autumn months when the weather is cooler." He didn't tell her a place called Lover's Bluff wasn't popular in West Ridge. Most of the women were married or too young for courting.

"It's so peaceful here. Actually, it's peaceful all over town." Her eyes sparkled and he thought he detected a hint of a giggle. "You do a good job of keeping the peace."

It didn't take much effort to keep the peace in West Ridge, for which he should be thankful. All the job required was for him to take a walk around town once in the morning and once at night.

"I'm not much of a lawman. Sometimes I think I do a better job as the city repairman." There wasn't much he couldn't fix. His father had been a jack-of-all-trades and passed much of his knowledge on to his boys. "Sometimes I feel like a fraud when folks call me sheriff."

"You're a wonderful sheriff. Everyone in town loves you." Her cheeks turned a light shade of pink. She lifted her chin as well as her brow. "What I mean is, I've seen how well-liked you are in town."

"Being liked is fine, but do they believe I can keep them safe?"

"Of course, they do." She shifted on the bench until she faced him. "Look at how you saved me the day when Brent showed up in town. You broke the case and helped capture those terrible men who caused so much grief."

For someone who avoided him like a plague most of the time, she sure was quick to stand up for him. He liked hearing her come to his defense. The memory of holding her in his arms filled his mind. His attention focused on her bottom lip, which she had pressed between her teeth. He leaned toward her, and her eyes grew wide.

Was that fear? What was he thinking? This wasn't the time or place to start sparking a woman who despised him.

He straightened and cleared his throat. "How are you all adjusting?"

"Good. We like it here." Her shoulders visibly relaxed, and her words tumbled from her lips as if she were in a hurry. "The twins have made friends at school, and they like their new teacher. Mr. Prescott says they're doing well with their letters and writing. Of course, Esther loves going to school every day. Hannah was a bit nervous at first, but she says she likes her teacher because he's very tall and, therefore, smart."

"What about Katie?"

"Katie?" Her face paled. The pink hue was gone. Her beautiful blue eyes flashed. "What do you mean?"

Whenever he mentioned the teenager's name, Maggie got defensive. Why? Had she taken Katie from her family? What would she do if he came out and asked her point-blank? He wouldn't be so bold, but he might as well take the bull by the horns.

"Do you think she's happy here?"

"I believe so. She hasn't complained, and

she loves to visit the Swensons. They've taught her so much about baking."

"Are you sure she doesn't have any family back East? Maybe an aunt or an uncle, grandparents even? They must miss her."

Maggie turned away from him and crossed her arms over her waist. He could sense the tension radiating from her, but he wasn't about to back off.

"Why don't you just tell me what's bothering you?" He ran his hand through his hair and sighed. "What is it about me you don't like?"

Maggie dropped her arms. She turned to him, hand over her mouth. Her eyes were wide, and her brows wrinkled. "Who said I don't like you?"

"You." The incredulous look on her face surprised him. "You show it every time we meet. Well, just about every time."

"No, it's not like that." She shook her head and placed her hand on his arm. "I like you, Owen. We all like you. You've been an amazing help getting us settled and starting the restaurant. We know we can all depend on you."

The gentleness in her eyes made his heart lurch. She was one moment cold and the next warm and inviting. Everything was fine so long as he didn't ask about Katie.

"Then what makes you so jumpy around me?"

There was a long silence, as if she were weighing her words or deciding how much to share with him. "You're a lawman."

"What's wrong with that?" He looked at his badge and then back at her. "Are you a criminal?"

"No, of course not." She laughed, but he detected a hint of uneasiness in the sound.

"I didn't think so." Was she? He thought he read people well, but no one was perfect. Still, it was hard to believe she had ever broken the law.

"It's not easy to explain." She kept her gaze on the waterfall, and the small space between them seemed to stretch for miles. "I'm sorry."

"Please don't do that."

"Don't do what?" She looked at him, her already furrowed brow deepened.

"Push me away." How could he have let the conversation get so out of control? Here he was baring his soul and for what? "All I want is to be friends."

He cringed at how juvenile he sounded. Was he back in grade school? How did he ever get to this point? He sounded like a lovesick schoolboy. As soon as he got back to the jail, he'd sit down and write his parents a letter. He did need to move on. His skills were wasted here, and there was no happy ever after for him in West Ridge.

"We are friends," Maggie insisted. Her words pulled him from his gloomy thoughts. "But I'm not ready to talk about it."

"When you are ready to talk, I'm happy to listen."

"Thank you." Maggie glanced toward the falls.

"It's getting late." He stood, and as much as he wanted to take her by the hand, he dusted off his pant legs instead. "We better get you back to the restaurant."

Buster led the way, stomping through the underbrush as he ran up the trail. They passed by an old weather-beaten sign posted to a tree years ago. Time had faded the writing, but Owen knew the words once printed in bright red. Lover's Bluff. They came to an uneven part of the path. He offered Maggie his arm. She took it, and his chest swelled with contentment.

19

Maggie glanced at the clock on the wall and sighed. There was half an hour until closing time, and their last customer left thirty minutes ago. The wind outside howled, and with it came torrents of rain. No more customers were likely to come to the restaurant in this weather. Mrs. Lamb had already retired to her room, on-call if needed. Katie and the twins were in their bedroom, and Belinda was at the Women's Church Committee meeting.

Maggie wasn't surprised when Owen didn't show for dinner. The walk this afternoon started pleasant but didn't end well. His sincerity had touched her heart and threatened to shatter the walls she built to guard it. He was searching for answers she wasn't ready to give. She had almost slipped and told him everything. Let him decide if she were in the right or not. But she would be taking a risk. The cost was too high.

She shook away the troubling memories from earlier in the day and focused on her family. This was a good opportunity to spend some time with the girls a little earlier than usual. They were almost finished with the book they had started reading last week. If time allowed, she should be able to finish the tale before their bedtime.

Maggie wiped her hands on the towel slung over her shoulder and headed toward the foyer to post the closed sign and lock up for the night. Before she could reach it, the door opened. A gust of wind blew into the foyer and whipped her hair over her eyes. Maggie stepped back out of the way to allow room for the man to pass. She brushed her hair back and deftly turned the sign to discourage other potential diners. Praying he wasn't interested in eating a big meal, she pasted on a welcoming smile for the customer.

Maggie peered at the unfamiliar man's back as he marched into the dining room. She eyed his clothing. Tall black boots and a woolen hat branded the unfamiliar man as a lumberjack. There were enough trees in the Ozarks to keep a woodsman busy for a lifetime. She didn't recognize this man as someone from town.

"Welcome to the Welcome Wagon Restaurant." She remembered her manners and greeted him as she followed his path into the dining area. Before she could direct him to a table, he swung around and Maggie gasped. "Mr. Maxwell."

"Where's Katherine?" His voice was deeper than she remembered, and the man's bloodshot eyes were wide and piercing. His nostrils flared, and his brows furrowed. She could smell the alcohol on his breath.

Maggie shuddered. A chill spread over her shoulders and raced to her feet.

At least six feet tall, he loomed over her. She peered at the man she had often thought of as Katie's cruel uncle. Mr. Maxwell's eyebrows rose as he waited for an answer. She took a slow, deep breath as she focused on how to reply to the man's request.

A low rumble emanated from deep in his chest.

She swallowed against the fear churning in her stomach. Somehow, she had to turn this situation around before it was too late. The worst-case scenario was for him to discover Katie was in this very building. Maggie pressed her lips tight and wrung her hands together. "What makes you think you will find her here?" Her voice trembled, giving away her fear. She closed her eyes briefly and prayed silently for help.

"Don't give me any of your foolishness. I've been to welcome wagon town after welcome wagon town, and they all tell me the same thing: Belinda Jones took my niece with her."

Maggie's heart skipped a beat. Mr. Maxwell thought Belinda was the one caring for Katie. His heavy boots pounded the floor as he came closer to her. "I asked you where she is."

Maggie kept a wary eye on him, aware he was growing more agitated by the moment. She chose her words carefully, as if she'd misunderstood who he was asking about. "I'm not sure where she is right now. There's a lady's meeting at the church, and I believe she was going to help with . . ."

Mr. Maxwell threw back his head and groaned. He balled his hands into fists and glared. "Don't tell me the woman's brainwashed her with religion as well as kidnapped her. Wait until I get my hands on Miss Jones. She'll pay. You'll all pay for this."

He spun on his heels and began to pace back and forth across the floor while Maggie fidgeted with the hem of her apron. Her mind was on Mrs. Lamb and the children in the back of the building. She prayed none of them would feel the urge to venture out into the dining area.

Mr. Maxwell whirled and headed back in front of her. She squared her shoulders and held her ground. Putting fear in the hearts of others gave men like him a sense of power. He smiled at her as if he thought she would fall under the spell of his control. "I don't have a lot of time to waste. When will she be back?"

"I'm not sure." She expected Belinda to return soon but didn't want to give any information to Katie's tormentor.

He took a seat at the table nearest to them. Under normal circumstances, she would have asked if he'd like to place an order or at least have a cup of coffee, but she wanted him to leave. He wasn't here for a meal.

"I'm sorry, Mr. Maxwell." She kept her voice soft and steady. It wouldn't do to upset him. Not until she figured out a way to get him out of here. "I didn't mean to sound so vague. I guess I'm a little shocked to see you. We were all under the impression something terrible had happened to you back in Missouri."

Her soft tone seemed to calm him. He stopped fidgeting and his gaze came to rest on her. "I remember you. You're the one taking care of her sick sister's kids."

Maggie nodded. There was no need to explain anything to this man. He was trouble, and the sooner she got rid of him, the better. As much as she wanted to escape his presence, she didn't want to lead him to Katie or Belinda.

"Would you like something to drink?"

"What have you got?" His face sparkled with interest.

"There's some coffee left and a pitcher of tea."

Mr. Maxwell threw back his head and laughed.

"Well, if you'll excuse me." She inched away from the table. "I have dishes to clean."

"Sit down." Mr. Maxwell slammed his fist on the top of the table. "I'm not leaving until Miss Jones or Katherine shows up, and you aren't going anywhere until one of them does."

Maggie took a seat at the table across from him. There was no point in trying to reason with the man. Belinda would return soon, but to avoid drawing attention to herself, she often entered by way of the back door. Maggie prayed Mrs. Lamb would sense something was wrong and make sure Katie didn't come into the restaurant.

Mr. Maxwell's sudden appearance was the

worst thing possible. What had he been up to while everyone thought he was dead? It couldn't have been any good. If only there were a way to get him to leave without seeing Katie. The sweet teenage girl had grown so much since their arrival in town. She had a more positive outlook on life and enjoyed being a child rather than a servant and scapegoat.

It was evident from their brief conversation that Mr. Maxwell was somewhat unstable and unbalanced. The angry man had no business anywhere near Katie, who was now part of her family. Someone needed to stand up to this bully, but she couldn't do it alone. She needed Owen's help.

Only, what would Owen do when he learned the truth?

The side door they rarely used opened, and Belinda stepped into the dining room. Mr. Maxwell jumped from his seat. He moved quickly around the table and hurried toward her. He reached her side two steps before recognition brought Belinda's look of horror.

"Where is Katherine?" he demanded with such force Maggie feared he would hurt her friend.

They had vowed to keep Katie safe but at what price?

Belinda gasped and started to turn. Mr. Maxwell grabbed her arm and spun her around to face him. "Where do you think you're going? No one's leaving until you hand over my niece."

"I don't know what you're talking about." Belinda drew back from him. As hard as she struggled to get away, he refused to let go of her arm. "Let me go. You're hurting me."

"I know Katherine is around here somewhere." He dragged Belinda across the room toward the tables.

Maggie watched in horror even as she prayed for wisdom.

"You can't keep her from me. I'm the only family she has."

Maggie's mind raced to find a way of escape. The front door was locked. The side door was accessible but on the other side of the building. Their third option, the door to their living quarters, would lead him right to Katie.

She was sure Mr. Maxwell was drunk. Their only hope was Owen. He always stopped in for a cup of coffee after making his evening rounds. Only, she had already turned the open sign. She prayed Owen wouldn't be deterred by her unfortunate decision to close early.

■ ■ ■ ■

Heavy cloud cover obscured any possibility of moonlight helping Owen as he finished his evening rounds. What had started as a scattering of raindrops quickly turned into a downpour. The gas street lamps gave a good deal of light as he made his way back to the jailhouse. A cup of hot coffee sounded good.

Who was he kidding? A visit with Maggie sounded good, even though she hadn't looked very happy with him the last time they'd parted ways. Trying to figure out people was a part of his job, but he'd been too pushy earlier up on the bluff. He regretted upsetting her, but if it got her to open up and share her feelings, it was worth it.

He walked up to the door of the diner. Someone had turned the open sign around. They must have closed early tonight. He peered into the window. There were still lights on inside the dining area. He jiggled the doorknob, but it was locked. He could just make out some movement. The women must be cleaning. He didn't want to disturb them.

He could make coffee at the office. The company wouldn't be as good, but there was always tomorrow. The howling wind filled his ears, and he hurried to his home. Inside his office, he stirred the embers in the stove and added some sticks to get the fire hot enough to heat the water.

After making sure Buster was fed and had plenty to drink, he sat at his desk to look over some notes while he waited for the water to boil. Other than the storm outside, it was a quiet night. At this rate, he'd be able to turn in early and catch up on his sleep.

The door flew open and Dale from the West Ridge Savings and Loan marched into the office. He removed his hat and shook the water off before making his way across the room to Owen's desk. "I just saw a stranger in town."

Up until the welcome wagon showed, they didn't get many strangers in West Ridge. Friends and relatives from out of town came to visit often, what with the river and all, but they could always be identified as belonging to someone who lived in West Ridge. The townspeople weren't opposed to visitors, but Owen and everyone else liked to keep an eye out for possible trouble.

Dale lowered himself onto the seat across from Owen. "He looked like a lumberjack."

"Would you care to tell me exactly what a

lumberjack looks like?"

"You know, they wear those tall heavy boots and thick wool hats."

"He could be visiting the Wilsons." The description fit some of Chuck's brothers who came out to fish ever so often in the summer. "They have kin who work at cutting trees for a living."

"That's right. I forgot about the Wilsons." Dale's shoulders visibly relaxed and he took a seat across from Owen. "You can never be too careful when you're in charge of keeping people's money safe."

"Just the same, I'll ride out to the Wilsons and check it out in the morning."

With the mystery solved, Dale crossed his ankles and leaned back. "I sure am glad we have those gals from the welcome wagon with us."

So was he, but for a different reason. He hoped. Dale was about his age and an educated man. He made a good living as the bank manager and lived in a modest house on Second Street. Owen sat up straighter. "So, you like the new restaurant?"

"Sure do. I make a point of going there almost every night."

Steam issued from the pot on the stove and Owen rose from his chair. "Would you like a cup of coffee?"

"No." Dale shook his head and stood. He put his hat on and headed toward the door. "I better get back to my paperwork."

Owen poured himself a cup of coffee and returned to his desk. While he waited for the brew to cool, he perused the newspaper, looking for any updates on the attack on the Missouri caravan. On the bottom of the front page was a paragraph about more members of the outlaw group being arrested. Apparently, Brent kept his word and gave names. Good news.

Owen kept reading. Among those still trying to connect with misplaced family members was the man searching for his niece, Katherine. The article described him as a retired lumberjack. A lumberjack?

Owen jumped from his seat and reached for his gun belt. It might not mean anything, but he had a bad feeling in his gut. He should have knocked at the first sign of movement inside the restaurant.

He put on his hat, and Buster started to rise.

"Stay." He didn't need the dog's help.

Owen wasn't sure his help was even needed, but over the years, he'd learned to trust his gut. Marching through his living quarters, he exited through the back door and crossed the alley to the back of the old church building. He tapped quietly before opening the door just wide enough to see inside. He didn't want to frighten anyone, nor did he want to alert anyone who might be causing trouble. The hall was empty and quiet.

With stealth-like movements, he made his way to the door Maggie and the others used to enter the dining room. He managed to push the door open a sliver without making a sound and peeked out. The hairs on the back of his neck rose and blood rushed to his ears.

Maggie and Belinda sat side by side while a man dressed as Dale had described towered over them. Red in the face, he glared and flailed his arms about as he ranted. The stranger didn't appear to be armed. There was a table between him and the women. Owen drew his gun and burst into the room.

"Put your hands up." He took long strides to cross the room.

The man stepped back, raised his arms, and stumbled. He fell onto a chair and had to grab the side of a table to keep his balance. They didn't have a saloon in town, but the man had clearly been drinking. His eyes rolled back, and he collapsed onto the tabletop passed out.

"Are you ladies all right?" Owen's gaze

trained on Maggie, who nodded.

Her face was pale, and her eyes were wide with fear. "We are all fine, thanks to you." She looked toward the door he'd used to enter the restaurant and arched her brows.

He'd explain it to her later.

"I don't know what might have happened if you hadn't shown up when you did."

"Do you know this man?"

"Well, sort of." Maggie blew out a breath. She seemed to be searching for words. "He was . . ."

"I remember him from the wagon train." Belinda cut Maggie off.

Maggie looked at Belinda, her eyes filled with confusion and surprise.

This was news to Owen. Another man from the wagon train? What were the odds? "Do you think he was in cahoots with Brent?"

"No, I don't think so." Belinda's eyes narrowed as she seemed to consider the idea. "Of course, I couldn't say for sure."

Maggie gave her friend a stern sideways glance and remained seated.

"Well, we'll sort it all out in the morning." Owen nudged the man until he opened his eyes and sat up. "You ladies try to get some rest."

"Thank you, Sheriff." The look of sorrow

on Maggie's face was heart-wrenching. Had he missed something? Before he could ask what was wrong, Belinda stood and blocked his view of Maggie.

"We appreciate all your help." Belinda smiled and nodded her head toward the lumberjack. "The sooner you get him out of here, the sooner we can get to bed."

"Come with me," he ordered the inebriated man. "I've got a nice clean cot for you to rest on while you sober up."

Maggie paced from one end of the long hallway to the other. Her worst nightmare had come true, and there was nowhere for her to hide or even run. "What will we do?"

"Nothing. There's nothing we can do." Belinda sat in a chair she'd placed in her open bedroom door. She was nibbling on the corner of her left thumbnail. "Don't worry so much."

"When he sobers up, Mr. Maxwell will talk." She couldn't help but worry, not for herself, but for Katie. There had to be something they could do. She didn't know of any lawyers in West Ridge, but there must be one in the county seat. A lawyer might have some advice for them. Why hadn't she thought of that in the first place?

"Who will believe him?" Belinda looked

over her hands as if to see which nail to attack next.

"Owen and everyone else who hears his story." Maggie stopped in front of Belinda's door. "I can't believe you let Owen think he might be one of the bandits."

"It was his idea." Belinda shrugged. "Anything to give us more time."

"That does make sense." Maggie nodded, but there was no telling how upset Owen would be when he realized they had purposely misled him.

Should she take the girls and Katie and run? Where would they go, and how would they get there? She was doomed. What she wouldn't give to go back to the moment beside the waterfall when she'd had the chance to tell Owen everything he wanted to hear. He may have found a way to help them, but now she would never know.

Mrs. Lamb, who had been in her room reading the Bible, stepped out into the hallway. They had told her about Owen taking Mr. Maxwell to jail. "Girls, I've been reading my Bible. I think we should all read and trust in First Peter, chapter five and verse seven and then call it a night."

"What does it say?" Belinda rose from the chair and joined them.

"Casting all your care upon Him; for He

careth for you." Mrs. Lamb quoted the verse without needing to look at her Bible. "We can't accomplish anything by worrying and fretting. Let's give it to the Lord and trust Him to work things out according to His will."

"All right, I'll do that." Belinda rubbed her hand across her eyes and yawned before she moved the chair back in her room and shut the door.

"Good night." Maggie hugged Mrs. Lamb and went to her bedroom. All three girls slept peacefully. Her heart broke at the thought of what tomorrow might bring. Maggie changed into her nightgown and crawled into bed beside Esther. The little girl mumbled something in her sleep and turned over. Maggie lay on her back with her hands on her face. How could she face tomorrow?

20

Owen pulled the cell door shut and turned the lock until the bolt clicked. He hung the keychain on a hook mounted to the wall. The prisoner was three sheets to the wind and fell asleep as soon as his body hit the cot. This was the second person to be a guest in his jailhouse this summer. Both men were strangers from out of town. Owen rubbed the back of his neck and yawned. This accounted for the residents of West Ridge being so anxious about outsiders. Strangers. The ladies from the welcome wagon had been a blessing to the community, although, they were remotely responsible for drawing the two no-accounts to the small town.

Owen took a seat and started to straighten his desk. He needed to clear off some space to work before getting to the arrest report. It was late, and as much as he wanted to lock up and head to bed, it was best to fill in the information while it was fresh in his mind.

He found the paper he was looking for and picked up a pencil. Buster snored from his place on the rug. Owen closed his eyes, just for a moment to let them rest.

"Let me out."

He raised his head and blinked. What was he doing sleeping at his desk? Owen yawned and rotated his shoulders. How long had he been asleep? The front window revealed a night sky turning hues of red in the east.

"You have no right locking me up." The sounds of slurred speech came from the cell nearest his desk. The prisoner sat staring at him. The man he'd arrested last night gripped the bars. The whites of his eyes were whiskey-soaked red. His hair was flat on one side and a tangled mess on the other. "What do you think you're doing by locking me up in here?"

Owen must have been asleep for a good while. Buster stirred beside him. The dog raised his head and let out a wide yawn. Owen picked up his pencil and searched for the form he had been about to fill out hours ago. "I'm making a list of your charges."

"Charges?" The man's mouth hung open with disbelief. "What charges are you talking about?"

"Disturbing the peace, for starters." Owen looked up and gave his prisoner a long hard stare. "Public drunkenness. That one will cost you."

"I've done nothing wrong." The man sounded quite sure of himself.

The judge would have a field day with this one.

"It's a free country. A man has a right to drink if he so chooses."

"Drink yes, but not make a spectacle of himself by harassing innocent women." Owen put down his pencil and turned his chair so he could get a good, clear look at the man. "How did you end up in West Ridge in the first place?"

"I've come to get my niece back."

Owen's jaw nearly dropped in shock. His thoughts flew to the article in the paper. A man looking for his teenage niece. Was Katie this man's niece? It explained all the secrecy if the ladies from the welcome wagon were protecting Katie from this drunkard.

He couldn't blame them for wanting to keep her safe, but kidnapping wasn't the answer. It wasn't kidnapping. Katie was almost a grown-up herself. Perhaps that was what they had in mind. Keep her safe until she was of legal age.

They should have confided in him. He

might have found a way to help. His badge. Maggie said she couldn't let him close because he was a lawman. It all made sense. "Your niece? Who is your niece?"

"Yes, my niece! Katherine, or Katie as those child abductors like to call her. I'm her guardian and they had no right to abscond with her when I was away."

If that were true, he had no reason to hold him. There was the charge of being drunk in public, which equaled a night in jail. But come morning, he would have to let the man go free. He glanced toward the window. It was morning.

Owen rose from his desk. His clothes were wrinkled but could wait. He pulled his hat from the wall and headed for the door. Buster stood to join him. "Stay."

His faithful companion settled down and rested his head on his front paws.

"Where are you going?" Mr. Maxwell's bellow was followed by a hiccup.

Owen ignored him. He was on a mission to uncover the truth. He'd been held at arm's length long enough. When he stepped outside, a bird twittered from a branch on the tree in front of the restaurant. His gaze scanned the street. Jessup was sweeping the boardwalk in front of the mercantile, and at the blacksmith shop, Rudy concentrated on pumping the bellows to increase the heat.

This was his town, and it was his duty to keep the peace and uphold the law. It was his job, plain and simple. Also, a part of his job was protecting the citizens who lived in West Ridge. Katie was one of those citizens.

Maggie had risen early to get the dining room ready for the breakfast crowd. She swept the floor with a heavy heart and pushed in chairs without caring how they lined up. Other than the familiar sounds of Mrs. Lamb arranging pots and pans in the kitchen, the restaurant was quiet.

A steady knocking sound came from the foyer. She set aside the broom. They didn't open for another forty-five minutes. She opened the door to let Owen in. His face was drawn and his shoulders slumped. His hair looked as if he hadn't combed it in days.

She wondered how long it would take for him to find out the truth. Dread had pooled in her stomach all morning in anticipation of this moment.

"Maggie?" Owen entered the foyer, and she shut the door behind him without bothering to lock it. He wouldn't be there long.

"Maggie," he repeated her name as he followed her into the dining room. "We need to talk."

"I don't know where she is." There was no sense in wasting time. She got right to the point. They both knew why he was here. Now she could face him and get it over with.

"What do you mean?" His gaze searched the empty diner and stopped at the door across the room.

"Katie isn't here." Maggie waved her hand toward the front and then the back of the building. "She's gone."

"Where did she go?"

"I don't know." She shook her head. Her heart was numb and her mind clouded. She had gotten very little sleep. Although, she must have slept sometime during the night because when she woke, Katie wasn't in her bed or anywhere to be found.

"When did you last see her?" Doubt clouded Owen's hazel eyes.

"After you left last night. She was asleep in bed. This morning she was gone." It didn't make any difference if he believed her or not. She was telling him the truth. There was nothing left for her to lose. "She must have heard the commotion and left when she realized Mr. Maxwell had found her."

"Where could she have gone?"

"I don't know where she is, Owen." She

had a good idea where Katie had gone; otherwise, she'd be worried out of her mind, but she wasn't about to share her suspicion with anyone, not even Mrs. Lamb or Belinda. What mattered was Katie could stay safe and out of the clutches of the monster locked up next door.

"Would you tell me if you did know?"

She couldn't answer. She didn't know the answer. The silence seemed to go on forever as he waited to hear what she had to say.

Finally, he spoke, his voice low and weary. "So that's it. You don't trust me."

"I trust you, Owen. Please believe me when I say I don't know where she is." The tears she'd been holding back all morning spilled down her cheeks. "There's only one thing I know for sure. You can't let that man take her away from here."

Owen stepped toward her just as the door to the diner flew open. Rudy ran into the room. He came to a skidding halt when he spotted Owen. "Sheriff, you need to get over to the jailhouse. Your prisoner in there is screaming his head off."

"All right." He took one final look at her and then marched out.

Rudy followed him.

She never should have let her guard down. It had been much easier to stand her ground when she set out to avoid him. He was gone now, maybe forever. Maggie locked the front door and went to the back of the building to collect the twins. There wasn't time to worry about what might have been.

Hannah and Esther were sitting at the kitchen table with Belinda. "Thank you for watching them."

The girls drew pictures while Belinda drank a cup of coffee. They'd finished breakfast and were dressed. "Was that the sheriff I heard?"

"Yes. Owen knows everything."

Belinda set her cup on the table and looked at Maggie. Her eyes were filled with concern. "Will you be OK?"

"We'll manage." She had money. It wasn't a whole lot, but the small amount she'd started with had grown considerably from tips.

"I wish you didn't have to go."

"It's better this way." She had her sister's babies to consider.

They weren't running from the law, not really. There weren't any charges against her. Katie had asked to join them, and they allowed her. They couldn't leave her alone in the wilderness.

"I don't know what else to do."

"I understand."

"Come along, girls." Maggie reached out her hands and the twins hopped off their chairs to join her.

"Are you sure you'll be all right?" Belinda started to gather up the drawing supplies left by the girls.

"Yes. We'll be fine." She took each of her nieces by the hand and they slipped out the back door. They stayed in the alley and made their way to the side street. She led them across the road and into the alley beside the bakery. Maggie knocked on the back door of the Swenson's Pastry Shop.

21

Owen stormed into the jailhouse. Mr. Maxwell ran a tin cup across the bars and yelled about his rights.

Buster's hackles were raised. The dog's growl was low and menacing. He stood at a distance from the cell.

"It's OK, Buster." Owen gave the dog a treat and motioned for him to lay back down before he turned to face the man making all the ruckus. "What is your problem?"

"I've got rights." Mr. Maxwell took one look at Owen and stepped back from the bars. He lowered his arms and retreated to his cot. "I need something to drink."

Owen was tempted to throw a bucket of water in the man's face. He wasn't in the best of moods, and Mr. Maxwell was at the center of his problems.

"Is everything all right, Sheriff?" Rudy stood in the doorway. His mouth hung open as his brow furrowed in confusion.

"Yes. Thank you for letting me know I was needed at the jail." Owen filled a cup until it overflowed. Water splashed over his hand and onto the floor as he carried it to the prisoner. Without saying a word, he waited for Mr. Maxwell to hand him the empty cup before giving him the one with water.

"Thank you." Mr. Maxwell mumbled and returned to the cot.

"Well, then," Rudy took a long weary look around the room as he reached for the door handle. "I guess I'll be getting back to the shop now."

Owen nodded and waited for him to close the door before taking a seat behind his desk. The prisoner's slurping water from the tin cup was the only sound in the room.

With a heavy sigh, Owen propped his elbows on the desk, folded his hands together, and pressed his thumbs against his lips. His focus wandered over the wall across the room. Wanted posters, a filing cabinet, and green curtains his mother made hung across the window. He had seen them all a million times. He closed his eyes.

Maggie didn't trust him.

One thing he strove to be as a sheriff and a Christian man was to be trustworthy. Without trust, one had nothing to build a relationship on, be it family, friends, sweet-hearts, or especially spouses. They weren't married, never would be, but she was the first woman to capture his heart.

Living in a community made up of mostly men, he didn't have much experience when it came to women. He'd be the first to admit his naivety, but some things just came naturally. Love was such an abstract thing. It wasn't something one found in an instruction book, and, like the falls over the Spring River, it wasn't something a man could easily hold back.

He lowered his arms from the desk and took a deep cleansing breath. There was a job to be done. He wasn't allowing a teenage girl to be put in harm's way, but he did have to carry out the law to the best of his knowledge. Since no help would be coming from Maggie or the other members of the welcome wagon, he'd have to question Mr. Maxwell and then depend on God to give him the wisdom he needed.

Anna Grace opened the door and allowed Maggie and the twins to enter the kitchen area of the shop. Katie was sitting at a worktable, gazing out the window. Maggie sighed with relief. She had a feeling she'd find the teenager here. The young woman spent most of her free time with the Swenson sisters and seemed to feel at home with them.

"Katie, why don't you show your little sisters how they can cut out cookies?" Anna Grace gave the girl a tender smile and then turned to Maggie. "We're baking cookies for the mayor's surprise birthday party."

"OK." Katie gave Maggie a timid look and then led the twins over to a large table where cookie dough had been rolled out and ready to cut.

The bell above the front door of the shop rang.

"You three can work here in the kitchen." Anna Grace patted Katie on the shoulder. "I'll be up front waiting on customers."

Before Maggie could figure out if she was expected to stay in the kitchen or follow Anna Grace, Sadie Mae pulled her aside. "We need to talk."

As soon as they were out of hearing distance from the girls, Sadie Mae glanced over her shoulder and then looked Maggie square in the eyes. "Who is responsible for those scars on that child's legs?"

"Mr. Maxwell." Tears filled Maggie's eyes. Did they think she was capable of such a thing? Of course not. Lack of sleep was making her emotional.

"Who is Mr. Maxwell?" There was a look of fire in Sadie Mae's eyes. It was a look Maggie never wanted to be the recipient of.

"A man who claims to be her uncle."

"Claims to be her uncle?" Sadie Mae stared at her in confusion. "What do you mean?"

"He was traveling with Katie's aunt on the wagon train." Maggie began to sense the Swenson sisters could possibly be the answer to Katie's problem. Strong, independent women, they'd built a successful business in a man's world in a town full of men. "He's a mean man, and he's here in town now to take Katie away with him."

"We'll see about that." Sadie Mae crossed her arms. "I know Katie's mother died a few years ago. What about her aunt?"

"She caught cholera and is the reason we stopped traveling." If only they hadn't had to stop. Perhaps not Sarah, but Chester would be alive today. But if that were the case, Katie would still be with Mr. Maxwell. Maggie shuddered at the thought. "Katie's aunt passed away the day before the attack on the wagons."

"Thank you." Anna Grace's friendly voice carried from the front of the building. "Have a great day!"

"Wait here." Sadie Mae motioned for

Maggie to stay with the girls while she went into the front of the store, where her sister was alone.

Maggie kept an eye on the girls from a distance. She didn't want to spoil their innocent play. They took turns cutting out cookies and placing them on one of several large trays.

Katie had her back to her, but by the laughter in her voice, Maggie could tell she was happy. She must have slipped out before sunrise to visit the Swenson sisters, who were up before dawn most mornings.

Sadie Mae tapped Maggie on the arm and motioned for her to come out to the front of the shop. Anna Grace flipped the open sign to show they were closed and locked the front door.

"Where is Mr. Maxwell now?" Sadie Mae asked.

"Owen put him in jail last night, but I don't know how long he'll be there."

Anna Grace pulled a key ring from her skirt pocket and handed it to Maggie. "Stay here with the girls. Don't leave and don't let anyone in."

Both women left the shop and stood on the top step until Maggie locked the door behind them. She had no idea what they had in mind or how long she was supposed to wait.

Maggie moved over to the window and pulled back the curtains to peek outside. Sadie Mae crossed the street and marched down the boardwalk until she reached the courthouse. She knocked on the door to the mayor's office, and after a few moments, she opened the door and stepped inside.

Anna Grace meandered down the street, stopping people she met. After speaking to them, she moved on to another person. In front of the bakery, she spoke with a woman Maggie recognized as being on the Women's Church Committee. The woman's eyes grew wide as she listened to whatever it was Anna Grace was telling her. She had a look of shock on her face. She quickly walked away until she disappeared into the bank. Anna Grace continued speaking with people on the street. The lady from the Women's Church Committee came out of the bank and hurried into the mercantile. Soon the street swarmed like a group of busy bees fluttering here and there, pollinating the air with something only they could identify.

Maggie watched in wonder. Her amazement grew even more when the street became empty. There was no one in sight. Had she imagined the whole thing? Across the street, the door of the jailhouse opened, and Mr. Maxwell stepped outside, grinning from ear to ear. The hair on the back of Maggie's neck rose. The horrible man climbed onto the bench of his buckboard and sat down. Owen stepped outside and scanned the empty street. He ran his hand through his hair and put on his hat before giving the quiet town a perplexed look.

Would he force her to hand over Katie? Was she willing to go against her sensibilities for the man she'd fallen in love with? Yes, she admitted to herself. She was in love with Owen, but no, she could not put a child in harm's way for anyone or anything.

Sadie Mae Swenson came out of the mayor's office and hurried down the boardwalk. She stopped when she reached Owen's side. Standing on her tiptoes, she whispered something in his ear. His face flushed dark red, and his hands fisted into balls as he listened.

He started to step forward, but Sadie Mae placed her hand on his arm and continued to share whatever news she had for him. Owen nodded and slowly walked toward Mr. Maxwell and his rig.

"Well, where is my niece?" Mr. Maxwell bellowed so loud Maggie could hear him from inside the pastry shop.

Owen walked around to the front of the wagon and took hold of the horse's reins. "Anyone here know where this man's kin might be?"

Rudy Brown stepped from the blacksmith shop. His powerful voice echoed in the air. "No, sir, Sheriff. I don't."

Mitchel Anderson came out from the telegraph office and yelled, "There's nothing on the wire."

Mr. Maxwell glanced around the street. Confusion marred his features, and his jaw dropped open. Maggie followed his gaze to where a crowd of people began to form at the western edge of town. They weren't talking or moving, just gathering. Men mostly, a few women, and some teenagers filled the pathway.

Maggie swallowed back a lump in her throat. She recalled the stories Belinda shared about mountain people taking care of their own. She wasn't sure she could go along with anything sinister. Would they harm Mr. Maxwell? Would Owen stand by and let them?

Maggie glanced toward the kitchen. All three girls were laughing as they continued making treats for the party. As much as she despised Mr. Maxwell, Maggie couldn't abide going against the law. But she couldn't allow a horrible human being like Mr. Maxwell to take Katie.

"Well," Mr. Maxwell was speaking loudly again, but not as demanding this time. "Then I guess I'll be going."

No one in the line budged. Maggie's heart raced. *Let him go.* Why weren't they letting him go? With him gone, it would give her time to take Katie and the girls away from here. Where, she didn't know, but there had to be somewhere safe for them to live until Katie reached eighteen.

"Just a moment," the mayor called from outside his office at the other end of the block and hurried toward the commotion. He had a board with a paper on it in one hand and a pencil in the other. "Sir, I need you to sign this before you leave West Ridge."

Mr. Maxwell's lips moved as he read the sheet of paper the mayor handed to him. His features grew dark and hard when he reached the end. He glared at the mayor.

"Is something wrong?" Owen remained stationed in front of the rig.

Mr. Maxwell looked up and glared at the sheriff too. The crowd started forward. Maggie sucked in a deep breath and held it.

"No, nothing's wrong." Mr. Maxwell

signed the paper and handed it to the mayor.

The line parted, and Owen stepped aside. The man snapped his whip and the team of horses fled toward the edge of town. Maggie watched until they were out of view. Mr. Maxwell was gone. She exhaled with relief.

Letting the curtain fall back in place, she pressed her forehead against the doorpost. Pent-up emotions surged to the surface. Tears welled in her eyes and ran down her cheeks. Her shoulders shook as all the fear and frustration she'd been holding back poured from her body.

The doorknob jiggled as someone unlocked the door. Maggie moved back. Owen stepped inside. He took one look at her and held out his hands. She fell into his arms.

"It's OK, Maggie."

Wrapped in his warm embrace, she could finally believe everything was all right.

"Please, don't cry." He ran his hand over her hair, brushing it away from her face before pulling a handkerchief from his pocket.

She took the cloth and wiped her tears.

Once she gained her composure, she let out a shaky breath. "I saw Mayor Todd hand Mr. Maxwell something. What did the paper say?"

"Oh, that." Owen's sly smile spread wide. He ran his thumb across her wet cheek. "Just a formality. He relinquished all claims on Katie and agreed never to return to this county. Sadie Mae tried to get the mayor to make it the whole state of Arkansas, but Mayor Todd didn't think that would go over well. Until she is of age, Katie is a ward of the city of West Ridge."

"Aunt Maggie," Esther called from the kitchen.

Maggie pulled away from Owen. She didn't want the children to see her like this.

"I'll go check on them for you." He put his hands on her arms and placed a kiss on her forehead before he went into the kitchen.

"It's Sheriff Owen." Katie sounded both surprised and happy at the same time.

Hannah and Esther giggled. The sound of their laughter put a smile on her lips. She loved them all dearly. There was no greater joy than knowing they were happy and safe.

"What are you all doing in here?" Owen feigned a gruff lawman's accent.

"We're making cookies." Esther's voice rang with pride.

"We have cookie cutters," Hannah explained. "Do you like my snowman?"

"A snowman in September?" Owen

sounded incredulous. "You must be mistaken. That looks like a fish I caught the other day in the Spring River."

22

As soon as Maggie had the girls tucked in bed for the night, she sneaked out to the foyer to be alone. The small room was far removed from everyone, and somewhat private when the restaurant was closed. She sat beside the window and watched the western sky turn shades of dark red and yellow. The long days of summer were coming to an end. Relieved this day was over, she thanked God for the way it turned out.

Katie was back with Maggie and the twins, and they didn't have to worry about anyone taking her away. In fact, Katie had had a long talk with the mayor and his wife. Maggie hadn't been there to hear the conversation, but Katie assured her she was happy with the arrangement. She would turn eighteen in November. Although she would be an adult and able to do as she pleased, she would never be alone. There was always room for her here at the restaurant. The Swenson sisters offered to train her to run the bakery. Regardless, Katie would always be welcome wherever Maggie called home.

Mr. Maxwell was gone forever. After all the morning excitement died down and the town returned to normal, Mrs. Lamb had insisted Maggie take a nap with the twins. Rest time was nice but short-lived. They had a big day planned for tomorrow, and the girls were too excited to sleep. There was to be a surprise birthday party for the mayor after church. The twins had spent most of the day baking and decorating cookies with Katie at the pastry shop. There were to be enough cookies for everyone in town to have at least three.

She needed to take a few moments to reflect on God's blessings. The Bible verse Mrs. Lamb shared the other night was on her mind. She cast her cares on Him and He took care of her needs.

The shadow of a tall man with broad shoulders moved across the boardwalk and paused right in front of the restaurant. A dog ran toward the base of the tree out front and barked. Owen must be making his nightly rounds.

"Would you like to take a stroll with me?" his deep voice was music to her ears. There hadn't been any time to be alone with him after the brief moment when she cried all over his shirt. It seemed as though she was forever ruining his clothes.

"Yes, I'd like that." She was happy to spend time with him, just the two of them. There was much she wanted to say and even more she longed to hear. He opened the unlocked door and joined her inside the foyer. Their gazes met, and she couldn't contain her smile.

Maggie hadn't thought about how she looked. She reached up to straighten her hair.

Owen took her hand and pulled her from the stool. "You look beautiful."

The sheriff of West Ridge guided her out onto the boardwalk in front of the restaurant and closed the door behind them. It was a beautiful night. The air was warm but not too humid. A spark of light appeared and disappeared across the road, followed by a half a dozen more splashes of light scattered along the base of trees and the grass. The fireflies were out in huge numbers tonight.

The windows of the pastry shop across the way were dark and peaceful. A gentle breeze blew in from the direction of the river and caressed Maggie's cheeks. High above them, the moon played peek-a-boo with a lightly clouded sky. Owen offered her his arm. She placed her hand in the crook, and they strolled along the empty walkway.

It was a lovely night for a walk, and she was happy to be alongside the town's sheriff. Still a bit of a mystery to her, he was a godly man, and she had no doubt she could trust him. She thanked the Lord for him and the Swenson sisters. Maggie shuddered at the thought of how things might have turned out if it weren't for the people who called the town of West Ridge their home.

Once they passed the jailhouse, they crossed the street to the alley beside the mercantile without speaking. It was a comfortable silence. They were headed for the bench beside the waterfall. As if he sensed their destination, Buster took off running ahead of them.

They stepped through the row of towering pines and into the clearing. Moonlight shimmered off the water falling from high on the bluff.

Owen cleared his throat. "From the bench, there's an amazing view of the sky since there aren't any buildings to get in the way."

There was a streetlamp beside the bench. She hadn't seen it the last time they were here. On that occasion, their visit had been during the middle of the day. The dim light cast a fairy-tale-like glow across the seat made of stone.

"Let's sit down." Owen stepped aside, letting her choose which side she wanted to take.

"It's a beautiful night." Maggie sat on the end nearest the light. She smoothed the wrinkles from her skirt before looking toward the sky. "You're right. The stars are much brighter from here."

"You should see them out on the river." Owen nodded in agreement, although his face was pointed toward the heavens. "On a clear night, you can see a million stars."

"The Spring River is one of the nicest rivers I've ever seen." She'd only been there a few times, but each visit had been enjoyable. "It's such a nice place to visit. I'm surprised we didn't see anyone else fishing there the other day."

"Lots of folks go fishing on the Spring River." Owen's arm brushed against hers as he turned his face to look at her. Their gazes met and held, and all her senses focused on him. "You just have to go at the right time of day."

"When is that?" she managed a whisper.

His gaze fell on her lips, and she swayed toward him. He cleared his throat and looked into her eyes as he moved closer.

"Early in the morning or late in the afternoon. It's best to go when the day is at its coolest."

"Is it good fishing?" She had a hard time concentrating on the conversation and wasn't making much sense, but he didn't seem to notice or care.

"There are plenty if you like catfish." Owen's warm, calloused hands enveloped hers, and Maggie's skin tingled with delight. "I don't have much time for fishing now, but we spent lots of time out by the river when I was a kid."

"We?"

"My older brother and me." Owen's gaze darted toward the falls for a moment before returning to her. "He's the one who taught me how to fish."

"Your brother, Jim, who lives up north?"

"Yes. He never cared much for the quiet life." Owen returned his gaze to the heavens and seemed to be searching for something. "He and his wife, Susan, live in Chicago. They have a little boy named Peter. He just turned one."

She followed his lead and turned her face upward. The clouds were gone, and the sky was filled with a spectacular array of shimmering lights.

"Have you ever looked at the stars?" There

was a dreamy quality in his voice. His tone was so intense, a strange weakness spread over her arms and legs. "I mean really looked."

"They're beautiful." She kept her voice low, so as not to spoil the moment. "I remember our first night away from the city. It was the first time I'd gotten a real look at the stars in the sky. The Milky Way is so beautiful. There must be millions and millions of stars in the heavens."

"Sleeping under them is the best part of camping." There was a twinkle in his hazel eyes when he glanced her way. His dimples deepened as a smile spread across his face. "When we were kids, my father taught my brother and me how to find the constellations. We turned who could find them first into a competition."

"I don't know many of the constellations." She did know how to find the Big Dipper but, at the moment, she wanted to know everything about Owen. What had he been like as a boy? "Tell me what it was like for you growing up in the Ozarks."

"Sure." He squeezed her hand, searched her gaze, and smiled before turning his face toward the forest. "One thing you have to learn is how to live off the land. It's important to know what is safe to eat and what to avoid. There's a lot of wildlife out here . . ." His eyes narrowed.

He was quiet for a long moment.

She placed her hand on his arm and his muscle tightened. "Owen is something wrong?"

"No." He took a deep breath and twisted on the bench until they were face to face. A dimpled grin covered his handsome features. They sat so close his warm breath caressed her brow. "Nothing is wrong. There will be plenty of time later to talk about how to survive in the wilderness."

The aroma from the leather from his vest and the soap he had used to shave his face delighted her. His gaze dropped to her lips and they curled upward on their own accord. He pressed his mouth to hers and she closed her eyes.

His strong arms wrapped around her, and he pulled her close. She raised her arms and draped them around his neck. Their kiss deepened and shards of delight pulsed through her veins.

Buster barked.

Owen pulled away from her. With his hands on her shoulders, he looked in her eyes and held her gaze. "We'd better get back."

She nodded and waited for him to release

her, but he raised one hand and brushed a lock of hair from her face. "The day you all rode into town, you rode into my heart, Maggie."

Before she could respond, a low growl came from Buster. Something in Owen's eyes hardened. He placed his hand on his waist, and a look of surprise thinned his lips. "I don't have my gun."

He took her arm and pulled her from the bench as he stood. There was concern in his voice. "We need to leave."

Maggie drew a quick breath. Her heartbeat pounded in her ears. "What is it?"

"Shhh. There's no need to panic." He tucked her hand under his arm and kept her close. They followed the path toward the back of the mercantile at a quick but steady pace. "Buster smells a mountain lion."

Maggie gasped.

Owen wrapped his arm around her shoulders, bringing her even closer. He kept his voice low. "We aren't in danger. Buster won't let the cat near us. It's the dog I'm concerned about. I need to get to my gun."

Once they reached the boardwalk, Owen took her hand and they raced across the street and into the jailhouse. The town was quiet at this hour of the evening. Owen's dog hadn't followed them.

"Will Buster be all right?"

"Yes. He can take on a wild cat, but I'd rather not have him tore up." Owen pulled a rifle from the wall and checked the chamber before he looked at her. "Wait here. I'll be right back. I just need to scare off the animal. We don't need any wild critters roaming so close to town."

Owen rushed out the door, and Maggie found a chair to sit on. This was her first time inside the jailhouse. She had spoken to Owen outside the building on occasion but had never stepped inside. The room was neat and organized, with just enough clutter to make it looked used. She raised her hand to her mouth and closed her eyes at the memory of his lips on hers.

When he held her in his strong arms, she experienced what it meant to be protected and cared for by a man. There was no other place she wanted to be other than beside West Ridge's heroic sheriff.

The sound of a gun blast shattered the stillness, and Maggie jumped. A long silence followed. It seemed like forever before Owen's footsteps sounded outside the door. She stood to greet him, but Buster entered the room first.

Maggie returned to the chair and gave the

dog a big hug. "You're a hero, Buster."

The Blue Heeler wagged his tail and let her pet him. Owen hung the rifle back on the wall, and then pulled something from a bag beside the stove. The well-trained dog sat still and waited for his master to hand him his reward.

"Good boy." When Owen spoke, the dog took the treat and lay down on his blanket, happily chewing on the bone he had so bravely earned.

"Is everything all right?" She searched Owen's handsome face.

The smile he wore filled his eyes with joy. "Yes. Everything is all right." Owen reached out for her hand and helped her up from the chair. "It's getting late. Let me walk you home."

It didn't take long to reach the building next door. Once they were in front of the restaurant, he turned her to face him and looked into her eyes. She searched her mind for something to say, but all she could think about was how much she liked being with him. She had held him at arms' length for so long, she hadn't taken time to get to know him, as well as the others.

"Has anyone ever told you that you have beautiful eyes?" He didn't wait for her to answer. Instead, he placed his hands on her shoulders and bent to give her another kiss. This one was shorter than the first but just as sweet.

Heat warmed her cheeks.

"Would you and the twins like to go fishing with me after the mayor's birthday party tomorrow?"

"Yes. We'd love to." She winced at the sound of eagerness in her voice. "But I've never been fishing before. I'm not sure what to do."

"Don't worry. I'll bring an extra pole along with us and show you how it's done. It's not hard. You just need to have patience." He reached out and tucked a strand of hair behind her ear. "We'll catch some fish and have a cookout right there by the river."

"The girls will love it."

They loved being around the sheriff. Their eyes brightened whenever he was near, and she understood why. "As will I."

"Great." He cleared his throat, shifting his weight from one leg to the other until finally, he crossed his arms over his chest and nodded. "I'll see you tomorrow then."

"Good night, Owen."

He didn't move from his spot, so she opened the door and slipped inside the foyer. The stool she had sat on earlier was as she'd left it. She couldn't stop the smile spreading across her face nor did she want to.

Did she dare hope there was a place for her and the children in Owen's heart? It was easy to imagine he cared for her. His love for the children was obvious. His kiss still lingered on her lips. As she made her way through the empty restaurant, all she could think about was how wonderful it would be to be loved by him.

23

Owen had never been happier in his life. He sat on the side of the riverbank with his favorite fishing pole. Buster ran up the path a piece, following the scent of something more interesting than the treats in Owen's pocket.

Hannah and Esther lay side by side on a blanket in the shade, sound asleep. Best of all, Maggie sat by his side with a fishing pole of her own.

She glanced toward the girls and whispered, "I think they ate too many cookies."

"Those cookies were pretty good." He'd had a few more than he needed as well. "I think the mayor was surprised this year for his birthday. There isn't much that gets by him."

"If he wasn't surprised, he did a good job of acting it." Maggie kept her voice low. She was turning out to be the perfect fishing partner. "The girls should sleep for quite a while."

His line grew taut and Owen tugged on the pole as the fish fought to get away. "I hope they're hungry when they wake up. This feels as if it'll be a big one."

After some back and forth, the battle became one-sided, and Owen pulled in one of the biggest catfish he had ever caught. He couldn't help feeling a sense of pride. Too bad his father and Jim weren't here. They were the ones who'd taught him to fish.

"Wow." Maggie's blue eyes danced with amazement. "That's the biggest catfish I've ever seen."

"I might have to take this one back with us to show off." He removed the fish from his line and hooked it to another line he had in the water to keep them fresh. "I guess we can eat whatever you bring in."

"But," her eyes grew wide with concern, "this is my first time fishing, and it doesn't look as if I'll catch anything."

"Don't be so sure about that. You're doing a wonderful job. Remember, patience is the key. You'll get the hang of it soon enough. Some days they're biting better than others. One time when the fish were biting, I caught three large catfish in less than half an hour."

"That sounds amazing. Mrs. Lamb will be happy to know you're such a good fisherman. She's mentioned adding fried fish to the menu."

Maggie grew quiet, and she seemed to be concentrating on catching a fish. Owen baited his line and threw it in beside hers. It didn't matter if they caught any more fish today. No one was likely to be very hungry after all the food they ate at the birthday party. Owen was content to be in one of his favorite places with the people he loved most.

Maggie sniffed and wiped the back of her hand across her cheek. When she turned to him, her eyes were filled with tears. His heart stilled and then raced to catch up.

"Owen," she blinked rapidly and sighed. "I don't know how to thank you for all you've done."

"All I've done?" He did bait her fish for her, but it hadn't been hard.

She wasn't the first girl to squirm at the thought of spearing a worm onto a hook.

"It seems as though ever since I arrived in West Ridge, all I've been able to say to anyone is thank you. There's so much more I want to say to you."

He sensed she wasn't talking about fishing. She set her pole aside. He opened his mouth to warn her it wasn't a good idea, but she turned those beautiful blue eyes toward him and reached for his hand.

"I was such a fool." Her gaze dropped to their fingers, and she pressed her lips together before looking back at him. "If only I had just told you everything from the start."

"I understand." He reached out and wiped a tear from her cheek. "You didn't know me from Adam and keeping Katie safe was too important to risk."

"Those are the same words I told myself over and over again, but we both know I should have confided in you."

He squeezed her hand and rubbed his thumb against her soft skin. "It's over now, and everything turned out fine."

"Thanks to you." She raised her free hand and started listing off names one finger at a time. "And the mayor, the Swenson sisters, and most everyone else in town."

"I heard from Mrs. Lamb that Anna Grace and Sadie Mae have hired Katie as their apprentice."

"Yes. She loves to bake." Maggie's lips tipped upward in a smile, and she blinked away the last of her tears. "I guess her mother worked in a bakery. She has many good memories from that time in her life. The love of baking seems to be in Katie's blood."

Maggie's fishing pole flew upward and cascaded off the rocks as it was pulled into the river by some unidentified fish. Her hand flew to her mouth. Her eyes widened in shock and then amusement. "Oh, I hope that wasn't your favorite pole."

It wasn't, but Owen took his pole and moved it to the other side of him. Her face filled with concern and he laughed before leaning over to give her a quick kiss.

Maggie marveled at how peaceful life was without the weight of worry heavy on her shoulders. Thus far she'd fully enjoyed their visit to the river. They only caught one fish and, according to Owen, it was too big not to show off back in town. It was indeed the biggest catfish she'd ever seen.

She apologized for losing his fishing pole, but he'd laughed off her concerns. The twins slept soundly next to her on a blanket under a shade tree. They hadn't gotten enough sleep in the past two days, so she was happy to allow them to catch up on their rest.

"I guess when I pulled that big catfish out of the water, the others swam off." Owen set his pole aside and left the riverbank. He joined her and the twins on the blanket.

Buster returned from scouting the area and came to lay down beside them.

"I don't think any of us are all that hungry anyway." She leaned back against the tree and raised her face at the first sign of a cool breeze from off the water.

Owen scooted closer to her and rested his head on the same tree trunk. He closed his eyes, crossed his arms, and let out a contented sigh. Maggie's heart was full, just the four of them, without a care in the world. She wanted to save this memory in her mind and carry it with her always.

"Maggie?" Owen moved away from the tree and hopped from the ground. He reached his hand out. "I want to share something with you."

She took his hand and he pulled her up. "I need to keep an eye on the girls. They might wake."

"We aren't going anywhere." Owen slid his arms around her waist. "I just want you to know I love you."

An array of emotions filled her heart. She and the girls were safe, they were home, and she was loved. Maggie rested her cheek against his broad chest, savoring the strength of his embrace. His chest moved with each breath he took.

She lifted her face to see the handsome features of the lawman who held her heart in his hands. "I love you too, Sheriff Owen Somers."

He tightened his hold on her, and she rose on her tiptoes to be closer. He ran his hand through her hair, and she closed her eyes. Owen pressed his lips against hers with such tenderness that shivers danced over her skin. Maggie placed her arms around his neck until their kiss deepened. He held her so close she believed nothing could ever come between them. His mouth left her lips, and he placed a kiss on her forehead.

"I love you, Owen." She liked saying the words out loud.

He kissed the top of her head before taking a step back. The moment he released her, she missed the warmth of his touch. He pulled something from his pocket. His hand was wrapped around the object and she couldn't tell what he held.

"Thank you for helping me keep my family together."

"I hope you'll let me do more." The somber look on his face caught her off guard until his smile widened. Owen held his hand higher for her to see. "I have something for you."

"What is it?"

"I know I'm not much, and in a town full of bachelors, a gal like you could have her pick." He smiled and opened his hand to reveal a ring. "Maggie Lynn, will you marry me?"

Heat crept up her face. The words every girl longed to hear, only for her they were spoken by the one she loved. Unable to speak, Maggie bit on her bottom lip and nodded.

He reached over and tucked a strand of hair behind her ear. "I believe I've been in love with you since the day I had the honor of swinging you down from the welcome wagon and you looked at me with those beautiful blue eyes of yours. If you'll let me, I plan to protect you and the girls for always." He stared at her for a long moment. "I hope you'll let me be a part of your family one day."

"Yes."

"Yes?" he raised one brow and smiled.

"Yes. Of course, I'll marry you."

"When?"

"The sooner the better."

"Will we have to live in the jailhouse?" Esther sat up and rubbed her eyes.

Hannah sat up too, blinking with confusion.

"The jailhouse might not be the best place to raise a family." The sound of Owen's laughter was like music to her ears. "But you don't need to worry."

Maggie covered her mouth with her hand. It was easy to forget little ones were listening.

Owen tugged on her hand. "Let's sit down and talk it over."

All four of them huddled together on the blanket.

Buster raised his head and whined.

Owen patted the empty spot beside him, and the dog joined them, his tail wagging.

"When my folks moved, they sold their house but bought all the land behind the jail."

"You mean the meadow with the deer?" Esther asked.

"When did you see a deer in the meadow?" Maggie scratched her head. She didn't recall seeing any wild animals behind the buildings.

"When Katie takes us to the outhouse every morning, there's a momma deer and two babies in the meadow."

"Yes, that's the correct place." Owen took the end of Esther's ponytail and brushed it across her cheek like a paintbrush. "I've been meaning to get started on putting a house on the property but haven't had any reason to rush until now."

"It sounds like a lot of work." And time. She didn't want to sound anxious, but having a home of her own had been a dream of hers for years.

"I've got a few friends who might be willing to help." He had a lot of friends. He was the most well-liked person she'd ever met. "How many rooms would you like to have?"

"It doesn't have to be too big." The heat rose on her face at the thought of adding babies to their family. "The twins have always shared a room. I don't know how well they'd do if they were separated. Katie will need her own room, of course."

"We can always add on when we need to." Owen leaned over and kissed her on the cheek.

The twins started peppering him with questions about the new house.

"Can we have a yellow house?"

"Yellow?" Owen tapped his finger against his chin before giving Maggie a quick wink. "I think I saw a can of yellow paint at the mercantile."

"I like green better." Esther grabbed a blade of grass and held it for them all to see.

Buster barked and wagged his tail with enthusiasm.

"So does the dog." Maggie laughed.

"Will it be bigger than where we live now?" Hannah's eyes widened with awe.

"Bigger than a church building?" Owen gasped with a great deal of exaggeration.

Maggie laid her head on the strong shoulder of the sheriff, her hero, the man she loved, and listened to the playful chatter around her. Her heart was full, and she was happy to be home.

EPILOGUE

Four months later.

"You look beautiful." Mrs. Lamb stepped back to admire her work.

Maggie looked at herself in the mirror. Her wise, and trusted, friend had somehow managed to tame her wayward curls, making them cascade in ringlets down the sides of her face and back.

"Thank you so much." Maggie twisted to get a better view of the back. "You make it look so easy."

"Are you nervous?" Katie sat in a chair, watching, ready to help wherever needed.

"A little bit," Maggie admitted. "But I'm more excited than anything"

"Owen looks handsome in his new suit." Mrs. Lamb spoke as she weaved strands of lace into Maggie's hair.

She hadn't seen Owen since last night at dinner. His parents and Jim's family arrived last week and had been staying with him at the new house. He had been right about friends being willing to help him build their home. The two-story structure had a wrap-around porch, four bedrooms, and the largest kitchen she had ever seen. She warned him if he were marrying her for her cooking skills, he would be disappointed. "When did you see Owen?"

"On my way over here." Mrs. Lamb stepped back and clasped her hands together. She was finished and, by the look on her face, was pleased with her efforts. "He was letting Buster out the back door."

"I also had to take a peek at the wedding cake." Mrs. Lamb turned to Katie and gave her a wink. "You did a wonderful job, young lady. It looks beautiful."

"Thank you." Katie blushed at the praise coming from one of her many mentors. "I hope Maggie and Sheriff Owen like it."

"I'm sure we will." Maggie hugged her. "You make the best cakes in town."

"I've been blessed with some amazing teachers." Katie pulled a box out from underneath a chair and handed it to Maggie. "I made something for you."

"For me?" Maggie opened the box. Something soft and white was wrapped in paper.

"Yes. You're the best friend I've ever had." Katie pushed the wrapping aside and took a bouquet made of silk flowers from the box. "I don't want to think about what my life would be like if God hadn't brought you into it."

The beautiful gift took Maggie's breath away. She reached out and gently touched the cloth petals. The soft life-like flowers, large and small, were perfectly shaped and held together in a white lace net.

"Mrs. Irvin showed me how to make them."

It wasn't easy, but Maggie somehow managed to hold back her tears. She didn't want to cry moments before she walked down the aisle. She took the beautiful gift from the incredibly talented teenage girl. "I will always treasure this, Katie. You're an amazing person with a strong heart."

A knock sounded on the door, and Belinda stuck her head into the room. "Is it safe for us to come in?"

"Yes. Come on in." Mrs. Lamb pulled the door wider.

Belinda had the twins with her. The little girls were dressed in matching pink-and-white dresses and wore brand new shoes. They were gifts from their new grandparents. Owen's mom and dad insisted that was what the girls were to call them.

Maggie looked around the room. They

were all together. The women from the welcome wagon. Taken in by a town of people in the backwoods of the Ozarks with whom they had nothing in common. Loved and cared for, they could never repay all they had been given. Food, shelter, and clothing were just the tip of the iceberg. They had been given a new start in life and learned the value of being good neighbors. And she had found the love of her life.

Her once bitter-and-resentful spirit had almost cost her the greatest joy in life. Being loved by a godly man like Owen. *Thank You, Lord.*

The pianist started to play, and Maggie's heart raced. It was time for her to become Mrs. Owen Somers. She raised her hand to her mouth and widened her eyes as she looked at her friends.

"There's no backing out now," Belinda teased as she opened the door.

Backing out was the last thing on Maggie's mind. Hannah and Esther came to stand beside her, and the three of them stepped out into the hall. A short walk to the corner of the building, and they'd be in the vestibule.

When the doors to the sanctuary opened, she was shocked to see the church full of people. She shouldn't have been. Her soon-to-be husband was the most popular man in town. She and the girls started forward.

Esther waved at the Swensen sisters, who sat in the back pew holding a spot for Katie, Belinda, and Mrs. Lamb. Across the aisle were Dr. Gentry and his brother. She hardly recognized Rob in a suit. There were so many people in the room, she couldn't see the platform. Hopefully, Owen was there waiting for her. Of course, he was. These people wouldn't be smiling so broadly if she'd been left at the altar.

Halfway down the aisle, they passed Mrs. Todd, who was dabbing her eyes with a handkerchief. Finally, up ahead, Owen stepped into view. Her heart swelled so much she froze. Her tall, handsome hero smiled and held out his hand. Before she could take another step, the twins broke away from her and raced to the front of the church to greet the man they had grown to love.

A ripple of laughter spread through the building and the music stopped. Owen's parents stepped forward and convinced Hannah and Esther to sit with them. Without the piano playing, she wasn't sure if she should keep walking. As awkward as it was standing four pews short of the altar, she waited. Finally, Owen came down from the platform and walked toward her. The music began to play once again, and Maggie met him at the front of the sanctuary.

"You look beautiful," he whispered and took her hand.

Pastor Irvin cleared his throat and motioned for them to join him. More giggles came from the crowd, but they were friendly and enduring friends sharing a memory which would be retold many times in the years to come.

Pastor Irvin cleared his throat. "Dearly beloved, we are gathered here in the sight of God and in the presence of these witnesses to join together this man and this woman in holy matrimony."

Owen took her hands in his and their gazes held. From here on they'd be together. It had all been part of God's plan. Maggie had a home and family she'd always dreamed of and a future with the man she loved.

A DEVOTIONAL MOMENT

Be not forgetful to entertain strangers:
for thereby some have entertained angels
unawares. ~ Hebrews 13:2

The turmoil that people experience can be attributed to worry and concern over what might transpire going forward. One is often at the mercy of others who mean to help us but still leave us wrought with uncertainty. But God assures us He will bring calm in the storm. He guides us, and sometimes gives us other people in our lives who have His spirit within them.

In **The Welcome Wagon,** the protagonist is weighed down by problems brought about by others. As she tries to resolve issues, more arise. God sends her to people who will help. Holding on to her trust in God and family, she has to figure out who to trust, and whom she can help, as she navigates through the troubled past to a brighter future.

Have you ever felt as if things in your life were out of your control, as if you were being tossed about on the wind? When this happens, it's important to take a time-out. Get away from the noise of life around you. Be still. Give yourself to God. He will give you the ability to see solutions and resolution to anything that besets you. While it may be traumatizing to walk through trials, God has promised to be with you and to help as you navigate through tribulation. You can be at rest, both mentally and emotionally, knowing that outer turmoil is temporary, that God will send you people who can help, and that He holds your heart.

LORD, HELP ME TO DISCERN PROBLEMS AND BE ABLE TO SOLVE THEM WITH YOUR HELP AS I WORK THROUGH WAYS TO HELP OTHERS. IN JESUS' NAME I PRAY, AMEN.

ABOUT THE AUTHOR

Taming the Wild West — two hearts at a time. Surrounded by the forest in the Ozarks, **Jamie Adams** writes clean and wholesome stories of romance, most of them set in the Wild West. Strong, independent women and handsome cowboys are her favorites to read and write.

The employees of Thorndike Press hope you have enjoyed this Large Print book. All our Thorndike, Wheeler, and Kennebec Large Print titles are designed for easy reading, and all our books are made to last. Other Thorndike Press Large Print books are available at your library, through selected bookstores, or directly from us.

For information about titles, please call:
  (800) 223-1244

or visit our website at:
  gale.com/thorndike

To share your comments, please write:
  Publisher
  Thorndike Press
  10 Water St., Suite 310
  Waterville, ME 04901